The Carfitt Crisis

and two other stories

BOOKS BY J. B. PRIESTLEY INCLUDE

FICTION

Adam in Moonshine
Benighted
The Good Companions
Angel Pavement
Faraway
Wonder Hero
Laburnum Grove
They Walk in the City
The Doomsday Men
Let the People Sing
Blackout in Gretley
Daylight on Saturday
Three Men in New Suits
Bright Day

Jenny Villiers
Festival at Farbridge
The Other Place: short stories
The Magicians
Low Notes on a High Level
Saturn Over the Water
The Thirty-First of June
The Shapes of Sleep
Sir Michael and Sir George
Lost Empires
It's an Old Country
Out of Town (The Image Men—I)
London End (The Image Men—II)
Snoggle

COLLECTED PLAYS

Volume I	Volume II	Volume III
Dangerous Corner	Laburnum Grove	Cornelius
Eden End	Bees on the Boat Deck	People at Sea
Time and the Conways	When we are Married	They Came to a City
I Have Been Here Before	Good Night Children	Desert Highway
Johnson over Jordan	The Golden Fleece	An Inspector Calls
Music at Night	How are they at Home?	Home is Tomorrow
The Linden Tree	Ever Since Paradise	Summer Day's Dream

ESSAYS AND AUTOBIOGRAPHY

Midnight on the Desert
Rain upon Godshill
Delight
All About Ourselves and other Essays
    (chosen by Eric Gillett)
Thoughts in the Wilderness

Margin Released
The Moments and other pieces
Essays of Five Decades
Over the Long High Wall
Outcries and Asides

CRITICISM AND MISCELLANEOUS

The English Comic Characters
English Journey
Journey Down a Rainbow
    (with Jacquetta Hawkes)
The Art of the Dramatist
Literature and Western Man
The World of J. B. Priestley
    (edited by Donald G. MacRae)

Trumpets over the Sea
The Prince of Pleasure and
    his Regency
The Edwardians
Victoria's Heyday
The English
A Visit to New Zealand

J. B. PRIESTLEY

The Carfitt Crisis

and two other stories

STEIN AND DAY/*Publishers*/New York

First published in the United States of America, 1976
COPYRIGHT
The Carfitt Crisis and *The Pavilion of Masks*
© J. B. Priestley 1975
Underground
© 1974 The Illustrated London News & Sketch Ltd
All rights reserved
Printed in the United States of America
Stein and Day/*Publishers*/Scarborough House,
Briarcliff Manor, N.Y. 10510

Library of Congress Cataloging in Publication Data

Priestley, John Boynton, 1894–
The Carfitt crisis, and two other stories.

CONTENTS: The Carfitt crisis.—Underground.—The
pavilion of masks.
I. Title.
PZ3. P934Car3 [PR6031.R6] 823'.9'12 75-34382
ISBN 0-8128-1890-3

Contents

Dedicatory Letter to Charles Pick, Chairman and Managing Director of Wm Heinemann Ltd.

Dear Charles,

I hope you will accept this dedication as at least some small token of my warm regard for you as an enthusiastic publisher and as a friend.

If any reader chooses to see these two novellas as an old writer's toys, I shan't take offence, even though the ideas that can be discovered in them are serious ideas important to us in the present age. The stories they tell were originally in dramatic form—though I have made many changes—and this has encouraged me to make an experiment in my manner of narration here, deliberately avoiding all but the barest description and refusing to offer the usual accounts, with which so many novels are over-loaded, of what my characters are thinking and feeling. This severely objective method, confining itself to what my characters say and do, may or may not be welcome, but at least it is a change.

Anyhow, I trust you will enjoy these novellas, a form quite new to me, and even if you don't, I shan't regret this dedication.

Yours ever,

November 1973.
Kissing Tree House,
Alveston.

J. B. Priestley

Author's Note

I ask readers to accept my assurance that no reference to actual persons, places, enterprises or institutions is intended here. We writers are compelled now to find and use names, and readers themselves would be the first to grumble if we began a work of fiction by telling them that 'X lived for many years in the town of Y'.

J.B.P.

The Carfitt Crisis

or
The New Man

One

IT WAS THE dull leaden middle of a Friday afternoon in November. Marion, wife of Sir Brian Carfitt, wearing a long velvety housecoat, was asleep, lying full length, deep in cushions, on an unusually large settee. Though twice the size of any Early Victorian sofa, it was half-pretending to be one, if only to make some sort of match with several genuine Early Victorian armchairs in the room. It was a long room and at each end it lost any pretence of being Early Victorian, for the end further away from the door to the hall had a radiogram and a television set, and the end quite close to that door had been transformed into a bar, with a curved counter, two or three high stools, and the usual tempting array of bottles behind. This was indeed the all-purpose sitting room of Fallowfield, originally a fairly large Sussex farmhouse before the Carfitts bought it and crammed modern technology into it, together with Early Victoriana for gracious living.

Marion Carfitt made several little movements and then gave a choking cry of alarm, as if she might be coming out of a frightening dream. She woke up and then raised herself, staring at nothing, not yet quite rid of the dream. After a minute or two she padded over to the bar, where she poured out about an inch of whisky, which she took neat. She was a rather tall woman, about forty, with the dark auburn hair that looks natural only on young girls, bewildered large blue eyes, and a soft but discontented mouth. In spite of the hair, the expensive housecoat, the neat whisky, she suggested immaturity, some childish quality.

When she had drunk half the whisky the telephone rang. It was close to the bar and its sharp demanding sound startled her. 'Yes, Fallowfield, Lady Carfitt speaking,' she told it, peevishly. But then her tone changed dramatically. 'Oh Joyce—thank God it's you! . . . No, I'll explain in a minute. Were you ringing up about tonight? . . . Well, about eight, I thought. It's just *us*, y'know. . . . Long dress if you like, my dear, and it'll be lovely to see you. . . . Well, if you can stand it, I'd like to explain. Two things really—both rather hellish. The first thing was—the death of a very dear friend. There's a notice of it in today's *Times* which I didn't see until after lunch. I knew him before I met Brian. . . . Well, I *was*—yes. And so was he, for nearly two years. . . . How clever of you to guess! Yes, it was Lawrence Blade, the painter. But, Joyce, don't mention him tonight unless we're by ourselves. . . . No, I hadn't seen him for ages, but even so that *Times* obituary notice knocked me sideways, and then I had to have a drink or two. After that I dozed off and just before you rang me I'd had a horrible dream. Most of it I've forgotten but I know that Brian was in one of his terrible rages and was pointing his shotgun and was about to shoot somebody. . . . Yes, I know, Joyce, but that last part of the dream, just before I woke up, was so clear, so real, so certain, that I'm still feeling all churned up—but better than I felt before you rang—bless you! . . . Yes, eight o'clock then. 'Bye, darling.'

She finished her whisky, picked up the bottle but then put it down again, took *The Times*, folded it carefully, and put it on a small table, and then wandered round the room doing some vague tidying-up. There were sounds suggesting that something was happening in the hall, perhaps at the front door, but she couldn't bother to go out and see and didn't even try to listen carefully. If things were happening, then let them happen. She went into the dining room, looked round as if she had forgotten what she was looking for, straightened one of its pictures, then drifted out again. A minute or two later, a monster walked into the room.

Marion cried out in alarm. The monster was wearing jeans and a wind-breaker but had an enormous shining-pink idiot face. At the very moment that Marion realized that this must be a mask, it was taken off and she found herself staring at a girl in her early twenties who was laughing at her.

The girl came closer, still laughing. 'Wasn't trying to frighten you. Just a fun thing.' She had an American accent.

Marion was furious. 'Well, who asked you to come here and do your little fun thing?'

'Hey, cool it, Aunt Marion. Can't you see it's me—Elvira?'

Marion stared at her, too astonished to speak for a moment. 'You mean you're Elvira Porter—my niece?'

'Wouldn't be here if I wasn't, would I? Only flew in this afternoon. Hitchhiked from the airport.'

Still staring hard, Marion went nearer. 'But I'd never have recognized you—'

'So what? How old was I when you saw me last?'

'It was when we went to New York—eight years ago—'

'Well, work it out.' The girl sounded impatient. She was quite goodlooking in a nervous, untidy, slightly ravaged fashion; perhaps because she was tired. 'I was fourteen then, just a kid. Now I'm twenty-two—a woman. And don't tell me that makes no difference.'

'But I'd a letter from your mother only the other week, and she never said anything about your coming over—'

'Because she didn't know. I'm impulsive—she must have told you that. Now listen, Aunt Marion, I'm only staying a few days. I like to move on. But if you don't want me here, tell me to beat it.' As Marion tried to say something, 'Or do you want to take a look at my passport?'

'Of course I don't, Elvira. But you can't blame me for being surprised—'

'And you can't blame me for sounding impatient. I'm eight hours in a plane. Then I have this immigration thing—big deal! Then I start hitchhiking—oh, I've money but I hate to spend it on transport. So I'm tired. I could use a bath.' Again Marion failed to interrupt her. 'Yes, Aunt Marion—sure the bath's all ready for me. But I've one or two things to say, so please will you first buy me a drink? Okay? Scotch on the rocks, then.'

'Of course. We'll both have a drink.' As she went to the bar, she continued talking. 'My dear, you're welcome to stay as long as you please. After all, you're the only niece I have and your mother's the only sister I have. But I must warn you, we don't know many young people.'

'That's okay. I'll find some. Even if that place we just came through—Thursley, is it?—looked like the original Dullsville. I won't be sitting around. I go out and give out. That's Pony!'

'Pony?' said Marion, hanging over her Scotch. 'You did say *Pony*, didn't you?'

'I did too. One of the things I wanted to say. About names. I'm only Elvira to my parents and some of the creeps they know. But ever since high school I've been Pony to one and all. Don't answer to anything else.' She swallowed about half of her Scotch on the rocks, just as if she'd been drinking it for years.

'Very well, Pony. And I'd better be *Marion*. *Aunt Marion* really does sound too stuffy.'

'How right you are, Marion!' For the first time since she entered it, she took a good look at the room.

'Like it?' Marion asked.

'Too much furniture and knickety-knacks for me, Marion, but a swell room. You could have fun here.'

'We could, no doubt, Pony, though I don't think we do.'

'Husband a creep?'

'Certainly not. The last thing you could call Brian is a creep.'

'That's fine. Now there's the other thing I wanted to say. I've brought a man with me.'

Marion didn't hide her dismay. '*A man?*'

Pony laughed. 'Yes, a man. And a nut, I'd say, but kind of cute. Now don't rush sex into this, Marion. Typical generation difference. We have sex when we feel like it while you're thinking about it all the time.'

'We are, are we? Well, let's keep to this man you've brought, Pony. If you're not about to sleep with him, why is he here? and who is he?'

'His name's Engram,' Pony replied sulkily.

'Well—?'

Pony jumped at once from sulks to wild impatience. 'Explanations! Explanations! If there's one goddam thing I hate it's making explanations or listening to 'em. It's why so many American men are so boring. They *explain* everything. Okay, Marion. I could use a refill, but you'll find Engram out there somewhere—looking for the kitchen when I left him.'

'Well—really!' Marion was indignant. 'I don't have to have a strange man in my house—looking for the kitchen. If you won't explain anything, then perhaps he will.'

She marched into the hall, turned right at the bottom of the stairs, flung open the door there, saw a light ahead of her and knew that somebody was in the kitchen.

'Well, I must say!' she began, all indignant challenge.

The man in there, who must be this Engram, turned and smiled at her.

Two

THERE WAS NOTHING hangdog or even apologetic about his smile. He might be a lunatic of course, but somehow he didn't look it. He had shortish unbrushed grey hair but few other marks of age, and his eyes, much lighter than his darkly tanned face, still looked young. She was determined to stand no nonsense from this impudent stranger but even so her indignation was beginning to evaporate.

'My name's Engram,' he said, still smiling. 'And I apologize for being here in your kitchen without your permission. And you are— let me see—'

'I am Lady Carfitt. And this is my house you're beginning to explore, Mr Engram.'

'Not *Mister*, if you don't mind. Just *Engram*. But hasn't your niece—Pony—explained why I'm here? No? Then of course *I* must explain. But do please sit down.'

It was a fairly large kitchen, modern, functional, very bright; it had one metal chair, for the cook to take to the central table; and one high stool. As soon as Marion sat down in the chair, Engram, with a quick easy motion, perched himself on the high stool. Marion felt vaguely she ought not to have sat down just because this man suggested it, but somehow she had done. Now she looked at him expectantly.

'I cadged a lift on a lorry that was going in this direction,' he began, in a tone that he might have used to a friend. 'We stopped for Pony, a born hitchhiker. This lorry put Pony and me off at Thursley. Pony decided she would take a taxi on to this house. As I was moving in this direction, I accepted her invitation to go along with her.' He paused to give her another smile. 'Clear so far, I hope?'

'Yes of course. Go on.'

'Now the only available taxi in Thursley was coming to this house, Fallowfield. Had been ordered. So it brought us here—'

Marion stared at him in disbelief. 'Now wait a minute! Nobody here could have ordered a taxi. Quite impossible.'

'Your Spanish couple did. I watched them go, taking all their luggage with them—'

'Surely there's some mistake. My God—they couldn't just have *left* like that. And without a word. I paid them only this morning. I don't believe you.'

Engram swung off his stool. 'Then all I can suggest is that you go upstairs and see if their belongings are still there.' He turned aside and began looking at the kitchen fittings as if he was already in charge of them.

Two or three minutes later she was back, furious but breathless. 'Yes—everything's gone. But why—why—just tell me why—they behaved like that? You didn't tell them to go, did you?' she ended idiotically. 'No—no—that's silly.'

'Very silly.' He was smiling again. 'I understand a little Spanish, which pleased them. They went because her cousin is opening a Spanish restaurant in Bournemouth. They were sorry to leave you, they told me, but disliked your husband and hurried away before he came back from the City.'

'Yes, I can believe that.' She was sitting again now. 'And they were always rather stupid, especially him. But where do you come in? Why are you here? Why are you looking round the kitchen?'

'Good questions,' he told her cheerfully. 'The taxi driver said I could catch a bus here that would set me on my way. That's towards a large country house about thirty miles from here. I have to be there on Sunday morning to attend a meeting and then give a lecture. But as I've nearly two days to fill in, it occurred to me you might like me to stay here to act as cook and butler—'

'You can't be serious, Mr—I'm sorry—just Engram. Don't tell me you're an unemployed chef or butler because I know dam' well you're not, whatever else you may be. So what's the idea?'

'Not to rob you, if that's in your mind.' But now Pony was at the door, whisky in hand.

'For God's sake, Marion, you can talk to him later. Just show me where I'm to take my bag—and a bathroom. I'm dying to go to the john. So make it snappy.'

Left to himself, Engram began to make leisurely preparations for dinner, chiefly concentrating on the pheasant that would have to be roasted. After a few minutes, a bewildered Marion joined him again.

'I don't know where I am,' she confessed. 'I've a niece from New York who seems to me a complete stranger. And now there's you, Engram—and I can't make head or tail of you.'

'It's quite simple so long as we don't try to complicate it. I've a couple of days to fill in. You need somebody. It amuses me to do some cooking and easy butlering now and again. You'll provide me with bed and board—'

'And some money?'

'No money. And I'll leave you to explain this to your husband when he comes home.'

'And that won't be easy. Somehow I believe every word you say, but God knows what he'll think. But I ought to know a bit more about you. I mean, what d'you *really do* ?'

'Try to keep awake, fully conscious. Give some talks. Stay away from offices, factories, warehouses, and the gross national product. So I decided years ago to acquire some useful little skills—much easier than most people think they are—carpentering, decorating, elementary plumbing, rather primitive gardening—and cooking— quite good within a limited repertoire.'

'A kind of highbrow odd-job-man—um ? And I'll bet you're never short of work whenever you want to do any. But what about insurance cards and all that sort of thing ?'

'I'm outside the system. Good for most people, but I'm not most people.'

'I've gathered that. Well then, what about those talks ?' As he smiled but shook his head: 'I see—*no comment*. All right then, what about dinner ? Two people—close friends—are coming.'

'I know. I read your note to the Spanish woman. Dining at eight-thirty. I suggest we keep to the *pâté*, then the roast pheasant, but instead of the crème caramel I make an orange soufflé, which I do rather well,' he continued cheerfully. 'A respectable clàret with the pheasant but no doubt your husband attends to that. He'll also have to attend to the cocktails. I'll be too busy.'

Marion couldn't help laughing. 'I only hope you're as cool with him as you are with me. He has a quick temper and he can be frightening at times.'

'I'll try not to be frightened. By the way, where is your telephone —I may want to use it soon—and where do you keep your liqueurs —for my orange soufflé?'

'In the same place,' she replied, quite gaily. 'I'll show you. Come along.'

Somehow it was all different when they left the kitchen for the sitting room. Marion immediately felt much easier with him. 'Here's the telephone, and there's the bar, where you can look for your liqueurs. Oh—what about this horrible thing?' She showed him the mask. 'Where did she get it from? And why did she come in wearing it?'

He took it from her and then dropped it behind the bar counter. As he spoke he was already looking for the liqueurs he wanted. He seemed to be the kind of man who could do two different things at the same time. 'She was carrying it on the way here. A man she talked to on the plane was standing next to her at the Customs inspection. He'd had to open his two cases, and he asked her if she'd like this mask and then gave it to her.'

'All right, but she didn't have to come in wearing it, nearly frightening the life out of me, did she? So why?'

'I can answer that two ways,' he replied, pulling out one of the bottles he wanted. 'If you want to be suspicious, then probably she wore it because the shock she gave you was helpful. When, after the mask, you saw a girl's face, it would be easier for you to accept it as your niece's.'

'That won't do,' she told him. 'I *was* suspicious but when I took her upstairs she showed me her passport and two letters from her mother—my sister.'

'Then it was just a childish trick. Don't forget she'd been in that plane from New York, full of excitement but having to keep most of it bottled up. And anyhow she's an irresponsible type, not at all a stable character.' He was now facing her, over the two bottles he had placed on the bar counter. 'Grand Marnier and Orange Curaçao. I may need both.'

'While you're there, wouldn't you like a drink?'

'No, thank you.'

'Don't you drink?'

'Certainly. But I don't want one at the moment.' He came round the bar counter and then leant against it, giving her a long enquiring look.

'And the trouble is—*I do,*' she said, as if replying to his own look. 'And I really mustn't. I've had two or three whiskies already, right in the middle of the afternoon—as if I were an alcoholic, which I'm not, though I suppose I could soon turn into one. It's all too easy, isn't it ?'

'It is if you want to blur reality.' He stopped there because she was obviously bursting to tell him something that was important to her.

'I had to have a drink because I'd just had a horrible dream— really a nightmare I suppose.' She was sitting down now, gazing up at him. 'It's just the last part—I've forgotten the rest—when Brian —my husband—was pointing his big double-barrelled shotgun at somebody and was going *to kill him.* And it was all so clear, so vivid, so *real,* not vague and confused like most dreams. Just as if I was seeing something *that was bound to happen.* What's it called, that kind of dream ?'

'Precognitive,' he replied, quite offhandedly.

'Yes, Joyce Roke who's much cleverer than I am—you'll see her tonight—said that. But how can you see the future if it's not there yet ?'

'Some possibilities are there.' He didn't seem particularly interested, almost bored. 'After all, you may have dreamt that dream just because you noticed your husband's shotgun this morning.'

'No, it's not in the hall cupboard. Hasn't been there for ages. I think he must have got rid of it—thank goodness! But then there was something else, before that dream, really much more important.' She stopped, looked away from him for a moment, then gazed at him searchingly, as if wondering whether she could confide in him.

'Go on. I'm listening.'

'Yes, you're a real listener, not like all those people who are just waiting to speak their own next piece. But I'm wondering if you're sympathetic—'

'Probably not. You must risk that.'

Impulsively she asked, 'Are you interested in painting ?'

'Yes, I am.'

'Then you might have heard of Lawrence Blade—'

'Certainly. Like his work. Somewhere between abstract and representation—rather like Nicholas de Stael. Not quite as good—but good enough.'

'Well, he died yesterday. It's in *The Times*.'

'Then I'm sorry.' This wasn't mere politeness; he really sounded sorry.

So it came pouring out. 'I'm more than that, Engram. Before I met Brian, I was in love with Lawrence Blade and lived with him for nearly two years. We were always desperately hard-up—and Lawrence wasn't easy to live with—but it was *wonderful*. I was alive all the time, even when I didn't know what the hell to do, when he'd gone storming out, cursing and blinding, and I was wondering what excuse to make to the grocer—you understand?'

'Yes. But don't start nursing your grief—'

Impatiently she cried, 'And don't you start giving me advice just when I want to talk.' But then she shook her head at herself, waited a few moments for a retort that never came, and finally, staring into her memories, began speaking slowly. 'As soon as I read that piece about Lawrence in *The Times*, I remembered so much. All of it heart-breaking. There was the time when he'd sold two pictures— we hadn't been together long then—and he said he must show me the North, where he came from. So off we went in a terrible old car that was always breaking down. Oh—we came in the end to a tiny place miles from anywhere, with great fells all round it. There was only a church, the little pub where we stayed, and a bridge over the river that wasn't much more than a stream.' She paused there, then with even more feeling: 'We stood on that bridge, our arms about each other, and dusk falling everywhere and the river that was only a stream occasionally flashing white and making a tune for us—and oh God!—I was never so happy in all my life.' She had been looking away from Engram but now she stared at him through gathering tears, waiting for any signal that he had heard enough. But he gave her a nod as if he wanted her to continue.

'And now he's dead, there's only one of us left to remember it— to keep it alive—with more and more emptiness and darkness, and time rushing it away until it's gone for ever. And how can we pray to God when this is what happens to us?' She ended with heavy sobs.

Speaking sharply for once, Engram cried, 'Stop! Stop!' Then as she began to recover herself, in what seemed to her a callous fashion he looked at his watch. 'Before you abandon yourself to despair, encouraging it, luxuriating in it, we might try a little experiment.'

He might have been a research chemist, entertaining a visitor, and still choked with grief she resented his tone and attitude.

He must have realized this, although she said nothing, and he went on, 'I'm not changing the subject. If the experiment succeeds, it might help you, whereas what you're feeling now is nothing less than a waste of life. What I want you to do is rather difficult, so please listen carefully. Will you?'

She merely nodded out of her bewilderment.

'Now try to recall, as clearly as you can, those moments on that bridge—'

'That won't be difficult. You ought to know that—'

'But I've not finished yet. Now comes the hard part. While you're holding that scene in your memory, instead of losing yourself in it, you must at the same time be deeply aware of yourself recalling the scene. Do you understand what I mean? You must remember those moments while also remembering yourself.'

'That's too complicated,' she muttered unhappily. 'I couldn't possibly do that.'

'You can try,' he said, coming closer and staring hard at her. 'At the worst it's better than crying. And I'll do what I can to help. You have to use your will instead of destroying it. Now then—you must remember the scene and remember yourself, here and now, remembering it. Try—try!'

There was a long pause while he watched her closely. At the end of it she gave a cry of joy and was jubilant.

'Oh—this is different. I'm not remembering. It's all still there. It's still going on—alive. Yes, Lawrence—it *is* a wonderful place and I've never been happier—oh—no!'

But this last was a cry of despair. As she spoke now she slowly opened her eyes and stared at Engram. 'It's gone now. No, it didn't leave me, I had to leave it. Not like simply remembering at all— quite different. We were there again—really there—on that bridge. Did you do it? Are you a kind of magician?'

'If I were,' he said smiling, 'I wouldn't need to use the telephone, which I ought to do now. Try it yourself some time when all's quiet and you feel ready to try it. But if you'd like to do something for me, while I'm telephoning, would you mind laying the table for dinner? You know where everything is—and what you want—and I don't. And I'll be responsible for dinner itself—don't worry about that. And you don't mind if I do use your telephone?'

[14]

She gave him a rather misty smile. 'You're making yourself responsible for dinner. You won't take any money. You seem to be working magic of some kind. And then you ask if you can use the phone—*really*! So now I'll lay the table, the least I can do.' And off she went into the dining room.

Engram glanced at a diary then dialled a longish number. He got the engaged signal and so moved away. He opened the door into the hall and then overheard a commanding voice saying, 'No, Tusker, I want to say something to you before you put the car away. We'll go in here.' He went back to the telephone and began dialling again. Two men came into the room.

Three

SIR BRIAN CARFITT was a thickset man about fifty, high-coloured, domineering, quick-tempered. Tusker, the chauffeur, was a coarse specimen, like a bad imitation, of a well-built goodlooking young man in his later twenties. They both seemed to bring into the room a beefy male principle.

Engram was still holding the receiver. 'Hello,' said Sir Brian bluffly, 'phone gone wrong?'

'Not more than usual,' said Engram.

'Oh—thought you were a G.P.O. engineer. Sorry! Visitor? Friend of my wife, eh?'

Engram put down the receiver. 'Not yet. Only known her about an hour.'

This brought a guffaw from Tusker, who was standing, cap in hand, in the middle of the room. His employer was immediately loud and angry.

'Shut up, Tusker!' He turned to Engram. 'Look here—I'm Sir Brian Carfitt—and this happens to be my house.'

'I know,' said Engram mildly. 'But I asked permission to use your telephone.'

'Dare say you did, though we're not running a public phone service, and I don't think you ever thought we were. So the point is—'

But now Marion rushed in from the dining room. 'Brian dear, *please!*' she cried hurriedly. 'I can explain everything and it's really very important. In the dining room.'

Her husband followed her out but called over his shoulder, 'You wait there, Tusker.' The dining room door closed with a bang behind him. Relaxed now, Tusker perched himself on the arm of a chair nearer to Engram, who had now turned away from the telephone and was lighting a pipe.

'Tell you one thing, mate,' said Tusker, who had one of those slovenly accents that do not suggest any particular region, just a lot of sluttish mean streets. 'His Lordship isn't goin' to like that.'

'Like what?'

'The pipe, what yer think. So watch it.' Tusker waited a moment. 'An' what's she goin' to explain to his bloody Lordship in there? Or aren't you tellin'?'

'She'll explain I'm here to be cook and butler tonight and tomorrow.'

Tusker produced a chortling sound. 'I know now, don't tell me. Them two Spanish onions—Garcia an' his precious Isabella—they've scarpered, haven't they? Knew they would, though mind you they were robbing these Carfitts blind. I can do a bit of fiddlin' at my end, but nothing to them two. Didn't know 'em, did yer?'

'Only caught a glimpse of them.'

'I'd 'ad enough of him, Garcia—a mean sod, very nasty temper,' Tusker began expansively. 'Ravin' bloody jealous of Isabella, younger than him an' ready for a bit extra from somebody—me for one. If I was in the kitchen an' he wasn't around, she'd brush up against me accidentally-on-purpose—tits hard as iron. Till he caught her one time. Then he gets me out in the passage, pulls out a knife yer could skin a bullock with—' and Tusker began illustrating this episode with his hands—'an' he says "You go into my wife, these goes into you—deep in the belly." Cripes!—an' he meant it. 'Appen to know where they've gone?'

'To a restaurant her cousin's opening in Bournemouth.'

'Then that's one place I don't go to eat in.' He lowered his voice. 'An' I might easy be in Bournemouth at that, 'cos I'm turning this bloody job up soon. Rather be back on lorries.'

Engram was regarding him with amused interest. 'Harder work, isn't it?'

'Might be—depends. But the great Sir Brian here's such a bastard. She's not so bad—and I'd say she's another one that could do with a bit more rolypoly, if yer worked at it. Hadn't that in yer mind, had yer?'

'Never occurred to me. But why don't you like him?'

'Don't like any of 'em, if it comes to that. Sod 'em all, I say. What they need is Chairman flamin' Mao. But this one here's a real bastard. Yer don't know how to take him. One minute nice as pie —an' next minute shoutin' an' bawlin' his bloody head off—an' if he could have yer flogged he'd be happy. An' listen—if I'd more money than I knew what to do with, I still wouldn't invest a fiver in his Fallowfield Investment Trust that he thinks makes him such a big shot—not a single quid I wouldn't. He's too erratic, that's what he is—too erratic.' He stopped but then remembered something. 'But here—listen—who's the blondie bird I saw lookin' out of a bedroom window just now?'

'Niece from America; likes to be called "Pony".'

Tusker made his chortling noise again. 'Didn't have a good look with the light behind her, but that's a pony I might have a nice ride on. What do *you* think?'

'I don't,' said Ingram. 'Not interested.'

'Maybe not—your age. But me—I believe in having it while yer can enjoy it.'

'Enjoy *what*, Tusker?' This was Sir Brian who had come in quickly and had caught the last words.

'Private conversation—if yer don't mind—'

'I'll tell you what I *do* mind, Tusker,' said Sir Brian angrily, 'and I've had quite enough of it. You must have had the Rolls out most of the afternoon—on your own.'

'Had to go an' see about that tyre, hadn't I?'

'Don't give me that, Tusker. I checked the mileage. Now this is the last time. If it happens again—*you go*.'

Tusker was angry now. 'I might go anyhow, like them two Spaniards who buggered off today—'

'That's enough from you, Tusker. *Out!*' And Tusker, muttering, went. After a sharp look at Engram, who was comfortably smoking his pipe, Sir Brian gave himself a large whisky and soda, hastily swallowed about a third of it, and turned to face Engram. 'Had to deal with that fellow first,' he said. 'Typical specimen. Now they've got everything they ever dreamt of, they hate our guts.'

'A lot of people now,' said Engram casually, 'hate their own guts too.'

'Do you?'

'No.'

'Neither do I.' Sir Brian sat down rather heavily, a Chairman of the Board or Managing Director at work, fixing the other man with a hottish brown stare. 'Now look, Engram—I'm supposed to call you Engram, I gather—my wife's just told me a curious story about you. And I'm afraid I don't believe it.'

'I thought you wouldn't,' said Engram cheerfully.

'My wife's a clever woman in her way but inclined to be a bit naïve. Led a sheltered life before I married her. But I tend to be rather suspicious and cynical. A financial man has to be or he'd soon lose his shirt. Now here you are. You're not looking for regular employment. My wife says you don't want any money. You've no insurance card or anything of that sort. I've no check on you.'

'None whatever.' Engram took the pipe out of his mouth, gave it an approving glance, put it back again.

'Damn it, for all I know you may have come here to make my wife. You could be an inside man, working for a gang of thieves. There might be financial espionage now, as well as industrial espionage, and you might be here to pick up information and report on my Fallowfield Investment Trust.'

'Why? Is it in trouble?' Engram sounded mildly curious.

'That's my business—not yours,' Sir Brian retorted sharply. 'Unless you're a shareholder. You're not, are you? Because that could be another explanation.'

'It could—except I don't own any shares in anything.'

'But I've only your word for it.'

Engram looked amused, not anxious. 'Well, why not take my word? Your wife did. And now she's looking forward to a good dinner while you're prowling round a maze of clandestine lovers, burglars' advance men, financial spies. And probably if I'd asked you for some money you wouldn't have been suspicious at all.'

'Possibly. So why the devil did you tell my wife you didn't want any money?'

'Because I don't,' said Engram coolly. 'I'm not in need of any at the moment. It'll be a pleasure to do a little cooking. And if you pay me money you'll think you're entitled to shout at me. And I'm not to be shouted at. I moved from that years ago.'

'What were you before? Clerk or something?'

'No. When I walked out, I was the youngest major executive in British Incorporated Stores and had just been given a seat on the Board.'

'British Incorporated? You mean—Charles Ferguson-White's combine?'

'I do—yes.'

'I don't believe you. That just won't wash. You're younger than I am—and you'd have been far too young—'

'Not at all.' Engram interrupted him for once. 'You've got our ages wrong. I'm sixty.'

'I don't believe you.'

Engram did not reply at once. He took out his pipe and stared at the other man over it. His manner and tone were now quite different, curiously impressive, although he did not raise his voice. Indeed, he spoke quite softly. 'Sir Brian, I think you're in trouble. That's why you're behaving so badly. And soon you'll be in even deeper trouble if you keep saying *I don't believe you*. I've been telling you the exact truth. Perhaps you're losing the sense, the taste, the flavour of truth. If so, you're hopping blindfold on the edge of disaster.'

Sir Brian tried to pretend this speech had had little or no effect upon him. 'Well, that's enough for now. We've a couple of guests and I want some dinner tonight. Use the phone if you like. Later I want the line kept clear—might be one or two important calls.' He hastily finished his drink and then continued in the same bluff manner. 'I'm going down to the wine cellar. After that, if you feel you can leave the kitchen for a few minutes, I'll be going upstairs and I'll show you your room—second floor, I'm afraid.' He was on his way out to the hall as he added this.

He had left the door open, but Engram now closed it and returned to the telephone. This time he reached the number he wanted. His tone was easier and more intimate than any he had used before.

'Alice, this is Engram. . . . No, Sunday's arrangements stand and you're still very kindly taking me to Charles's place. . . . Well, yes, Alice, there *is* one change of plan. I've agreed to cook and bottle-wash here, a house called Fallowfield, belongs to one Sir Brian Carfitt—and it's on the main road about two miles west of Thursley. . . . Yes, really on the way to Charles's place. But this is the point, my dear. Would you mind calling for me quite late on Saturday night? . . . You sure? Bless you! . . . Yes, better warn Charles. . . . No, Alice, I've planned nothing at all, no experiment in disturbing this time, though of course it might be necessary. But so far I'm just curious. And that's why I don't want to leave earlier tomorrow.

And you *really* don't mind its being so late? ... Good! 'Bye, my dear!'

Then he collected the used glasses, finding a small tray for them under the bar counter, and as he moved with the tray towards the hall door, he playfully assumed the solemn face and pompous walk of an old butler. Then, dismissing the role, he laughed quietly.

Four

MARION AND JOYCE, wife of Dr Alfred Roke, went into the sitting room, leaving their husbands to sit over the port and talk business. They sat fairly close together on the sofa-settee. They were both wearing long dresses—a light grey and green for Marion, a dark crimson for Joyce—and they looked and felt splendid. Joyce was shorter than Marion, a brunette with sharp eyes and a sharp nose, a clever woman who only pretended to be silly to make her husband feel better.

'Coffee shouldn't be long,' said Marion. 'I've had to leave it to Engram. I don't feel I can start ringing for him.'

'You can ring bells to salute him for that super dinner. But I still can't make him out. And obviously Alfred didn't believe a word you said about him. You'd have to put a lot of Engram into test-tubes to convince Alfred.'

'When I tried to explain about Engram to Brian, he said I only believed such rubbish because I'd led a *sheltered life*. My God!—after living with Lawrence Blade on and off for two years!'

'You said upstairs you might tell Brian now—'

'I'm going to, my dear.'

'All wrong! Don't think of it.' Joyce was emphatic.

'But now that Lawrence is dead—'

'Could be worse, if anything. Just shut up about everybody and everything, except for idiotic female gabble. I've never told Alfred a single dam' thing about anybody,' Joyce went on, amused. 'Every time he goes off to a conference, he thinks I'm sitting at home, waiting for one of his postcards. So don't be silly, Marion. You let Brian still imagine you've had *a sheltered life*. And who taught him that ridiculous expression—his grandmother? But so far as there are any sheltered lives, we know who lead them—the men. They don't even need women to close the doors and windows and bandage their eyes. They're just natural self-deceivers.'

'I'll bet Engram isn't,' said Marion, rather defiantly.

'Hoy—hoy! You've fallen for him already.'

Marion refused to respond to the playful manner. 'No, it's not like that. Something quite different.'

'My dear, you had that proud tone of voice that's always a give-away. *I'll bet Engram isn't*. Unless of course it's that orange soufflé. Another of those and I'm halfway there myself, darling.'

'Oh—stop it!' Marion spoke sharply. 'Alfred's not here, so you don't have to talk like that, Joyce—'

'Rather a bitchy remark—'

'Well, why don't you be serious, Joyce?'

'What about? After that outburst on the phone about Lawrence Blade dying, and then your shotgun dream, precognitive perhaps, you haven't told me a thing. Yet you make me feel that you think something exciting, mysterious, wonderful, has happened. Of course it may just be you're a bit sloshed and Soufflé Engram's gone to your head.'

'I don't feel sloshed. I've come to terms with Lawrence's death. The shotgun's gone. And Engram seems to clear my head, not go to it.' Then she obviously checked herself and kept silent for some moments. 'I can tell you something you can be serious about, something I suddenly felt when you were talking. We're supposed to be close dear friends. *Darling Marion! Dearest Joyce!* But do I really like you? Or you me?' She hesitated.

'Don't stop,' said Joyce. 'Let it all come out.'

'Well, I can't *bear* Alfred—never could.'

'Fair enough! I don't know how Alfred feels about you, but I know he thoroughly dislikes Brian. And though Brian's not as dreary as Alfred—and occasionally makes a swift stealthy pass late at night—in my book he's just an insensitive bullying egoist. And that just about wraps up our cosy quartet of kindly thoughtful neighbours and close friends—'

'What are we doing then?' Marion demanded urgently.

'Conveniently passing the time. Trying to look as happy as the people in the advertisements who've just bought something. Looking soon for computers to allow us the price of a new outfit or a holiday in Bermuda. Finally hoping for a nice transplant kidney, liver or heart.'

'Don't talk like that. Now I know you're not satisfied.'

'But I am.'

'You *can't* be.'

Joyce did not reply at once, just gave Marion a long look. 'I'm now able to say I'm satisfied because I'm well past expecting anything. I've settled down to enjoy the super-market Good Life, as the idiots call it. Twenty years ago I came out of the university with a good degree—and expectations a thousand feet high and lit up all night. Then I soon began to feel dissatisfied. The expectations were now about twelve feet high and hardly lit up at any time. Later I stopped even feeling dissatisfied because I knew I couldn't expect anything worth having—'

Marion stopped her. 'How can you say that when you've two children? Look at me!'

'Oh—yes, the kids were adorable when they were little. As if they belonged to some other and better planet. But now they're growing up, on earth as it definitely isn't in Heaven. Rupert—thirteen now—is going to be Alfred all over again. That'll be two of them.'

'But Jill,' Marion protested, 'she's not like that—and she's sweet—'

'She turns that on for you. No longer for me,' said Joyce, increasingly bitter. 'I'm stuffy old Mummy, always finding fault. And look at her! Seventeen now—with a woman's body and a woman's urges and the mind of a child. And even already I sometimes catch a certain look, slyly suggesting she knows all about sex and I don't. All right, I could be wrong about that. But look what's waiting for her—that glorified farmyard and loony bin—the Youth racket.'

'Joyce, you're being altogether too pessimistic and cynical.'

'And you're ready to be too sentimental, with a little help out of a bottle.' As Marion, shocked, tried to break in. 'No, Marion, I oughtn't to have said that, even if we all decide we rather dislike one another. At least we can keep some manners, and that was an unmannerly illbred thing to say to you in your own house. I'm sorry, my dear.'

Marion hesitated and then said in a rather muffled tone, 'Perhaps we could be friends—really friends—if we tried and yet stayed honest. . . . I wish I could ask Engram.'

'Oh—no, not while I'm around. I'll take his cooking and be grateful, but no mysterious Oriental wisdom, if that's his line.'

'It isn't,' Marion snapped at her. 'And I could have done without the snub.'

Engram came in from the hall carrying a coffee tray with four small cups on it. He was now wearing a houseman's jacket that had been made for somebody else and didn't fit him.

'Oh thank you, Engram!' cried Marion, obviously pleased to see him. 'You've brought the men's too. Quite right. It's time they joined us.'

Engram put down the tray on a little low table, which he moved closer to Marion. From his entrance he had done everything with an ironical slight exaggeration of a butler's manner. And Joyce had been watching him carefully. Now she caught him before he could go.

'I must tell you something, Engram,' she said brightly. 'That was a lovely dinner, and thank you very much. You must excuse this, Marion. But Engram, I'm not so happy about your butler bit. It's obvious you're playing a part and I can't help feeling you're over-acting it.'

He offered no sign of embarrassment. 'You're quite right of course, Mrs. Roke. I always overdo it. As a carpenter, decorator, plumber, electrician, I'm entirely convincing, even occasionally using local dialect or accents. I rarely have to attempt a butler—'

Marion had to cut in. 'You don't have to be one here, y'know. Only the cooking.'

'I'm sure,' said Engram coolly. 'But I can't resist trying to buttle occasionally. And of course it's ridiculous, so I'm always tempted to overplay it. Always unwise too because I'm also tempted to be mischievous—showing off, really. Not good.'

Marion was about to say something but Joyce got in first. 'Lady Carfitt seems to think you're a very wise man, Engram, though she hasn't explained why—'

'I'm glad to hear it,' he murmured.

'But is it wise to go about playing parts?'

'It's not a game, you know, Mrs. Roke. Most of the time I'm earning my daily bread. And there's no harm in consciously playing parts. What's unwise and dangerous is to be for ever playing parts inside yourself and not even knowing you're doing it. So instead of being one real person, you're just a bad repertory company.' He

[25]

reverted to the butler manner. 'Will that be all at the moment, Lady Carfitt?'

'Yes, thank you! But *do* stop that!'

'I'll do what I can,' Engram replied with mock gravity, and left them. Marion poured out coffee for Joyce and herself. Joyce was looking thoughtful and said nothing.

Marion waited and then, not without a touch of malice, said, 'Didn't get much change out of Engram, did you, Joyce?'

This was ignored. Still thoughtful, Joyce said, 'No chance to-night, I imagine, of talking to that man alone. When is he leaving?'

'Late tomorrow night, he says.'

Joyce gave her a frowning look. 'But he won't have to cook dinner tomorrow night. You're going with us to the Jarmans' party —buffet supper—remember?'

'I know. I told him. But even so he insists on staying late.'

'Did he say why?'

'No, he didn't,' Marion said abruptly.

But Joyce was persistent. 'Have you asked him?'

'No I haven't. And I'm not going to, Joyce. And I think that's enough of that.'

'Oh—is it? Sorry!' Joyce took a sip of coffee, tried another sip, then gave Marion a long speculative look. 'What are you afraid of?'

Marion shook her head and then apparently decided that any wild answer would have to do. 'Oh, my dear—I'm frightened of all sorts of things that wouldn't worry you at all. I'm not brave, I'm not clever, I'm ready to believe almost anything, films can make me cry—even television. And if I'm feeling very sorry for myself—like today—I drink whisky in the afternoon—'

'Well, as long as you don't start in the morning—'

'The men are coming in—'

Joyce's husband, Dr Alfred Roke, arrived first, tall and thinnish, with a tediously monotonous voice and a manner in which conceit and timidity were unhappily mixed. Sir Brian was both looking and feeling expansive, having dined well and had a good deal to drink. He went at once round to the bar. 'Joyce, brandy—cointreau—what?'

'Brandy please, Brian,' she told him.

'Cointreau for you, Marion?'

'No—nothing, thank you.'

'Ate too much of that soufflé, did you? Brandy for you of course, Alfred?'

'I'll risk it, Brian. Though I read the other day that old French peasants say that when their worst enemy visits them, they give him their best brandy.'

'Why do they do that?' Marion had heard it before, but she was the hostess.

'They think it shortens his life,' said Roke triumphantly.

'We seem to have shortened this bottle,' said Sir Brian, pouring it out. 'I must get another up.'

Knowing that no serious conversation was possible during this passing of glasses and coffee cups and nodding and smiling, Roke waited a while and then said heavily, 'Now, old man, just let me make my point. I'll put it this way. After all, I'm a scientist—'

'Or you were—*once*—' And this was from Joyce, sharp, malicious, clean out of her conjugal role.

Her astonished husband's '*What's that?*' was almost a squeak.

Joyce was back in her familiar role in a flash. 'Oh—darling—just one of my teasing remarks! But never mind your silly old point now. What I want to know is—have you men seen Marion's mysterious American niece yet?'

Brian got in first. 'Haven't set eyes on her, Joyce. One of those blondes with long straight hair, I'm told. Your type—eh, Alfred?' He winked over his cigar at Joyce.

'Tell you later, Brian,' said Roke in lighter mood. 'Older than Jill, isn't she, Marion?'

'Five years at least. And you've not seen her because she went straight out of the house, without saying a word, while I was upstairs changing. So I don't even know where she's gone.'

'What about the mastermind, Engram?' Joyce asked. 'Doesn't he know?'

'Well, he hasn't said anything, my dear. And here's a curious thing. I insisted upon laying the table for dinner, just to help Engram. And this was quite early, before I went up for my bath. Now I knew very well Pony was here—'

'*Pony?*' cried Roke, hugely bewildered.

'Leave it, Alfred,' said Joyce hastily. 'Go on, Marion.'

'But—will you believe it?—though I'd shown that girl her room not half an hour before, I laid the table for four, as if I'd forgotten that Pony existed.'

'*There!*' But Joyce's exclamation was derisive.

Roke had worked it out. 'Perhaps the poor girl had come down,

[27]

caught sight of the dinner table and saw she'd been overlooked, and that's why she went out. Joyce, perhaps Jill could show her round.'

Marion jumped on that. 'Oh—no, Alfred—I really wouldn't advise it—'

'And that's enough for me,' said Joyce hastily. 'It's *out*, Alfred darling. Just forget it.'

'Why? I don't see it. Do you, Brian?'

'What? Oh—no! Or do I mean *Yes*—'

'You see,' said Joyce, 'he's not even thinking about it.'

'I don't have to think about it?'

'Brian, that's rude,' said his wife.

'Sorry—didn't mean to be. Well now—' and Sir Brian took out his cigar and replaced it with some brandy—'as I told you, I haven't met the girl yet—*but*—' and it came like a smash at tennis—'*but*—she's American, five or six years older than your Jill, has to be called Pony, arrives here uninvited and without notice, doesn't stay in for her very first evening, and Marion obviously dislikes her. So if you want my opinion, Joyce and Marion are right and you're wrong, Alfred. Keep young Jill away from her.'

'A typical example, in my view,' said Roke, 'of the force of mere prejudice. In Amalgamated Pharmacies we meet it and have to reckon with it over and over again. Take a comparatively simple instance—the anti-narcosis compounds of considerable value to the medical profession even if they have been widely misused outside it—'

But he had lost his audience if he had ever had one. Engram came in, carrying a long narrow parcel carefully wrapped. All except Roke looked eagerly towards him.

'I apologize for this interruption, Sir Brian,' Engram began.

'No—no, that's all right—'

'We're loving it, Engram,' said Joyce.

'But a young man from Thursley has just delivered this,' Engram went on, 'together with a note.' And he handed this over to Sir Brian, and then returned to where he had been standing, still holding the parcel.

After glancing at the note, Sir Brian said, 'Yes, just what I thought. Unwrap it please, Engram.'

The Rokes watched with idle curiosity the large double-barrelled shotgun, as good as new, emerging from its brown paper. But Marion stared with some intensity as her husband, smiling with pleasure, went forward to take charge of the gun. He made sure it was not loaded and then he brought it up to his shoulder and pointed it in one or two directions.

Marion could stand it no longer. 'Oh—no—no!'

'Now what's the matter?' And Sir Brian put down the gun.

'It's a dream she had,' Joyce explained hastily. 'Marion, it's all all right now—look!'

'Dreams are nonsense,' said Roke, 'but all the same, old man, never point a gun like that—'

'I know more about guns than you do, Alfred. You saw me make sure it wasn't loaded—'

'All the same you could have made a mistake—'

'No, I couldn't, so just dry up.' He gave the gun to Engram. 'There you are! It lives in that first cupboard in the hall. I usually keep it loaded—may need it in a hurry and there are some cartridges in there—but I'll attend to that. What I would like you to do is to go down into the cellar and find another V.S.O.P. brandy like the one I've just finished. I'd go myself but I've a little radio interview coming on soon, and I want to hear it. All right?'

'Well—nearly,' said Engram, who was now holding both the gun and all the wrapping paper. 'I'm a little uncertain about the brandy—'

Marion saw her chance and jumped at it. 'Like this one,' she said, grabbing the empty bottle. 'You go ahead.'

Once outside in the hall, she whispered, 'Engram, I'm frightened. You know what I mean.'

'Of course. But you may have seen in your dream what you've just seen now—your husband simply pointing the gun—'

'No—no—no. Not like that at all. He was in a furious rage, ready to kill somebody. I *knew* he was. Don't you understand?'

'Yes, if you feel so sure.'

'Well then, what can I do?'

'Nothing probably. You'd better leave it to me. Can you trust me?' But he asked the question as if he hardly expected an answer to it. 'Remember—I'm not leaving until late tomorrow night.'

'Was that—?' But she checked herself. 'I must get back. Yes, I trust you,' she added hastily.

Five

THEY WERE TALKING about the radio programme when Marion returned. Alfred Roke, nothing if not methodical, had found it in *The Times*. 'This is it, isn't it? A series called "Your Money and Your Life".'

'That's the one,' Brian told him with some satisfaction. 'Short interviews with industrialists and prominent City men. Just sound radio of course. All quite painless. After I'd agreed to do it, chap came round yesterday at the office with a tape recorder. Nothing to it. How much time have we, Alfred?'

'About three minutes if they're punctual.'

'I'd better make sure we're on the right channel and all that.' He went to the radiogram, switched it on, made various adjustments but kept the volume so low that only he could hear anything. Roke had followed him round, and was now standing a few feet away, a kind of dithering nervous assistant. Their wives, still sitting fairly close on the sofa-settee, had to turn their heads to see them, which they did for a few moments but then looked at each other and pulled little derisive faces.

'What line are you taking, old man?' Roke asked.

Brian straightened up, grinning. 'Oh—no! You don't get *that* in advance, buster—'

'Quite right,' said Joyce obviously ironical. 'It would take all the *excitement* out of it, Alfred darling.'

'And you can cut the sarcasm, Joyce darling,' Brian told her sharply. 'You and Marion are dam' glad to spend the money when it comes in. But *you* can take it easy, Alfred old man. You and Amalgamated Pharmacies may be in for a pleasant surprise.'

'If of course they're all listening,' said Joyce.

'Quiet now! This is it.' And he brought up the volume and the announcer's voice, as easy and smooth as treacle, could be clearly heard. 'Continuing our weekly programme "Your Money and Your Life", a series of interviews of well-known and influential business-men, Henry Glemmer talks tonight to Sir Brian Carfitt—'

Glemmer was on now. 'Sir Brian, as founder and Chairman of the Fallowfield Investment Trust, you must have had many years experience in the City—'

'Well yes, I think you can safely say that, Mr Glemmer—ha ha!' Brian replied unctuously. And Joyce, unseen by the men, pulled a face at Marion.

'Ha ha!' Glemmer echoed dutifully. 'Now I wonder if you've listened to many of our "Your Money and Your Life" interviews, Sir Brian?'

'I'm a busy man, remember, Mr Glemmer. But a fair number I would say, especially during the last few weeks.'

'Ah—that's very interesting,' said Glemmer who didn't sound keenly concerned. 'And it brings me to my first question. Have you found yourself agreeing or disagreeing—not so much with the individual arguments as with the general tone of the interviews?'

'I'm glad you asked me that, Mr Glemmer, because there's a point here I want to make at once . . .'

But at this moment there was another point that Brian, alive in his own sitting room and not so much tape in the studio, had to make at once. Engram had come in with the brandy, and, seeing him, Brian shouted a harsh command, 'Stop there and keep quiet, man.'

Engram did exactly what he was told to do, holding the brandy bottle and never making a move. His face revealed nothing, but his eyes seemed very bright as he looked at Marion and Joyce, who were facing him.

. . . 'In my opinion—' this was Brian on the radio—'the general tone of these interviews has been altogether too down—too pessimistic—and so liable to discourage investment . . .'

But then, to both women, as they told each other afterwards, it all went into gibberish. *Jibble jabble jubble jobble jabble* for Marion. *Feeny finny-finny foe fancy fonsy fizz-fizz* it sounded to Joyce. And so it went on, and they began giggling.

Finally, they overheard, coming through the gibberish, Alfred Roke saying solemnly, 'Sound point that, Brian.' This was too much. Both women abandoned all control and screamed with laughter.

Roaring well above his radio self, Brian damned and blasted the pair of them, then switched off the set.

'They ruined the talk and you were making one or two good points,' said Roke. 'What's the matter with them ?'

'How the devil do I know?' said Brian angrily. 'How does anybody know what's the matter with women ? They don't know themselves. Suddenly start behaving like idiots.' He noticed Engram now. 'For God's sake, man—put down that bottle and clear out.'

Marion sprang up. 'Brian, you can't shout at him like that. I'm sorry, Engram.'

'Better find a glass case for him,' Brian muttered.

Having put down the brandy bottle, Engram turned and looked hard at Sir Brian. He spoke very quietly. 'I told you earlier, when I refused your money, I was not to be shouted at. Now *stop shouting.*'

'All right, all right, I was too rough. Lost my temper all round. But don't start giving me any advice. I don't want any.'

'Possibly not,' said Engram. 'But you're going to need some very soon.' And out he went, smoothly and quickly.

Roke cleared his throat importantly. 'May be a good cook and handyman, but that fellow gets above himself. I'd take him down a peg or two.'

Joyce flashed a look at him. 'Alfred—you make me laugh—'

This set the smouldering Brian off again. 'No—no—no—it wasn't Alfred who made you laugh—*I* did it—and God knows why when I was talking sound commonsense. You and Marion screaming your heads off!'

With ironical sweetness, Joyce said, 'You mean our *silly* little heads off, don't you ?'

'If that's how you want it—yes, *I do*. I didn't expect you and Marion to understand what I was talking about, but at least you could have kept quiet. Like a pair of hysterical schoolgirls.'

'An exact description, old man,' said Roke. 'And Brian was making some good sound points. Not tight, are you, Joyce ?'

'She isn't,' said Marion impulsively. 'And even I'm not. Brian, we couldn't help laughing because you and the interviewer suddenly started talking gibberish—'

'Nonsense! We were speaking plain English—'

'Well, it sounded to us like *gribble grabble robbleton rub-rub*—'

To which Joyce, giggling a little, added, '*Diddleton duddleton daddleton doo-doo*. Then you switched off.'

Brian was indignant. 'I was making a point about possible re-flation—'

'A sound point too, in my opinion,' said Roke, 'But I know what happened, old man. Seen it happen before with Joyce. One of them started some stupid women's joke—probably about sex—and then off they went, giggling and giggling until they couldn't control themselves.'

'Alfred,' said Joyce, 'don't be a bloody fool.'

'Cool it, Joyce,' said Brian. 'Alfred—more brandy or a whisky?'

While the men went into a drinks huddle, Marion and Joyce stared at each other, moved nearer, and began whispering.

'I've just thought of something.' This was Joyce. 'It was when Engram came in with the brandy—and Brian ordered him to stay there and keep quiet and so he stood looking at us—that Brian's radio talk sounded to us like gibberish.'

'I've wondered,' Marion whispered. 'Yes, somehow it must have been Engram.'

'And it must have been some sort of hypnotism. My God, Marion, you'll have to watch that man. When am I going to talk to him alone? It's too late tonight. We ought to go.' And Joyce looked at her watch.

Brian was looming over them. 'Now what about a drink? Joyce —Marion?'

Joyce got up. 'Sweet of you, Brian, but I really think we ought to go. It's getting late and I want to make sure Jill's at home. Besides, we're all a bit on edge—'

'And that's why a drink would help—'

'Unless it makes us edgier,' said Joyce. 'You're ready, aren't you, Alfred?'

'Yes, come along,' said Roke. 'And many thanks—Marion— Brian! Superb food—drink—and everything!'

'Our pleasure,' cried Brian heartily. 'And if you must leave us, you must. Though I'll admit I may have some work to do before I turn in.'

While Brian was outside talking to the Rokes before they started their car, Marion slipped along to the kitchen, where she found Engram washing dishes.

'I'd help you with them,' Marion told him, 'but I must have a serious talk with Brian before I go to bed. So will you please keep out of the sitting room ?'

'Yes of course.' For once there was no smile. In fact he looked rather melancholy.

'It was you, wasn't it, who turned the radio talk into gibberish for us ?'

'It was—and I'm proud of it. A stupid waste. Just mischief and showing off. I did warn you, though. I mean, about the butler thing. Yes, I'll keep out of the sitting room. But remember, your husband's a very worried man. Almost desperate, I'd say.' He returned to his dishes.

'Oh—yes—well, goodnight, Engram.' She was out of the kitchen in time to follow Brian into the sitting room. She watched him pull out the small writing table, put his brief case on it, bring out some papers. Then he looked up. 'Thought you were turning in, Marion.'

'I want to talk to you first, Brian.'

'Won't it keep ? I may have to take a very important call from Sam Foley, and anyhow I have some work to do—'

'For Heaven's sake,' cried Marion with some passion, 'just try for a few minutes to forget Sam Foley and your Fallowfield Trust—and listen to what I have to say—'

'Cool it then.' He waited a moment and then spoke not angrily but with great emphasis. 'But don't start telling me to forget Sam Foley. I wish to God I could. And the Trust. But you might as well know now we're living with a bomb ticking under the floor. On Monday it might go off and blow me and Sam Foley and the Fallowfield Investment Trust into the headlines and then into one law court or another. That's how dangerously we're living, girl. These next two days it's touch and go—and probably *go* unless we're lucky as well as clever.'

'You're not frightening me, Brian. I know you *are* clever.'

'Maybe—and many thanks! But I'll tell you something that'll surprise you, Marion. I'm not as clever as I thought I was. So it may have to be luck. And that could be running out. Want a drink ?' He was already moving to the bar.

'No. And you don't either.'

'Seems to me I do.' He poured one out to prove it. 'Well—go on—'

'I'd rather wait until you've settled down, to listen quietly, Brian. Please!'

He took his drink and then sat down, not too far away, not too close to her. 'Well—I'm listening.'

'Now I'm wondering how to begin—'

'Oh—a confession is it?'

'Sort of one. I know I haven't chosen a good time to come out with it. But I'd never have any peace of mind now if I didn't tell you the truth, Brian.' After a pause it came out with a rush. 'A man died yesterday. His name was Lawrence Blade. He was a painter, quite a good one. I knew him before I met you. I fell in love with him. For nearly two years—on and off because there were quarrels —I lived with him. I knew he'd no intention of marrying me, but I didn't care, I was so much in love with him.' Her voice was going out of control, so she waited. 'Then he said he'd had enough and was going to live in Paris. After a few days I went to find him, though I didn't even know where he was living in Paris. It took me a week to find out, one of the worst weeks I ever remember—'

'So that's why you never wanted to go to Paris?' And he looked more amused than concerned.

'Yes, it may be all very glamorous and delicious if you're in the right mood and in the right company, but it seemed to me just greedy, brutal and heartless.'

'You may be right at that,' he told her.

'I found Lawrence at last. He was already living with an American girl, another painter, and they made it quite obvious that I was just a bloody nuisance. I crawled back home—'

'A very nasty experience,' said Brian, who had already given her a sympathetic nod or two. 'Take it easy, Marion. I know the rest. Your father died and left you a little money. You joined your cousin Violet, who had a flat in Knightsbridge, where I met you—'

'And where I was Cousin Marion from the country,' she said bitterly, 'who of course had led a sheltered life.' Then, a sudden outburst. 'My God—I can't remember now if it was Violet or you or me who first trotted out that phoney pseudo-Victorian *sheltered-life* nonsense—'

It was then that Pony, looking bedraggled, burst in. 'Hi!' It was aimed straight at Brian. 'You must be my Uncle Brian. I'm Pony. Back from Dullsville. Thursley, where the action isn't. Hitch-hiked there and returned here on the back of motorcycle. Marion, no

[35]

breakfast—can't face it—but I can always take some coffee about eleven. You two staying in tomorrow night?'

'No we're not,' said Marion, trying not to look and sound disgusted. 'We're going to a party given by some people called Jarman. I don't think you'd enjoy it.'

'Are you kidding? I'd have to be gagged and bound. 'Bye for now!' She had never really come into the room, and now she vanished.

'Cheeky little piece, I'd say,' Brian remarked.

'If not worse. I oughtn't to say it, but I can't bear her. But never mind her, it's you I'm thinking about. I thought I understood you, but now I see I don't. I nerved myself to confess about Lawrence Blade, certain you'd be furious. But you're not even mildly surprised.' She stopped, to give him a long suspicious look. 'That's it. You must have found out.'

'I did. And of course from Violet. Somebody once said that if you give 'em time men always blurt out their own secrets and women always tell other women's. I even went to have a look at Lawrence Blade. Got a man I know to take me round his studio. You didn't miss anything there. Hadn't weathered well at all. Bloated and boozy—'

She said hotly, 'If I'd been still living with him, he wouldn't have been.'

'Possible but unlikely. Most men go their own way, women or no women.'

'But if you knew, why didn't you ever say anything to me?'

'No point in it.'

'But if this is true,' she persisted, still with some heat, 'why did you go on talking this ridiculous rubbish about my having lived a sheltered life?'

'Extraordinary, isn't it?' He managed a grin that was also rueful. 'Why, when I was first talking to Engram, when I thought he'd been kidding you, I told him you were a clever woman in your way but inclined to be a bit naïve, because you'd led a sheltered life before I married you. There's a sort of parrot in my head that insists upon repeating this dam' nonsense. I know very well you're not a clever woman, though no worse for that, and I'd known for the last four or five years that before you met me you'd gone lolloping in and out of bed with a boozy painter—'

'All right, sneer away,' she cried. 'But it doesn't make any real difference. I've been thinking all day about Lawrence, remembering the best parts of our life together. And then Engram—this was just after he arrived—told me something, made me see something—' she checked herself. 'No, I'm not going to talk about it. And we won't mention Lawrence Blade again.' Now her voice lost its sharp edge and she looked at him in a different way. 'After all, when you found out, Brian, you never said anything, didn't reproach me, didn't show any jealousy. And I'm thankful and grateful for that, Brian. Apart from these outbursts of temper that have been much worse—and I know it's because you're worried about money—you've been a good generous husband—and I've tried to be a good wife—and we've shared the disappointment about children.'

He didn't receive this unpleasantly but there was a rather too obvious suggestion of being patient. 'Yes, Marion—and I agree with all that. But we can save it for another time.' He glanced at his watch. 'There may be a call from Sam Foley coming through any minute now.'

Cooler now. 'Well, I'm going. And I'm making up the bed in your dressing room.'

'Quite right. I may be up late.'

Six

AFTER ABOUT FIVE minutes the call from Sam Foley came through. 'Yes, Sam, I'm here. What news? . . . I know it was that kind of dinner. You warned me. But didn't you have a quiet word with Laster? . . . I see. Bloody stuffed shirt! Doesn't look hopeful there, does it? . . . *Which* figure? . . . Wait a moment, I have it here.' He hurried across to consult one of the papers out of his brief case. 'Sam, I make it round about a hundred and eighty-three thousand. . . . I know it isn't . . . Well, I'm trying golf tomorrow too. I've a guest card from the Goreworth and there might be a lot of money playing there tomorrow—at least three merchant bankers to my knowledge. Keep your fingers crossed, Sam, and I'll cross mine for you. . . . You needn't tell *me*, for Pete's sake. I'm living with it day and night. . . . Well, get yourself a drink. That's what I'm about to do. . . . 'Night, Sam.'

He left the telephone for the bar and had poured out a lot of whisky and not very much soda when he found that Pony was almost at his elbow. 'Hi!' she was saying cheerfully, 'what about one for me?'

She was wearing a rather threadbare dressing gown over pyjamas, but she had obviously tarted herself up for this appearance and looked far more attractive than she had done earlier.

'Thought you'd gone to bed,' he grumbled. 'But I can't refuse you a drink while I'm having one. No Coke here, though.'

'Coke up yours, big boy! Scotch on the rocks if you have any ice.' As he made the drink, she chattered away. 'No action tonight. No

[38]

speed, no acid, not even a few joints.'

'Joints?'

'Pot, reefers, grass, marijuana—'

'Here's your drink. And, Pony, if you talk like that in public around here, you could soon be in real trouble.'

'That's what Jock said, but I've been around in the States and can take care of myself—'

'Who's Jock?'

'Jock Tusker—your driver—'

'And my driver not much longer,' said Brian, annoyed. 'Hadn't taken one of my two cars out, had he?'

'No, I told you how I got to Dullsville and back. Picked me up in a bar. Stuffy, though he's not. Talks big about tomorrow, Jock does.'

'He could be lying. He often is.' He took his drink across to the writing table. 'Now if you'll excuse me, Pony, I've some work waiting here.'

She went to stand close to him, putting a hand on his shoulder. 'Now listen—I'm disappointed in you, man. When I looked in earlier I said to myself "This Sir Brian's quite something and he's not really related to you, Pony." And I'm a girl who can take an older man.'

'Take him *where?*'

Her hand crept from his shoulder to his neck. 'Wherever he wants to go, if we're all in the mood. But so far you talk as if you're stuffy or chicken—or both. Don't be like that. Ree-lax.'

'Cheeky young devil, aren't you?' He gave a short laugh. 'What are you trying to do—seduce me?'

'I might start trying at that. Just to make *something* happen.'

He took it lightly, half laughing. 'I wouldn't advise it. To begin with, I'm old enough to be your father.'

'Don't give me that one.' Her hand was now caressing his cheek. 'You're not my father, just another attractive man. We don't want our own generation all the time, y'know. They're not *that* good neither, most of 'em—'

'But they haven't got business problems, worrying them, weighing them down—'

'No, but a lot of them have their own problems—worse for a girl—keeps them getting you into bed like trying to pass an exam. Besides, like I told you, what you ought to do now is—*ree-la-ax.*'

Swiftly and very neatly she kissed him.

'By the way, Pony,' he said rather hoarsely, 'in my circle we kiss but don't tell.'

'Then here's something not to tell.' And this time the kiss was a long one, and while one of her hands was on the back of his neck, the other was wandering.

Rather out of breath he disentangled himself and tried to recover a little age and dignity. 'Well—well! I only met your mother once, Pony, but I'd say you neither look like her nor behave like her.'

'You can say that again. I look and behave like my father's family —and—boy!—they're *wild*. Another thing. We don't stick around. Take me—I'm restless. Even if there's some action tomorrow, I might be off again in a couple of days. Paris maybe—or Rome— know some groovy ones in both places.' Standing apart from him now, but with her dressing gown wide open, she gave him a challenging stare. 'Hell!—we're wasting lovely time, man. You want it. I have it for you. And if you'll do any real work now, I must be slipping. You know where my room is, opposite end of the corridor from where you ought to be.'

He said nothing but nodded several times.

'Okay!' she said, smiling. 'I'll finish this drink upstairs. You can have quarter of an hour to kid yourself you're doing some work. So—be seeing you.'

Brian shuffled his papers around without really applying his mind to any of them. Wanting to talk rather than to work, he was not sorry to see Engram, who said, 'If it won't disturb you, I'll begin clearing up in here.' He looked completely at ease, smoking a pipe.

This may have shaped Brian's opening remarks. 'I don't understand you, Engram. It would hurt my pride to go round as you do —living on tuppence—doing odd jobs—taking orders from all kinds of silly sods.'

Engram emptied two small ashtrays into a larger one. 'I don't do very much domestic work of this sort. But it doesn't hurt my pride. A wise man said we all have two giants who go in front of us— changing everything to please us, but making it all unreal. They are Pride and Vanity. I'm trying to bring them down from giants to dwarfs.'

This made the other man impatient. 'That's all very fine and fancy, Engram. But here you are, staying up to empty ashtrays and wash glasses, just bumming around, and here am I, younger than you, a clerk once, responsible for big sums of money, given a knighthood, a well-known respected figure in the City—'

Engram did not speak sharply. 'Well, if that's what you want. And it lasts—'

Brian stopped him. 'Now, wait a minute, Engram. Either somebody's told you something or you spend a lot of time reading the financial sections—'

'Haven't looked at them for years. Hardly look at newspapers at all. But I told you earlier you're a very worried man, running into trouble.'

There was now a lightning change of mood. 'My God—I am! Look, Engram, I'd say you're close-mouthed, and this is in the strictest confidence. If I can't raise a quarter of a million by Monday morning, I'm going down the drain. I've just three or four chances left, over the week end.' Then he returned with a jump to his earlier mood. 'But even so, I'm leading a man's life—a dam' sight better than drifting around doing somebody else's housework.'

Engram spoke very gently. 'Even in the last minute, two quite different Brian Carfitts have talked to me.' He paused while the other man began putting his papers back into the brief case. 'No more work? What are you going to do now?'

Brian looked up with a grin. 'Believe it or not, Engram, I'm about to enjoy myself. Never mind how.' He glanced at his watch.

Engram relit his pipe. 'And believe it or not,' he murmured, 'that makes a *third* Brian Carfitt talking to me—quite different from the other two—'

Brian had finished his drink. 'What *is* this nonsense? What are you trying to tell me, Engram? And keep it fairly short because I must leave you in a minute.' He was standing up now and the two men were facing each other. There was challenge in the air between them.

This time Engram spoke with a touch of severity. 'I'm trying to tell you how far away you are yet from being anything like a complete person. It's just as if you had in your head a disorganized radio repertory company, all of them snatching the microphone to give their own performance of Brian Carfitt.'

As he left his writing table, Brian said sourly, 'And *I* think that's a lot of balls.'

Calling cheerfully as the other made for the door: 'And that makes the *fourth* Brian Carfitt we've had—'

Over his shoulder as Brian reached the door: 'And again—*balls!*'

Moving easily and efficiently Engram did all it was necessary to do in the sitting room, and then went to the pantry for some final washing up and putting away. A few minutes later, Marion appeared, wearing an apricot dressing gown but not looking like a fugitive from bed.

'I suddenly remembered I hadn't said anything to you about breakfast, so I had to come down,' she explained rather hastily. 'We don't have anything cooked—just toast and coffee, and I'll attend to that, so you don't have to bother at all with it. We'll have to talk about lunch sometime during the morning of course. And that might be rather important because we're not dining here tomorrow but going out for one of those buffet suppers that are usually rather unsatisfactory.'

She ended out of breath. He had nodded a few times to show that he was listening but, without saying a word, he continued to stare at her expectantly.

'All right, you win,' she said finally, bitterness breaking out. 'It's true about breakfast, but I really came down to tell you that Brian's just gone into that wretched girl's bedroom. Nice, isn't it? My own niece—half his age—and he's only just set eyes on her. My God—I can't understand it. Can you?'

'Oh yes, quite easily.' His manner was quite casual. 'A full-blooded man, crammed with food and hazy with drink, feeling desperately insecure—why, a girl like Pony, who takes sex as some people take aspirin, could seduce him in ten minutes. And not his own niece really.'

'Now you're defending him,' she complained.

He handed her two coffee cups to put away. 'I'm not defending him. I'm not prosecuting him. I'm explaining him.'

'Perhaps that's easier than being married to him.'

'Of course. Two more cups, if you don't mind.'

After a pause. 'I hope your room's comfortable, Engram.'

'Hardly know it yet. But I'm sure it will be.'

Her hesitation now made her meaning quite clear. 'Shall I—go up with you—and, well, make certain it's comfortable?'

'No,' he told her gently. 'You don't really want to make love in my room. You want revenge. It never works.'

She turned away to do something to the shelf where the coffee cups had gone. 'You're right. I'm being silly. I'm often silly. Not like Joyce Roke.'

'On a long term view you're better situated. You're still open. She's folded herself up.'

She gave him a long wondering look, then said simply, 'Engram, I believe you're a magician.'

He laughed. 'I wish I was. Then I'd have said to those dishes, plates, glasses, cups, "Go clean and dry yourselves and put yourselves away."'

'Now you're laughing at me, Engram. And really I was being serious. I want to know—why—' But there she stopped.

'Why what?'

'No, I'm not going to ask that question tonight. I might not like the answer. And I don't want to be lying awake half the night—wondering and worrying. After all, we'll have to meet in the morning to talk about lunch. But I'll risk another question. Are you really *friendly*—not just laughing at us? And I mean Brian as well as me. I know he shouted at you when you'd told him not to. But then you played that gibberish trick—that was you, wasn't it?—and ruined his radio talk and put everybody into a bad temper. Somehow that seemed to me *unkind*, not like you were before when you showed me how to bring alive that scene with Lawrence Blade on the bridge. So are you or aren't you really *friendly*, Engram?'

'I hope I am, Marion,' he replied carefully. 'I don't choose to live with people for two days just to laugh at them. I'm not proud of that gibberish trick, as you call it, but then I've already told you that. It was a childish waste of power. But as for the bad temper, it's not always harmful to encourage that, even though it's always harmful to indulge in it. But—as you say—we'll have to meet in the morning, and now it's late. So off you go, back to bed, while I take a final look round to see everything's in order. Goodnight, Marion.'

'Goodnight, Engram. And—thank you.'

Seven

IT WAS ABOUT eleven o'clock next morning, Saturday, when they met again, this time in the kitchen, to discuss lunch. Brian had gone off to his rich men's golf club. Pony was presumably still in bed. 'I've explored your magnificent 'fridge and looked round the larder,' Engram was explaining, 'and for what I've planned I don't think you'll have to run to Thursley for anything.'

'I'm glad to hear it,' said Marion. 'I hate shopping at Thursley on Saturday morning. But of course if I have to, I'll go. I have my little car. What have you planned then?'

'Hors d'oeuvres. Open a tin of sardines. You have some tomatoes. We finish the paté. Perhaps a couple of sliced hard-boiled eggs. Good enough?' After she had nodded and smiled, he went on: 'Then for our main course I thought I'd try a *lasagne à la bolognese*, which I usually do quite well. Do you know it?'

She didn't think she did.

'Layers of noodles—and I see you have some—alternating with layers of minced meat, chopped onion, tomato purée, a touch of garlic perhaps—cheese on top—and of course baked in the oven.'

'Can I watch you prepare it, Engram? Then perhaps I could try it later. I've never learnt to cook properly. Where did you learn?'

'I just picked it up. Some members of our group—men and women—are superb cooks. It's very ironical that while we're regarded from the outside as a number of vague crackpots, we're actually unusually efficient, able to tackle anything, from a building to a banquet. Well, let's make a start.'

[44]

There followed the oddest morning Marion had ever spent. She was bursting to talk seriously to Engram but at the same time wanted to play her part as his cookery assistant or pupil. In between trips to the 'fridge and the larder and the pantry and all the preparations in the kitchen, taking care not to question him when his mind was obviously concentrated on his immediate task, eagerly she took what chances came her way.

Brian was discussed first. 'I ought to tell you, so that you'll not be disappointed, after taking so much trouble,' she said, 'that Brian may not come back to lunch from that rich golf club. He can lunch there, and he may want to do.'

'That doesn't surprise me. He's gone there to look for money, and it might be easier to find at lunchtime.'

'Do you understand that world?'

'Yes, I was in it—once. In another existence, it seems now. Time for another layer of noodles.'

It was two or three minutes later when she asked another question. 'He's very worried about money, isn't he?'

'You might as well know. Brian's feeling desperate. I'd already guessed it, but he told me so last night just before he went up to Pony's room. Incidentally, that's one reason he accepted her invitation—and I'm sure she invited him—just because it was at least something he *could* do, to prove his manhood. Probably about nine-tenths of promiscuous sex is a mixture of insecurity and vanity. Now for more of the meat paste.'

A little later, she said, 'Please go on about Brian. I think I understand him, but he doesn't tell me enough. For instance, I didn't know he was feeling really desperate.'

'Like a lot of people now, he lives in a bad place in his inner world. He faces out all the time, never looks inside. He's never even tried yet to begin forming some central self. He can talk and behave like four quite different men in as many minutes. I told him so but of course he didn't listen. Men of his type never listen, they simply start shouting.'

'As he did at you. And that's why you dislike him.' Out of a certain loyalty to her husband, a challenge entered her voice.

'No, Marion, I don't dislike him. I'm not talking out of dislike. I'm trying to explain him, in terms of my own particular beliefs. What else can I do if you ask me about him? By the way, if he doesn't come back to lunch, we'll have to be greedy and eat most of

[45]

the *lasagne* ourselves. Now what about a suitable cheese? What have you got? Try the larder if you don't remember.'

'I must. Isabella ordered all kinds of things I never asked for. I don't think she was dishonest but I'm sure he was.'

When the cheese problem was finally settled, she risked another question, her voice trembling a little. 'Please tell me this, Engram. Would Brian kill anybody?'

He replied very slowly. 'Not unless there came a moment when one Brian Carfitt swept all the others away.'

'Just mad temper.'

'If you like. The real killers, psychopaths, are quite different. To them other people aren't real, just things to be destroyed. Brian's not like that at all of course.'

'I know that. He can be very kind and considerate. Only he is beginning to lose his temper far more often.' She waited a moment, then in a low voice, almost a whisper: 'Could he kill himself?'

'I don't think so,' he said carefully. 'People who do have usually carried the seeds of self-destruction in themselves for years. Some of us believe they pay a heavy price for suicide in their after-life, when they may keep returning over and over again to the moment when they decided to blot out themselves, looking for an extinction that never arrives. But Brian—well? It's always possible that a proud man, with no inner resources, entirely dependent on the world's opinion, when he finds everything crashing down, facing humiliation, perhaps a prison sentence, may decide to jump into the dark, hoping that's the end of him.'

'But that couldn't happen to Brian, could it?' And she gripped his arm.

'It could. But I hope not.'

'Engram—please—please—won't you help him? I believe you could. You could, couldn't you?'

'Well, I can try.' He left it at that although she waited for him to go on. When he turned aside, she went away as if suddenly remembering something she had to do.

It must have been half an hour later when she faced him again. She came straight out with the question that he knew had been in her mind all morning.

'I have to ask you this, Engram,' she began earnestly. 'Why have you decided to stay here until late tonight? Is there something you want to do here while we're out?'

Eight

IT WAS EARLY evening. After a bath, leisurely if far from being luxurious, in the staff bathroom at the end of his landing, Engram got dressed, no longer wearing the houseman's coat, lit a pipe and drifted at ease downstairs. The door from the hall into the sitting room was wide open, and he saw that Brian, in a jersey, old pants, bedroom slippers, was at the telephone.

'Joyce,' Brian was saying, 'hope you weren't in the middle of dressing. . . . Well, it's about tonight. This so-and-so of a chauffeur of mine is missing again, but then he's under notice and I'll kick him out in the morning—if he does turn up. And—you know—I've stopped driving if I'm going to do any drinking, and I don't suppose the Jarmans' party will be exactly dry. . . . Well, yes, Joyce, that's just what I want you to do. It'll be no trouble will it, just picking us up and bringing us back afterwards ? . . . O—ho, Engram! You're getting as bad as Marion. Yes—he'll be around. Told me he wasn't going out. . . . You do ? Then I can take a bit longer cleaning up and changing. . . . 'Bye now, then!'

Engram went in. 'Thought I overheard my name.'

'You did,' said Brian. 'Joyce Roke is coming to pick us up and doesn't mind waiting for a few minutes if she can have a nice little chat with you. What do you do to these women ?'

'They think I'm a mystery man,' said Engram, smiling.

'Well, you are, aren't you ?'

'Not at all. Do I offer her a drink ?'

Brian grinned. 'So long as it's a Campari and soda or a Dubonnet

[49]

and not some socking great dry martini.' Then he looked solemn. 'Now this is important. I may have a call from Sam Foley, who's my Number Two in the Trust. This may be Saturday night, but we're still on the job. Now I don't want Sam to ring and get no reply. You *are* staying in, aren't you?'

'Oh—yes. I'll be up in my room working on some notes. I have a talk to give in the morning.'

'That's okay so long as you leave your door open. The point is, there's a phone on your landing near your stairs. You can take any call there, so long as you make sure it's switched through from here. Look—if you don't mind—I'll show you. I'll also give you the number of the Jarmans' house in case Sam rings up while I'm over there. All right?'

'Why not?' It seemed to Engram unnecessary and stupid but he felt he ought to humour a deeply worried man. Five minutes later he returned from the top of the house to the sitting room to find a visitor who had not troubled to do any bell-ringing or knocking. He was carrying a record album and was taking a look at the radiogram. When he turned to face Engram, the latter saw that he was a tallish youth, slackly put together, who had a pasty face and a lot of hair all round it. The youth nodded and said 'Hi!'

Engram nodded and said, 'Good evening!'

The youth pointed to himself. 'Len Tabbs. Call me Len.'

Engram pointed to himself. 'Engram. Call me Engram.'

'You Pony's uncle?'

'No, not anybody's uncle.'

Len put his record album on the radiogram. 'Told to come here. Bring some of my pop discs. Got some smashing pop discs. Like to hear one? It'll sound okay on this machine.'

'No thanks.'

Len seemed to be surprised. 'Why not?'

'Various reasons,' said Engram. 'Too noisy. Too monotonous. And somebody will be calling shortly.'

'I'm too early? Trouble is—haven't got a watch. Where's Pony?'

'Not here, and I don't know where she might be. Perhaps Tusker's taken her somewhere—trying to find—and I quote—grass, speed, acid, even horse. Have I got them right?'

'Spot on. Asked me to bring some good discs, they'd do the rest. Then we have ourselves a ball if this machine can belt it out, and I don't see why it shouldn't if I give it plenty of juice. Better try it, though.'

'No, Len, I told you. I don't like it, and anyhow we'll have another visitor soon. I may be wrong, but I can't help feeling that Mrs Roke might not enjoy hearing you belt it out.'

'Hold it there.' Len pulled a face. 'Did you say *Mrs Roke*? She must be Jill Roke's Mum, and I'm not letting her catch me here. Had a proper sodding turn-up with her about young Jill. Are you broad-minded, Engram?'

'I try to be, Len.'

'Well, she isn't—Mrs Roke. She's got a nasty tongue and a nasty temper. She'd make war not love any time, she would. Typical! And she's like the rest of 'em. She doesn't know she's finished—*out* —just waiting to be nailed down and buried—'

Engram relit his pipe. 'She certainly didn't seem to know that when she was here last night. After all, she's only about forty—'

'Well I ask you, man—*forty !*'

'No use asking me, Len. I'm well over forty. Apparently I ought to have been nailed down and buried years and years ago.' He perched on the arm of a chair. 'And I don't know what you're going to do about this, Len.'

'How d'you mean?'

'Well, you can't win, can you?' said Engram cheerfully. 'You're facing the wrong way. Soon you'll be thirty. Then you'll be forty— finished—*out*.'

'Listen,' said Len anxiously. 'And never mind that bullshit. What's the quickest way out? 'Cos as soon as I hear Mrs Roke ringing at the front door, I'm pissing off—sharp!'

'Well, the very quickest way would be through the french windows there.' And he pointed to the curtains.

Len went to poke his head between the curtains, and then seemed more at ease when he came back. 'That's okay. Out like a shot! Then I can keep an eye on the front to see her go.'

'One thing we've overlooked though, Len,' said Engram mischievously. 'What if Mrs Roke doesn't ring the bell but walks straight in?'

'Go on! She'd never do that.'

'But you did. No bells, no knocks—and I find you in here looking at the radiogram—'

'But that's different, isn't it?' Len protested, quite indignantly.

'I see Pony and Jock Tusker in the George last night. She tells me to come here with my discs. We'll have the place to ourselves, she says. Okay—so I walk in. No bells, no knocks, none of that with us. You lot don't understand. We've burst out. We're on our way—'

'You are?' Engram said as if surprised. 'Where are you going?'

Len now seemed to be quoting some favourite orator. 'To a free life. You lot put yourselves in prison. We've let ourselves out. You couldn't do that. You'd be frightened. We know how to live without fear.'

'You do?'

'We do. Man, we really do.'

'But what about you and Mrs Roke?' said Engram.

'Aw—come off it! That's different, isn't it? I'm not frightened of her. But she can make trouble. And I don't like trouble. For instance, my Dad's a dentist, and this Mrs Roke sees him sometimes.'

'Don't you get along with your father?'

'Are you kidding? All he understands is teeth. And that's a life, isn't it? Looking at rotten teeth all day long. And then tearing off to his borders and his greenhouse, as if they'd got teeth. And mean as hell to me now. If it wasn't for Mum, I'd never have a penny—no discs, no films, nothing for the George or Coffee Corner.'

'You don't—er—work at anything—earn any money, Len?' Engram enquired mildly.

'Not at the moment. Just looking round. And ever since I had that argument with that silly old sod at the Labour Exchange—' But then the front door bell rang. 'She's here. Be seeing you!' And off he dashed, through the curtains, out of the window.

Joyce Roke, wearing a long outdoor coat, asked Engram how he was, and then moved briskly into the sitting room.

'I'm empowered to offer you a drink,' said Engram smiling. 'Something light was suggested, as you're driving. Dubonnet—Campari and soda—that kind of drink—'

'Dubonnet, please.' She unbuttoned her coat and sat down. 'And I wish you'd give yourself something, and not wander off somewhere. I dashed over specially so that we could talk.'

'A most handsome compliment,' said Engram while he poured out two drinks. 'We're leading a quiet life here at the moment.'

'So I gathered from Marion, who of course has been telling me all—over the phone. Oh—you're having a drink too. Good! Sitting down, I hope? Also, good! Now we can talk. Is it going to last?'

'The quiet life? Probably not.'

Her sharp eyes flashed; her sharp nose twitched. 'And you're waiting for it to blow up—um?' As he made no reply, she tried again. 'Perhaps you came here to blow it up?'

'Certainly not,' said Engram, no longer smiling. 'Why should I? I came here by accident—'

'But with this girl—Pony—'

'Completely unknown to me an hour before we came here together.'

She looked hard at him. 'Yes, I know. Marion's told me all about that. And I've never set eyes on the girl. But let's suppose something, Engram. And let me add I've been thinking about you ever since last night. Not like Marion, who adores you—'

'Not really. She's just been inventing exciting feminine chat to keep you interested over the telephone. Some women can't resist it.'

'I know, though you shouldn't. But now let's suppose something. Let's suppose that as soon as you'd talked to this girl, Pony, on the road, before you got here, you realized she was a kind of catalyst—one of those fatally destructive personalities who break up any little society that receives them. So you have to see what happens here after Pony arrives.'

'Just mischievous curiosity?' Engram shook his head.

'Curiosity certainly. I'm not quite sure about the mischievous part of it, because I'm not quite sure about you. I'm wondering if you're a white magician or a black magician.'

Now he smiled. 'I can help you there, Joyce. I'm not a magician at all.'

'Well, don't let's waste time arguing about the meaning of magician. I have a problem.' She hesitated for a moment. 'Do I or don't I tell the poor Carfitts what I believe—that you realized this girl was a destructive personality—a group breaker-down—so you insisted upon staying on just to see what would happen? You're in the lab and we're the rats and mice.' As Engram mildly tried to interrupt her. 'No, let me finish this. It's the only theory that fits the facts. Don't tell me you stayed on because you'd nowhere to go and like to do a little cooking. Rats and mice to that! Then again, you have to leave tonight—but *late tonight*. So why late tonight?'

'Surely that's quite simple,' he told her. 'I can't stay the night because I'm due elsewhere fairly early in the morning. So I stay as

[53]

late as I can.'

'To do *what*? No, don't answer that or we're just going round in a circle.'

'People usually are when they talk.'

'So I'll say again—you insisted upon staying just to see what would happen after this girl, Pony, the disaster, came here.'

Engram replied quite gently. 'But you're an intelligent woman, Joyce. Can't you see it's far more complicated than that? Pony the disaster arrived in what was already a disaster area. Both the Carfitts were facing a crisis. Marion because her old lover, probably the one magic man in her life, had just died. Brian because he's trying to rescue his Investment Trust and his whole financial career from ruin. And there's a further complication—'

She cut in eagerly: 'I know what you're going to say. Marion told me. The wretched Pony, probably because she hadn't any dope, proceeded at once to seduce Brian—no great feat but despicable in the circumstances. Oh yes, I'll grant you the Carfitt crisis and the disaster area.'

'Thank you! But there's still another complication. I happen to know something about Pony that nobody else knows *yet*.'

'What is it?' She waited for a reply but when none came, she said impatiently, 'All right, keep it. I suppose being secretive is part of your game.'

Emphatically for him, Engram said, '*I'm not playing a game*.' And he looked hard at her while saying this, so that she had to say something herself to escape embarrassment.

It was time for a lighter touch. 'Anyhow, though Alfred and I keep popping in and out, we Rokes are obviously not involved.' He was fiddling with his pipe and said nothing, so she was impatient again. 'Tired of talking to me, Engram?'

He looked up and smiled. 'Not at all, Joyce.'

'Well then, we Rokes aren't involved, are we?'

'I don't know.'

'Oh—come off it!' she cried. 'You've just called me an intelligent woman, and I can look after myself. As for poor old Alfred—' She checked herself and stared at him. '*Jill*? You're thinking about Jill, aren't you?'

'I'm not,' Engram replied coolly. 'But now *you* are.'

'I'm not worrying about Jill. She may not look it, but she's still only a child.'

'I can't agree or disagree,' said Engram, 'never having seen her.'

'Tonight she's staying in for once, probably adoring some pop idiot on the telly.' Because he said nothing, she made several impatient little movements, and finally, clearly feeling uneasy, she went to the telephone and hastily began dialling. 'Alfred? Me, darling.' She spoke in a falsely bright tone. 'Hope you're not all ready now and impatiently waiting, because the Carfitts aren't down yet. . . . Of course I will. Is Jill glued to the telly? . . . *What!* . . . Going to Maureen? Alfred, you believe anything that child tells you. . . . Don't you see she just waited until I'd gone. . . . Perhaps. And then again perhaps not.' She banged down the receiver, still very angry.

She spoke to Engram because she had to speak to somebody. 'And if I ring up this wretched Maureen's parents and ask if Jill's there—and she isn't—I'll feel a complete fool.'

'Have another drink.'

'Certainly not,' she replied crossly. 'And just remember, Engram, *you* started all this.'

But he was firm with her. 'I did nothing of the kind—and you know it. I never even mentioned your daughter. The worrying maternal Joyce took over from the confident Engram-baiting Joyce—'

'Oh—I know all that stuff. Too many different warring selves and no central controlling self—'

He pointed his pipe at her. 'You *know* it but you don't feel it. You're the opposite of Marion Carfitt, who feels but doesn't know—'

'If you have to give a lecture tomorrow morning,' she said sharply, 'don't start it now.'

'You're quite right of course.'

'And don't be so damned *smooth*.'

He shook his head. 'You're hard to please this evening, Mrs Roke.'

'Chiefly because you've made me wonder and worry about Jill—'

'I never even mentioned her name—'

'You didn't need to. Simply by refusing to answer, you made me force myself into a corner—'

'Where your fear for your daughter was waiting for you. Something with tentacles in the dark.'

Now she hit back. 'Because I refuse to idolize you, as Marion does, you're trying to frighten me.'

[55]

She expected an indignant protest but none came. Engram surprised her by giving the matter some thought before he replied. 'No, I don't think so,' he said slowly. 'I don't blame you for it, but it's not true.'

Maddened by this, she exclaimed fiercely, 'Whether it is or not, don't imagine I'll allow you to turn my Jill into one of your guinea pigs.'

He waited, wonderingly, before replying. 'Joyce, among your performers there's a madwoman. I've just seen and heard her.' He gave her a sharp look and spoke sharply. 'Now listen to me. The Carfitts will be down any moment. I know nothing about your Jill and I shan't be using her or anybody else as a guinea pig. It's true I may have to try a certain experiment, but if I do it will take far more out of me than it will out of anybody else.'

'So it ought. It'll be *your* experiment. But I'm not impressed by this mystification. You can keep that for Marion. She's never been among the wise men, the gurus, the prophets—and I have. And they always left me unconvinced. Which is what you're doing, Engram.'

He ignored that. 'Well, just remember I'm not thinking about the Roke family. All that I can do, I'll do for the Carfitts. If there's a crisis.'

He stopped there because Marion, a cloak over her long dress, came into the room. 'Hello, Joyce darling! Sweet of you to call for us, and I hope we haven't kept you too long. Brian will be down in two minutes. He's having trouble with his silly electric razor. Do you use one of those things, Engram?'

'No. I enjoy lathering my face. Can I get you a drink, Marion?'

'I think not—thank you. For some reason or other—and I can't imagine what it is—I feel curiously excited about going to this Jarman party.'

Joyce made a face. 'Then you must have forgotten what the last one was like.'

'You know, Joyce, I was thinking upstairs that you and I are much too critical of people. We ought to *enjoy* them more. What do *you* say, Engram?'

'I don't say anything—except that I'm going to cut a few sandwiches for myself.'

'Do you like sandwiches?' Marion asked.

He turned at the door, smiling. 'Not much. I must try to enjoy them more.'

After Engram had gone, Marion said, 'We might as well wait in the hall. It'll save time.'

'No, just a moment,' said Joyce hastily. 'Marion—the Jarmans are generous with their booze. Can you stop Brian drinking too much, if you have to?'

Marion looked and sounded dubious. 'I can try. The trouble is —as soon as he's had too much already, he's angry if you suggest he's had enough. There you're lucky with Alfred.'

'So lucky there are times when I long to see him good and plastered, ready to make love anywhere—the back garden or somebody else's bathroom.' Then she frowned. 'I'm cross with him at the moment. I made Jill promise to stay in tonight—she could watch television—but as soon as I was out of the house she asked her father if she could go and see her friend Maureen—and then of course she was off like a shot.'

'Well, perhaps she *is* seeing her friend Maureen—'

'Not if she was off like a shot. Nobody ever hurried like that to see Maureen. And now I'm worried. And Engram didn't help—'

'He doesn't know Jill, does he?'

'No, that's not the point. But he created a sinister atmosphere—'

'Joyce, I simply won't have that. Whatever Engram is, he's not sinister. Honestly, now you're being sillier than I ever am.'

'A seventeen-year-old daughter brings out my silly side,' said Joyce. 'And I can't help wondering what the artful little monkey is up to.' They went into the hall just in time to see Brian bustling downstairs.

'Sorry, sorry, Joyce!' he shouted. 'Ought to be on our way, I know. One quick drink—'

But the women cried him down.

'All right,' said Brian. 'But where's Engram? Must have a word with him.'

'I'll fetch him,' said Marion hastily. 'No shouting for him tonight.'

When she returned with him Brian said, 'Engram, you're sure you've got this telephone thing straight? If you hear the phone on the landing, you nip along to answer it. If I'm urgently wanted, then you explain and give 'em the Jarmans' number, which you've got. Right?'

'Right,' said Engram. 'Anything else?'

'Yes, there's this.' Brian went to the hall cupboard and brought out the big shotgun.

Marion was alarmed at once. 'Oh—no!'

'Cool it, Marion,' said her husband. 'I'm not going to shoot anybody. Point is this, Engram. You'll be at the top of the house. If there's any breaking and entering—and there's been a lot of it lately—you haven't much chance of getting to this gun in time. And if it's left down here, they could find it first and threaten you with it. So I suggest you take it upstairs with you. It's loaded, by the way.'

Still agitated, Marion spoke eagerly. 'Oh—yes, please do that, Engram. Take it up and keep it by you. And then—then—well, it won't do any harm, will it?'

'All right, Marion,' Brian said impatiently, 'you don't have to get all excited—'

'How do *you* know she doesn't?' Joyce asked, rather grimly.

'Look—I'm talking to Engram now.' He offered the gun. 'Here you are. Take it with you when you go upstairs.'

'No,' said Engram. 'If we're exchanging orders, then you put it back in the cupboard. I'm not a shotgun man. I'm far more afraid of shotguns than I am of burglars.'

'Oh—well, if that's how you feel.' And Brian went to the cupboard with the gun.

Marion caught hold of Engram's arm, to plead with him. 'But Engram, can't you see—have you forgotten—'

'I haven't forgotten anything, Marion,' he told her.

Brian was bustling again. 'Come on then, must push off now. We're forgetting poor old Alfred, who must be wondering what's happened to us.'

As soon as they had gone, Engram went back to the pantry, found a large plate for his sandwiches, looked about for a bottle of claret that had been opened, filled a glass from it, and was able to find room on the plate for the glass as well as the sandwiches. Before taking it upstairs he went along to the sitting room. Len was back, and, standing near the radiogram looking through his album of records, was a dark and rather pretty young girl. Jill Roke?

Len was pleased with himself. 'Watched 'em go. Lovely. This is young Jill Roke—our Jilly-Dilly—'

She looked up from the record album. 'Hello,' she said, rather uncertainly.

'Hello!' said Engram. But then he had to attend to Len, who had taken him further away from the girl and the radiogram, almost back to the door into the hall, as if there were confidences to be exchanged.

'Now what about you?' Len asked in a low voice.

'What about me, Len?'

'Well, I mean to say—when the other two come and we get started—you're not going to keep coming in, are you?'

'No, I'll be up in my room, working on something.'

'That's okay then.' Len was almost down to a whisper. "'Cos I meant to tell you before. I'm harmless, but if Jock Tusker gets steamed up he's apt to be rough and tough. And don't forget he's finished here. Told me that last night. So he's not going to care a fart, Jock isn't. As for that Pony—smashing bird of course—but seems to me halfway up the wall. I mean to say—I've got some sense, y'know.'

'Then you take care of it, Len.'

'I have an idea you think I'm all wet.'

'Wettish, I'd say—wettish. But you could be dried out, Len.'

'And then be like my Dad and his pals. No bloody fear! Tell you another thing about him. When he's not scraping teeth or arsing about in his greenhouse, he's a Rotarian. Told me once, when he'd waited up just to shout at me, I'd never be a Rotarian. "Are you kidding?" I asked him—quiet, y'know—no shouting. I let him do the shouting.'

'Quite right, Len. There's too much shouting.'

'There are some super records here,' Jill called out. 'Can I play some?'

'Not yet, kid. The man and me are talking. You can be picking out some of your favourite numbers, Jilly.' He turned to Engram. 'I'll tell you my main trouble. Okay?'

'Yes, but keep it short, Len.'

He was very solemn. 'My main trouble—and this is what is messing me up—is that I can't find my identity. Who am I? Don't know. And there's thousands of us just the same.'

'There must be by now,' said Engram. 'I've heard and read this so often. The search for identity.'

'That's why we can't settle down, the way you lot did,' Len said earnestly. 'We have to have *experiences*—all special, y'know—to try to find ourselves.'

Engram regarded him blandly. 'One way, I'm told, is to work

[59]

flat out for twelve hours—and then go on to work another six hours. Or do a twenty-mile walk, and then as soon as you get back home, turn round and do *another ten miles.*'

'Sodding murder! You can lose that lot, man.'

'Why, they'd be special experiences, wouldn't they?'

Young Jill surprised them both by calling out, half laughing, 'He's having you on, Len.'

'Not me! I rumbled him from the start. Here—I'll get a disc going.'

'Well, keep the door shut,' Engram told him. And he closed it carefully himself as he left them.

Nine

IT WAS JUST after eleven o'clock when the Carfitts invited the Rokes to share a nightcap with them. They could hear the noise when they entered the house, and as soon as the sitting room door was opened, it was deafening, with the radiogram blasting away. There was only one small light on, and nothing could be clearly seen. But as soon as Marion switched on the other lights, she gave a shriek of dismay. The room looked half-wrecked. A small table and two chairs had been overturned; a curtain had been torn, a large vase with flowers was lying on the floor; and there were broken bottles and glasses on the bar counter. At the far end of the room, all of them in various stages of undress, Pony, Tusker and a strange giggling young man were in some sort of obscene tangle, and not far away, crouching on the floor, white-faced and whimpering, was Jill Roke.

Now several things happened all at once. Marion was crying, 'Look what you've done! Look what you've done!' The Rokes were calling to Jill. In a fury of energy, Brian switched off the radiogram and then, shouting 'I'll show these bastards—my God I will!', hurried out of the room. The giggling young man pointed at Roke and said, 'Piss off, Dad!' And Tusker, goggle-eyed and standing up now, though uncertainly, bawled, 'Len, why don't we do the old sod?' But by this time Brian, roaring with rage, was back, carrying his shotgun: 'I'll show you why—you bloody scum! Look out, Marion!'

But as he raised and pointed the gun, Marion gave a scream, turned and tried to take it away from him. In the struggle, the gun, pointing to the ceiling, went off. The sound, very loud, shocked them all—except Marion who had been flung aside and was sobbing —into momentary silence and stillness. But then Brian brought down the gun to point it at Tusker.

'*Stop! All of you—stop!*' Engram had arrived unnoticed, and his command—for it was a command and not an appeal—had such a curious intensity that it seemed to freeze them.

He took the gun away from Brian, who appeared to be dazed and quite unable to resist him. He gave the gun to Marion, now on her feet again, and said to her sharply, 'Put that gun away, Marion.' He then moved to Roke, staring hard at him, then to Jill, who stopped whimpering, and from her to Len, to Pony, to Tusker, who all answered his stare vaguely and helplessly. As he moved down the room again and passed Brian and Roke they turned their heads stiffly to look at him. It was as if all six were hypnotised and were awaiting instructions. But this did not apply to Joyce Roke nor to Marion, who had now come back.

'This is all your fault,' cried Joyce angrily. 'Why did you allow it?'

'Yes—why—why—?' said Marion. 'I'm furious with you, Engram.'

'I told you this morning that you would be,' he replied coldly. 'But I didn't undertake to stay here as a children's nurse. Both of you keep quiet—and listen.' He moved forward and after running a hand across his forehead, for he was now sweating hard, he waved it in a large signal to the six as if to unfreeze them. There followed a scene that neither woman was ever able to forget. Brian and Roke spoke and behaved exactly like schoolboys of twelve or thirteen. Jill, Len, Pony and Tusker were now like spoilt children between three to five years of age, and spoke or chanted in sing-song and jumped and bounced up and down as such children often do.

Brian was saying, 'Rokie—I say, Rokie—did you see what happened? That man took my gun away.'

'Then he's a rotten stinker,' said Roke. 'Though it serves you jolly well right, Brian—'

And all the four, chanting and bouncing: 'The man took his gun away. The man took his gun away.'

Boy Brian said, 'You shut up, you silly little idiots.'

And boy Roke said, 'Buzz off—and play at trains or something.'

To which infant Len replied, 'We don't want to play at trains.'

And the other three infants joined in and chanted, 'We don't want to play at trains.'

Brian to Roke: 'You fat-headed chump, how d'you mean it served me right—about my gun?'

Roke jeered at him: 'Served you right, 'cos you were showing off —swanky swanky Brian Carfitt—'

The infant four now began a chorus of 'Swanky—Swanky— Swanky—Swanky—Swanky—' that continued while Brian and Roke, as small boys so often do, started to push and pummel each other.

Infant Tusker sang triumphantly, 'They're fighting—they're fighting—'

'Scratching and biting' came from Pony.

But Jill, as the youngest infant, was now rather tearful. 'But they're *fighting*. I'll tell Mummie—I will, I'll tell her—'

This took Joyce to Engram's side, where she dug her nails into his arm. 'Engram, stop it now, please—*please!* I must rescue Jill.'

Still sweating hard and now looking exhausted, Engram nodded and moved rather stiffly into the space between the two men and the four young people. He looked round at them, made a broad chopping movement of the hand, looked round at them again, then found his way to a distant chair and sank into it, his head in his hands.

'It's all right, Jill darling,' said Joyce as she went to her daughter. 'I'm here. Coming to take you away. But let's put the rest of your things on, darling.'

The others were out of their boy and small child characters but were not moving or talking, as if they had not yet quite recovered. But when Joyce, helping Jill to dress, demanded fiercely to know what had happened to the girl, Len, though mumbling, was able to answer her.

'She had a bad trip, that's all. Nothing else. Pony slipped some acid into her coke.'

'That's all? Terrifying the child!' Joyce cried savagely. 'If I've my way, you three are going to take a bad trip to the police station shortly.' She took hold of Jill. 'You'll be all right now, darling. You stay here, Alfred. She thinks she's going to be sick. I can cope.' Half-carrying Jill, she went out, followed by Marion, who had opened the door for her.

Len and Tusker, with Pony slumped between them, apparently fast asleep, were now mumbling at each other. Brian and Roke were exchanging puzzled glances. Engram still had his elbows on his knees and his head in his hands.

'Heard Joyce say quite clearly, "Taking Jill away",' said Roke in a bewildered low tone. 'But what happened before that?'

Brian was sharing his bewilderment. 'Oh—you as well! Seemed to hear myself talking some sort of rubbish. Like a dream.'

'Glad it happened to you too,' said Roke confidentially. 'Thought I must have blacked out. That would have meant serious heart trouble.'

'We need a drink, Alfred.' And as he went to the bar, 'God's truth!—look at this shambles!' After a little trouble, he found the brandy and two glasses. Len and Tusker still mumbled at each other. Pony hadn't stirred. Engram had taken his head out of his hands but showed no sign of paying attention to what was happening. Marion, having returned and finding herself cut off from everybody, began rather vaguely tidying up the nearer part of the room in which she could move around.

Having swallowed some brandy, Brian looked at Len and Tusker and called very sharply, 'You fellows stay there! Don't move!'

'Horseshit!' Tusker growled out. 'Who's going to stop me if I do move?'

Brian replied to this with sudden ferocity. '*I am.* If I have to smash a bottle over your head, Tusker.'

'Listen to Sir Bighead talking tough!'

Brian was less ferocious but there was venom in his speech. 'Now you listen, Tusker. You're still doped-up, and I think I could take you. But if you do bash your way out, then you're in a hell of a mess. I tell the police at once. There'll be half a dozen serious charges against you—'

'But not before I've put the boot into you.' And Tusker made a slight move.

'No, Jock—no!' Len was alarmed. 'For Christ's sake, go easy!'

'*We must all go easy.*' This was Engram, speaking without any force, quite mildly.

Brian whirled round on him. 'You—Engram—how could I have forgotten? The phone call from Sam Foley—did it come through?'

'No, it didn't.'

'Are you sure? I mean, with all this going on?'

'And letting it go on,' Roke put in.

'I know, Alfred. I'll attend to that later. But are you absolutely

[64]

certain, Engram, no call came for me?'

'Of course I am,' said Engram. 'I've told you, Carfitt.'

A desperate Len spoke up now. 'Listen—while you're dishing out the blame and talking about the police—what about her—Pony? A niece staying in the house, don't forget. Who made Tusker go all over the county, looking for a pusher? She did. Who set up this speed-and-acid party here tonight? *She did.*' As Roke, who was furious, tried to interrupt him. 'All right, Roke. Cool it. Don't go on as if the kid had been gang-banged. She just swallowed some acid she didn't know about and had a bad trip.'

'That's all, so don't blow up, Dad.' But then Tusker added, with a very unpleasant leer, 'Mind you she'd already started to strip, just to show us what she'd got—'

Roke was very angry. 'Well, I know something that'll take that filthy grin off your face. I'm phoning the police—'

But Engram stopped him before he reached the telephone. 'No, you can't do that, Roke.'

'Look—what's-your-name—Engram, I've never understood who you are or what the devil you're doing here.' Roke was as angry as ever. 'But one thing I *do* know—that this is now *my* business and not yours—'

'Alfred, I wouldn't be too sure about that.' This was Marion, who had just come in. 'And anyhow Joyce asked me to tell you that Jill's feeling better now and she wants to take her home.'

Still angry, Roke waved this away. 'As it's your niece who may have been chiefly responsible, you'd better keep out of this, Marion. And I'll tell you what I was about to tell this Engram. I'm sending for the police because it's *my* daughter—hardly more than a school-girl—who was lured here—to be given dangerous dope—to do God knows what—*my daughter.*'

'And you don't half own her, do you, Dad?' Tusker jeered.

Engram stopped Roke from replying. 'Certainly it was your daughter. But now you're so angry, you can't think. You bring the police in and these men and Pony are charged and arrested, then *your daughter* will be in it up to her pretty little neck. In court, out of court, in court again. You set these wheels in motion and then you can't stop them. You'll be putting your Jill through a mincing machine.'

'I shan't allow that. I'll stop it somehow—'

'You can't, y'know, Alfred. Engram's right. Here—finish your drink. Joyce is waiting for you.'

'And wanted you to hurry up,' Marion told him.

'I'm going,' said Roke. 'But what's going to happen to these fellows?'

'We'll have to let 'em go—eh, Engram?' said Brian.

'Yes, of course,' replied Engram. 'Only sensible thing to do. And Pony's more to blame than they are.'

'Well, I suppose so,' said Roke glumly. 'But I'd prefer a society that put fellows like these for the next three years in a penal work colony. Goodnight, Marion, Brian.' And he left them.

Brian turned to face Len and Tusker. 'All right, you two. Clear out—and think yourself lucky. And when I say *Clear out*, Tusker, I mean *now—tonight*. Pack your things—and get out. Your friend can help to carry your bags to Thursley. It'll be good for him after all the dope and sex he's been having.'

Tusker didn't move, but growled, 'Not witty—shitty!'

'Come on, Jock,' said Len, anxious to be off. 'We're well out of this.'

'I should think you are,' cried Marion, as they began to move. 'Look at this room! *Smell* it!'

'Tell your niece, not me,' said Len, passing her.

'Don't fail to give me as a reference, Tusker,' Brian called out when they were at the door. 'I'd enjoy telling somebody what I thought about you.'

Tusker turned at the door. 'Shove it, Carfitt! I wouldn't give *you* as a reference. Very soon, nobody would.'

As soon as they had gone, Marion pulled a face. 'Ugh! I disliked him from the very first. What about opening a window?'

'I suggest one of these french windows,' said Engram. He opened the curtains and then a window, but didn't return.

'He must be taking a breath of fresh air,' said Marion. 'And I don't blame him.'

'Nobody would,' said Brian. 'But what about tonight's little orgy, set up right under his very nose. Must take some blame for that, mustn't he?'

'No, that was Pony's doing.' As she went on, Marion sounded uncertain. 'I don't know about Engram. He may have known all about it, but then he may not, sitting upstairs. Sometimes he talks as if he knows what's going to happen—'

Alfred Roke had come back. 'Joyce spoke too soon. Jill's been

[66]

sick again and now she's falling asleep.'

'Joyce could bring her in here,' Marion said.

'No, Joyce is against that. Said it might have a bad effect on Jill. The car's quite warm and they're comfortable, and Joyce says she'll hang on out there for the next ten minutes or so until Jill's soundly asleep. So here I am, if you don't mind.'

'We don't, Alfred,' said Brian. 'Have another drink?'

As Roke shook his head, Engram returned. 'There's a touch of frost in the air and it's a glorious night of stars. I'd been indoors too long. Except in the very worst weather it's always better outside than you think it's going to be.'

'Never mind about the weather,' said Roke sharply. 'Brian, I want to know what's going to happen to that young woman, who's probably just pretending to be asleep. Surely you're not going to let her stay on here. If this were my house, I'd be telling her to pack up and clear out—*now*.' He was now louder and angrier. 'And don't look at me like that, Marion. I've just taken another look at my young daughter, who was enticed into this house, *your* house, and given some dangerous lysergic acid by *your* niece—'

'Stop shouting,' said Marion. 'We couldn't help it.'

'Of course we couldn't,' said Brian. 'Calm down, Alfred.'

Marion appealed to Engram. 'Say something—please, Engram.'

He looked at Roke. 'It really would be better if you left this to me.'

'Too much has been left to you already,' said Roke roughly. 'So why would it be better?'

'Because, for one thing, I know more about this girl, Pony, than you do.'

'I dare say. After all, she brought you here, didn't she?'

'That was accidental,' Marion put in hastily.

'How do you know it was?' Roke asked.

'Because both of them told me—'

'Do you believe everything you're told?'

Marion had had enough of him. 'Don't be silly.'

'Abuse doesn't answer my question.'

'Well, does this?' Marion said hotly. 'Whatever Engram has told me I've believed at once. He can afford to be truthful, because he's real.'

'That doesn't make sense to me,' said Roke, with a tight little smile. 'I'm real, aren't I?'

'*No.*' After that emphatic denial, Marion turned away, ostensibly

[67]

to do a little more tidying up, but really to break off the talk. Without speaking, Engram offered to help her, but she waved him away. 'No, thank you, Engram. I believe you're tired. Sit down and smoke your pipe.'

As he sat down and began to smoke his pipe, Roke turned his back on him and addressed himself exclusively to Brian, though there could be no pretence that Engram couldn't hear them.

'I'll be frank with you, Brian,' said Roke. 'I think far too much has been left to this man already.'

'I don't quite see it like that, Alfred, but I've had a question to put to him ever since we came back. It's part of my worry about the phone call that never came through. He swears it didn't, and he may be right. But I still want to know how those four young idiots were able to stage their pop-and-dope party right under his nose.'

'If you want my opinion, he didn't merely allow it, he deliberately encouraged it.'

'No, you're going too far now, Alfred. After all, he and I agreed he would be staying up in his room, to take my phone call. Are you listening, Engram?'

'Naturally,' said Engram coolly. 'You wanted me to listen, didn't you?'

'I did,' Roke told him angrily. 'And now I want an answer to a plain direct question.'

This brought Marion in. 'I wish you'd shut up, Alfred. You don't understand anything—'

Roke was quite fierce. 'I understand what happened to my daughter. Engram, did you or did you not know that Jill had come here?'

'Of course he didn't,' Brian said hastily. 'He was upstairs in his room—'

Roke was fierce again. 'I want *his* answer, not yours. Well, Engram?'

'Oh—yes, I knew about Jill.' Engram seemed quite at ease. 'I was still downstairs when she arrived. I had some talk with Len Tabbs. And she listened.'

Roke almost screamed with rage. 'And you hadn't the sense and decency to tell her to go home. Next thing we'll learn is that you were supplying them with drugs.'

'You'll only learn it from yourself,' said Engram. 'The drugs came with Pony and Tusker, and I'd gone upstairs before they arrived. But I knew they'd gone looking for drugs and would probably find them.'

'*You knew—you knew.*' Roke went closer, almost in a frenzy. 'And did nothing. I could knock your damned head off.'

'No, you couldn't, not even if I was standing up. Why don't you try to behave like a grown-up man?'

It was Brian's turn. 'No, Engram, you can't talk like that. It's you who haven't been behaving like a responsible man. Did you want to see those youngsters doping and rogering—or are you just simply irresponsible?'

'I'm not always as responsible as I might be,' said Engram slowly, thoughtfully, clearly not taking offence. 'But in this particular instance, I knew exactly what I was doing. There was a small risk, but it was worth taking. Brian might have shot somebody, but he didn't —and I don't think he'll give way to that impulse again. As for you, Roke, your Jill came to no real harm and from now on she'll try to find better company. We're well rid of Len and Tusker, and without finding ourselves involved with the police and the law courts. There's still Pony, but I'll deal with her. As Marion knows, I arranged to stay late here tonight, just to cope with the situation that I knew was building up. I may not be as responsible as I ought to be. But you two men seem to me completely and ruinously irresponsible. You can't help it because you identify with every foolish thought, every gust of feeling, that comes into your mind. You aren't real integrated persons, you're a football crowd. So you don't understand anything and don't know what you're talking about. And while I don't want to be offensive, I must add that I'm tired of you.' He got up.

Marion was alarmed. 'Engram, you're not leaving yet?'

He turned at the door, smiling. 'No—not time yet. I thought I'd make some coffee.'

'Oh—good! Need some help?'

'No, thanks. But I must know who's ready for coffee.'

Roke said heavily. 'You can leave me out. And Joyce of course. Never touch coffee myself after eleven o'clock.'

'Then there'll be only Brian, you and I, Engram,' said Marion.

'*And* Pony. She'll want some.'

'You're very forgiving. I wouldn't offer that wretched niece of mine a drop.'

'I should think not,' said Roke.

[69]

'No, she'll need some,' Engram told them. 'And incidentally, Marion, I don't think she is your niece.' That little bombshell took him out of the room.

Marion was all excitement. 'Brian, did you hear that?'

'No,' said Brian. He was pouring another brandy for himself.

'Don't be silly. You must have done.'

'Then why ask me?'

'I don't say that fellow, Engram, isn't clever,' said Roke thoughtfully. 'But if you ask me, he's a clever professional charlatan.'

'Well, I'm not asking you, Alfred,' said Marion. 'What do you say, Brian?'

'I don't say anything,' said Brian, sniffing his brandy.

'Oh—do stop it, Brian!'

Now he came to life. '*Stop it! Stop it!*' he began stormily. 'What the hell d'you think I'm doing—trying to be funny? Look—and this applies to both of you—I'm not thinking about Engram and this nuisance of a girl—and who's a charlatan and who isn't. I'm asking myself over and over again what's become of that phone call Sam Foley promised to make. I spent yesterday and this morning and lunchtime today being politely but very firmly turned down by some merchant bankers. But I'm not the charmer in our outfit. That's Sam Foley, and he agreed to take over today, at his golf club and elsewhere, to turn on the charm. Our last chance. Now where is he—and what's happening? Is he still dining out where the money is? Is he sitting, more than half-stoned, in some night club? Or after drowning his disappointment, did he pass out hours ago? You may think you don't care, Marion, but that's because you don't realize what's at stake—this house, for a start. As for you, Alfred, *you* ought to understand. You may be a scientist, but for the last ten years you've been in big business. So *you* must understand what I'm feeling.'

He drank about half the brandy he had poured out. Roke gave him a disapproving look, saw that Marion was staring at him and then hunched his shoulders in an obvious shrug.

Marion clearly didn't like what she had seen. 'What did that look and that shrug mean, Alfred? Just that you think Brian's drinking too much?'

'Let it pass,' he said to her very quietly.

But Brian had overheard him and now was truculent. 'She may let it pass, but I'm damned if I will. I said something to you, and you heard me. Well, Alfred?'

'Well—*what*? Don't get on your high horse.'

'If that means anything, you'd better explain it.'

Marion looked at them and listened in despair. Engram had been right about them. Brian was now aggressive and Alfred Roke irritable and impatient.

'Go on—go on,' said Brian.

'You might as well know,' said Roke. 'You've been wondering and muttering all the evening about your phone call. I don't think it'll come now. And if it did you wouldn't like it. Very bad news, I'd say.'

'That's what you'd say, is it?' Brian was very angry. 'Well, what the hell do you know about my business? You're in laxatives and headache powders, not in the City.'

'A minute since you said I was in big business,' Roke reminded him unpleasantly. 'Well, we are. And among other things, we have a financial board. I was asking yesterday what chance you had of rescuing your Fallowfield Investment Trust, and I was told you hadn't a hope.'

'Did you tell them I was a friend of yours?' Brian was furious.

'No, I didn't. Wanted a candid opinion.'

'Well, now you're getting another candid opinion, Roke. You obviously aren't a friend—'

'Oh—no, Brian,' Marion cried. 'Why not?'

'*What*? Actually dining here with us last night, and never saying a word, not the least warning, not even a hint, when he believes I'm almost down the drain. *Friend?* Don't make me laugh.'

Joyce walked in. She was obviously ready to go and began talking at once. 'Jill's fast asleep now, Alfred. All snug on the back seat. I must say there's a heavenly smell of coffee drifting out of the kitchen. Engram, I suppose.'

Roke said promptly, 'I told him you wouldn't want any.'

'I'll bet,' said Joyce.

'You can have some, Joyce.'

'No thanks! Time we took that child home. You too, Alfred. You're looking peevish.'

'Well he might!' said Brian, who was still very angry. 'Joyce, what does it feel like to be married to Judas Iscariot?'

'If I'm married to Judas, then you're Jesus and this is the Garden of Gethsemane—and that I can't buy. I'd also call that a pretty dam' stupid remark, Brian. You tight or something?'

This annoyed Marion. 'Oh—don't *you* start now—'

Roke was already making for the door. 'Come along, Joyce.'

'You're a happy bunch, aren't you?' This was Pony, wide awake, loud and clear. 'Dullsville squares at play.'

Hearing this voice, Joyce immediately turned round and went closer to Pony. 'Oh—so you're conscious at last, are you? Well, I'm Jill's mother and I feel like giving you a good hard slap.'

'Don't try it, Mummie dear,' said Pony. 'I've lived rough and you'd be in for ten minutes scratching and biting, kicking and hair-pulling. Now, who said something about coffee?'

'You have a nice sweet girl there,' Joyce said to Marion. 'Good-night!' In the hall she nearly bumped into Engram, who was carrying the coffee tray. Holding her side of the tray for a moment or two, she spoke across it, for once entirely serious, deeply earnest. 'Engram, I'll read the books again. I never see your name about—'

'You never will, Joyce. We're against it.'

'Well, I'll try to track you down, Engram, just to come and listen.'

'I hope you'll do that, Joyce. But they're waiting for this coffee. Goodnight.'

'Goodnight, Engram! And *au 'voir*.'

Ten

PONY HAD ATTENDED to an armchair that had been knocked over. She was now perched on an arm of it, with her feet pressed against the other arm, to keep a balance. She greeted Engram's arrival with enthusiasm. 'Coffee—coffee! At last the marines have landed.'

Marion gave Engram a reproachful look. 'Did you have to bring a cup for her?'

'Yes. She'll need some coffee.'

'You can say that again, Engram,' cried Pony.

This cheerful impudence infuriated Marion. 'He can say something else again—that he doesn't think you are my niece.'

Instead of everybody talking at once now, nobody said anything until the coffee had been handed round and a few cautious sips of it had been tried. There was then what almost looked like a miniature trial scene. Perched high on her chair, Pony faced both Engram and Marion, now sitting down and staring up at her. With his coffee and brandy on the bar counter, Brian leant negligently against it, often more than half turned away from the others, his attitude tending to suggest that his mind was mostly elsewhere.

It was Pony who ended the silence, in a tone of nervous bravado. 'Feel like hitting the hay,' she announced. 'I'll drink the rest of this up in my room.'

'Oh—no!' said Marion, all sharp accusation. 'If Engram's right, you won't have a room.'

'He's only guessing, Aunt Marion—'

'*Aunt Marion* again, is it? Doesn't even start to ring true. Engram?'

[73]

'Pony,' he began quietly, 'there are two ways of doing this. Don't choose the hard way or you'll be in really deep trouble. If you'll stop bluffing, if you'll be honest, I'll do the best I can for you.'

'Thanks a lot!' said Pony. 'But I don't know what you're talking about.'

Engram said, 'I asked you to stop bluffing,' and then he got up and went to her, holding his hand out. 'The letter, Pony.'

'What letter? I still don't know what you're talking about—'

'This is your last chance, Pony. *The letter*. I know you have it.' He looked round at the two Carfitts. 'It was an American airmail letter addressed to Marion. It came late this morning when Marion had gone upstairs, so I left it on the hall table. Pony came down about ten minutes afterwards, and the next time I looked in the hall, the letter had gone. I knew Pony must have taken it.'

'Then why in God's name didn't you say so earlier?' This was Brian and he was angry.

'For many different reasons—as I believe Marion will understand—but one of them will do for you, Brian. Pony went out and stayed out, and this is the first chance I've had to question her. Now Pony—*the letter.*'

'Okay—you win,' said Pony wearily. 'I lose—as usual.' She produced from a pocket in her jeans a folded American airmail letter, and as she handed it to Engram she continued, still wearily, 'Why the hell I didn't tear it up at once, I don't know. Guess I want to be a loser.'

'In some games the losers can win,' Engram told her. He gave the letter to Marion, who immediately began to read it. Pony, who was now standing behind her chair, made a move as if about to leave, but Engram stopped her. 'No, Pony, no! If you don't stay here, it'll be much worse for you.'

Both curious and impatient, Brian said to his wife, 'Must be from your sister. Isn't it?'

Distressed, crying a little, Marion replied, 'Yes, it's from her. Here—you read it.' She held it out, and he left the bar to take it from her.

Leaning against the bar counter, he glanced through the letter and then said in an undramatic staccato fashion, 'Elvira died in a car crash on the tenth. Somewhere in Missouri—can't make the name out. Must have been killed instantly. Been attending some pop festival in San Diego, California. Driving across country to

Chicago, to catch a plane to London. Some confusion about identity at first. Supposed to have been another girl with her. Elvira didn't like driving a long way alone.' He handed the letter back to Marion and pressed her shoulder. 'Sorry about this, Marion. Bad luck!' He looked at Pony and said harshly, 'Were you that other girl?'

When Pony didn't reply, Engram said, 'Of course she was.'

Out of her distress, Marion cried, 'I was a fool not to trust myself. When she first took off that mask and said she was my niece, I didn't believe her. And I've never really *felt* she was my niece.' Suddenly indignant, she looked at Pony. 'My God—that was a wicked thing to do. You must be thoroughly corrupt—really *evil*.'

'I don't suppose so, Marion,' said Engram. 'Very few people are, especially in their early twenties. Now Pony, tell us the exact truth. No more lies.'

She offered him two quick nods. 'You know something, Engram? I never did lie to you. All I said was that I'd just come over on the plane—and that was true enough.'

'All right,' Brian growled. 'Get on with it. Who are you, anyhow?'

She took a moment or two to brace herself, and then addressed all three. 'I'm Bridget Moore Molansky. Mother's Irish, Dad's a Polack. They live in Dayton, Ohio, and they're okay if you like 'em dull and square. As for me, I've been a loser all the way. But you don't want to know about that.'

'I must say, *I* don't,' said Marion coldly.

'And I wouldn't want to tell it,' Pony told her. 'But listen—this is just what happened. I'm in San Diego for this pop festival. I've had a fight, been told to get lost, and I'm broke. I meet this Elvira Porter —same age, don't look very different. She's got a good old Buick, and now she wants to make Chicago soon as she can. Will I spell her driving? Y'know, take it in turn to save time. Fine! I'm tired of the Coast so I'll take a free ride to Chicago. I don't like Elvira and she doesn't like me—but so what? Sometimes I think nobody likes anybody any more. It's gone out—like lace pants and home cooking. How about a refill of coffee with some brandy in it this time?'

'You'll get no brandy from me,' said Brian.

'How you've changed, haven't you, Sir Brian?' She held out her cup to Engram, who filled it. 'Thanks, Engram! Well, we've been on the road two days. I've taken us through Tulsa, Oklahoma, and when we swap over she's crossing the Ozarks on the way to St Louis.

I'm lying on the back seat, bushed, and soon fall asleep. Me—I like to keep to the big roads, trucks or no trucks. She always wanted to try side-roads and short cuts. And now she tried one too many. I wake up to the end of the world. We've hit a tree—she must have skidded at seventy—and when I know I'm still alive, I see it's a shambles. I won't give you the details because you wouldn't like them. But Elvira's dead, the car's a write-off, and when I've stopped screaming I realize I'm on an empty road, going from nowhere to nowhere, with about sixty cents in the world and the sun ready to go down. Elvira's left her handbag on the back seat. I take out of it her passport, a plane ticket Chicago–London, a folder of American Express cheques, and about thirty dollars in cash. So I grab one of her cases, the smaller one, and start running along that road, the way we were going, and the further I go the more I'm now Elvira Porter. About two miles further on there's a crossroads. I get a lift down to the main road. Wait for a Greyhound—and the rest was easy.'

'What about the passport photograph and the signature on the American Express cheques ?' Engram asked.

'Still easy. I pull my hair over my face, the way she had it, and any dumb creep could imitate that signature.'

Both Carfitts were angry. 'And now you could be arrested,' said Brian, 'and finally sent to prison under about five different serious charges—'

Marion cried, 'You're a thief as well as—as—everything else.'

'Guess I am at that,' said Pony. 'But what would you have done in my place ? Use your imagination.'

'Nothing you've done,' said Marion heatedly. 'I'd die first.'

'I've thought of that, more than once, long before Elvira Porter came along. Didn't I tell you I've always been a loser ?'

'What is it you want, Pony ?' Engram enquired quite gently.

'What is there, if you're not a creep ?'

'Am I a creep, Pony ?'

'No, you're not, Engram—and I don't understand about you. But you're not Bridget Moore Molansky neither—not bad-looking but no beauty, no talent, not quite stupid but not really clever. Okay—there were girls no better than that who are living like queens today. But they had one thing I haven't got—and that's luck.'

'Do we want all this ?' said Brian.

'A little more of it wouldn't hurt us,' said Engram. 'Go on, Pony.'

'What have I left behind? Forty years in Dullsville, waiting for your husband to claim his pension, then waiting to die. I'll take five years of what I've got now, though some of it's rough. All I ask for is to get nicely stoned, a few laughs and some dreamy sex. You're no narrow-minded creep, Engram, so what's wrong with that?'

'Almost everything, Pony.' He spoke easily, gently. 'You're facing the wrong way. You're like somebody who keeps walking into a cupboard instead of turning round and finding fresh air—'

Brian charged in, speaking roughly. 'What the hell's the good of all this when we ought to be sending for the police?'

'I don't see what else we can do,' said Marion, though she sounded uncertain.

'For Christ's sake, Engram, don't let them do that.' Pony's bravado had gone. 'If I'm put inside, with butch lizzies all round me, I swear I'll kill myself.' She looked at both Carfitts. 'And don't forget that before that I'll have told all—spilt the lot—'

The Carfitts exchanged meaningful glances and then looked enquiringly at Engram, who for the last minute or two had been quietly inching himself nearer the window curtains.

'Let's forget about the police, Brian,' he said. 'Other people's luck can run out as well as Pony's. I don't know what we can do with her, but why don't we invite Len Tabbs to join us? He's been breathing heavily behind these curtains for the last few minutes. Better come in, Len.'

Len did, advancing cautiously between the curtains.

Brian groaned. 'Not this fellow again!'

Len ignored him and appealed directly to Engram. 'How about this? If you'll have a heart and let her go, she can come with us. Out of the way—on the road.' He looked round, then continued hastily. 'It's like this. While Jock's getting his gear together, I go down the road and phone this bird I know in Thursley. Bit older than us—but okay. She's had a flaming row with her boy friend. She's ready to go anywhere, do anything, and she's got a four-seater that's on the way here now. I'm broke but she's got bread and so has Jock—I don't know about Pony here—'

'Watch me!' cried Pony. She pulled out a folder of American Express cheques and tossed it to Marion. 'There's all the travellers' cheques. I only cashed a hundred dollars. And now I'm broke. Passport's upstairs. I'll just collect one clean shirt and panties, another pair of jeans and my toothbrush. Can I go?'

[77]

Engram looked at the Carfitts. 'Let her go.'

Marion seemed confused. 'I don't know. Brian?'

But before he could answer, the telephone rang, shrill and demanding. Brian pounced on the instrument. 'Yes, Molly? Brian here. Hold on a second.' He shouted at Pony and Len: 'Get the hell out of here, the pair of you!'

They hurriedly exchanged a few inaudible whispers, then Len vanished between the curtains and Pony rushed towards the door into the hall. Marion and Engram kept still and listened to Brian at the telephone.

Eleven

'YES, MOLLY, I guessed that's what had happened to Sam. . . .
Well, if he's awake now, I want to talk to him and I don't care what
shape he's in. . . . *Important?* God Almighty—doesn't Sam ever tell
you *anything?* Get him to the phone if you have to carry him. . . .'

Waiting, with the receiver at his ear, Brian did some heavy breathing, tapped a foot, and glared all round at everybody and everything.

'Now then, Sam,' he began hoarsely, 'what happened and why
didn't you phone me? . . . No, I'm not stoned. *You are,* you great
ape. . . . *Who* laughed at you? . . . *All* of them? Then you must
have been at least half-stoned by that time. . . . *Spain?* Did you say
Spain? . . . I don't know what you're talking about, Sam. You're
still drunk and dreaming. Get Molly to the phone again. . . . Go on
—go on—tell her I'm not making any sense out of you—'

As he waited, Brian said to Marion and Engram, 'Sam knows
what I want but is too drunk to reply properly. His wife's sober but
doesn't know what I want.'

'You might be ringing up Western Civilization,' said Engram.

But Brian was speaking into the telephone again. 'Sorry about
this, Molly, but I'm not making any sense out of Sam. What was
that about being laughed at? Some Irish clowning? . . . *Business?*
Good God! . . . You're sure it was afterwards he started drinking
hard? . . . I see. But what was this nonsense about Spain? . . .
Tomorrow? Tell Sam he can't do that. . . . Holiday be damned!
He's not taking you on a holiday. He's *running away.* He's ratting
on me. So I hope you have a nice holiday—and he drops dead.'

Brian banged down the receiver, wiped his brow, then shakily added more brandy to his glass.

'That was a horrible thing to say, Brian,' Marion told him, 'really horrible.'

As if he had not sufficient energy left to be angry again, Brian spoke in a curiously dead tone. 'Even a quarter of a million, if we could have raised it by Monday morning, would have saved us. Now we go down the drain. And Sam Foley, my own man in the Trust, will be in Torremolinos and will stay there, probably having salted something away when I wasn't looking.'

Having taken a drink, he left the telephone and sat down heavily, a man in complete despair.

Marion tried to sound hopeful. 'It can't be so bad, can it, Brian? We'll have something left—'

'I doubt it. They'll take the lot, strip me clean. The trouble is, I've never been as clever as I thought I was. If it wasn't for two stupid moves, I might be sitting on a million now. Bloody fool!'

'I've known a few men who sat on millions, but I never remember envying any of them,' said Engram. But then they could hear the front door bell. 'Marion, answer that, please. It'll be Alice Brock calling for me. Tell her I'm all ready but I need a few more minutes here.'

Ready to go to the door, Marion said hastily, 'It's for Brian's sake, isn't it?'

'Yes—and yours.'

After she had gone, Brian said, 'Engram, probably the best thing I can do now is to take that gun and blow myself out of this bloody mess.'

'It doesn't work. And stop thinking about yourself, Brian.'

'As a matter of fact, I'm not,' he said slowly. 'Believe it or not, I'm thinking about those thirty thousand people—mostly badly-off —who put their savings into my Fallowfield Trust—'

Engram sounded urgent for once. 'Hold on to the Carfitt who spoke then. Stop all the other Brian Carfitts who want to talk—'

But Brian cut in impatiently. 'Look—man—I'm not in the mood—'

'Damn your moods!' And now Engram spoke with great force. 'Keep thinking about those thirty thousand shareholders. I'm going to try something I've never tried before. Just stand there—and keep quiet. We exist in what we might call a cube of Time, but usually attend to only one dimension of it—its length. But what if I can make you experience all of it.' As Brian tried to interrupt him, Engram cried, 'For God's sake, man—keep quiet. Look at me.'

Engram remained rigid, concentrated. After a few moments Brian vaguely moved his head and his hands, then his face began to work, and finally he stared, his eyes wide with bewilderment and horror, and gasped out some clues to what appeared to be happening to him.

'God's truth. Where am I? . . . I've shot somebody—Tusker— the police are asking questions. . . . I'm putting a gun in my mouth and my finger's on the trigger. . . . Why no! I'm going through the office, telling them myself we can't go on. . . . Now I'm somewhere else—another office—answering questions, questions, questions. . . . Somewhere else again now—one old man—seen him before somewhere—why it must be old Ferguson-White . . .'

'Hold it, hold it!' Engram called triumphantly . . . 'And remember those thirty thousand shareholders. Now, Carfitt, you're talking to Charles Ferguson-White. Look! Listen!' And Engram sat down and sketched the posture, facial expression and voice of a tough old man. Describing the scene afterwards to Marion, Brian swore that he no longer saw and heard Engram but old Ferguson-White.

'So, Carfitt,' Engram said in a hard old man's voice, 'having gone round the City, cap in hand, you're trying me—eh? Why? Just tell me why?'

'Because there are thirty thousand people who put their savings into my Fallowfield Trust—'

'And didn't know Sir Brian Carfitt couldn't carry corn—'

'And *I* didn't know. I was nothing like as clever as I thought I was. I made a few bad mistakes.'

'Know you did. Could have told you but you'd never have believed me. But what are you thinking about now, when you're trying to scrape together another quarter of a million—'

'I hope you'll believe me,' said Brian humbly, 'when I tell you I'm thinking about those thirty thousand people.'

'Then you'll do, Carfitt. Take a walk round my garden. I may have sums and some telephoning to do. I think you'd need a bit more than quarter of a million, my boy. Now off you go.' And Engram, his sketchy impersonation at an end, jumped out of his chair.

The joyful relief began to fade out of Brian's face. Out of the daze

[81]

that followed he realized that it was Engram he was staring at. Slowly and unhappily he said, 'And I thought I was talking to old Ferguson-White—getting somewhere—and it was you all the time.' Then he exploded. 'What a lousy rotten trick to play when I'm feeling like this—hopeless. You're going, so clear out now. *Out— out!*'

'I'll be gone in the next few minutes,' said Engram coldly. 'But we're soon back to shouter, aren't we? You probably shouted yourself into this mess, but you'll never shout your way out of it.'

Brian had dropped into a chair, a hopeless figure. 'No need to rub it in. It would take a miracle now.'

'All despair now,' said Engram. 'Well, we can neither shout for miracles nor groan for them.' He did not go on because Marion joined them.

'What's this?' she asked, sounding cheerful.

'Leave it,' Brian told her. 'You'll know soon enough.'

'That was Alice, I take it?' said Engram to Marion. 'Is she waiting in the car?'

Marion was enthusiastic. 'Yes. And isn't she a lovely woman? That white hair and that young eager face! And those great eyes! Are you in love with her?'

'Not at all,' Engram replied, smiling. 'But she's a close friend. She runs one of our groups.'

'I know. She told me.' Marion held up a card. 'She's given me her London address. *And* where you're going now—Charles Ferguson-White's house—'

Brian looked up sharply. '*Ferguson-White?* Is that where you're going? *His* place?'

'I told you last night,' said Engram cheerfully, 'I'd worked with him, years ago. Now we're old friends. Like so many very rich old men, Charles is all too often bored and melancholy. He doesn't believe half I say, but the other half fascinates him.'

'Then you weren't fooling me?' said Brian eagerly. 'You think I might have a chance to talk to him? My God—if only I could!'

'I'll tell him about you, then you and Marion can drive over for lunch. That's why I gave you a kind of rehearsal.' And Engram gave Brian a long hard look. 'Show him your usual whirligig of contradictory characters—start shouting or moaning—and the old man will tear you to pieces. Show him one decent responsible Brian Carfitt, and he'll help you. I've had it in mind ever since last night.'

He turned to Marion. 'I must go. Don't bother about seeing me out. Start talking to Brian. No more useless negative emotions about Lawrence Blade. Create conscious love. Begin tonight.' He spoke to them both at the door. 'See you both tomorrow. No, don't move. I've gone.' And he had, before they could move.

Indeed, before they could do anything, they heard the front door close and then the sound of the car starting up. As it roared away, Marion went to sit down nearer her husband.

'Engram said he wanted us to talk, Brian, and I want us to. We haven't really talked for a long time.'

'I'm for it, Marion. But I must warn you I'm still feeling dazed and shaky. While you were out, Engram—and how he did it, I'll never know—made me see everything that might happen to me. Imagine those possibilities, already lined up! My God—that's an experience!'

'It must have been terrifying. But it came right in the end, didn't it?'

'Wonderfully—so long as I remember not to make an ass of myself—'

'You will remember. I think Engram's some kind of magician. I told him so twice, but he only laughed and said he wasn't. I still don't know—and probably I'll never know—whether he came here by accident or not. But let's leave all that now, Brian.' She waited a moment and then went on, rather cosily: 'Tell me about Molly and Sam Foley—and what they said to you on the phone. I never really trusted Sam Foley but I always liked poor Molly—'

Then they talked and talked.

Underground

Underground

RAY AGGARSTONE TOOK the Northern Line from Leicester Square. It was some time since he had gone anywhere by Underground. Either he had used his car or had taken taxis for shorter journeys. But now that he was almost ready for what he liked to call, to himself but not to anybody else, the *Big Getaway*, he had sold his car for just over four hundred quid. Just showed you how useful it could be to chat somebody up, in this case that stupid sod who was always in the Saloon bar of the King's Arms. While waiting on the crowded platform at Leicester Square, Ray told himself once again that he was careful as well as very clever. For instance, after that car deal and with a few drinks inside them, some fellows would have boasted about the Brazilian setup and the flight to Rio, but not Ray—not on your life! He had told this stupid sod exactly the same story he had told his mother and his wife, Cherry, now waiting for him somewhere near the end of this Northern Line. 'Going to France, old man—Nice actually—where I've bought into a very promising property deal. Smart work, if I may say so.'

But of course he hadn't shown him the letters he'd concocted to show his Mum and Cherry, now ready to part with eight thousand between them, about all they had. They were both so excited about his plan for them to join him at Nice within the next two or three weeks, like a pair of idiotic kids, they left *business* entirely to him, Mum's clever handsome son, Cherry's dominating, fascinating if occasionally unfaithful husband. Serve them right when he vanished with the two cheques he was going to collect – the silly cows!

No train yet but more people arriving on the platform. He changed his place, bumping and shoving a bit, if only to show these types what he thought about them. A run-down lot in a running-down country! He could never come back of course, not after those two women finally decided he'd robbed them blind, but he didn't want to anyhow. He'd had it here all right—finish! He couldn't blame Rita and Karl for sneering and jeering, even though now and again they got his goat, specially Karl. But that was early on, before they began to talk business.

The train came along, already more than half full. And because he hadn't stood near the platform edge, though he pushed and shoved as hard as anybody, perhaps a bit harder than most, of course he didn't get a seat—not a hope! So there he was, standing and swaying, wedged in with a lot of fat arses, smelly underclothes and bad breath. Looking around, disgusted, he couldn't imagine now what had made him come down here when he might have hired a car, travelled in comfort and also impressed Mum and Cherry. So, to stop cursing himself, he began thinking about Rita and Karl again. After all he'd be meeting them in Rio in two or three days, and he began to wonder how things would work over there. Every time Karl, who was her husband all right, had gone to Manchester or Leeds and had stayed the night, he'd had Rita, a hot brunette if there ever was one, who'd start moaning if a finger touched a tit. Did Karl know, just guess, not care—or what? Anyhow, what Karl, a real businessman in the German–Swedish style, did know was that his friend, smart Ray Aggarstone, would be shortly financing most of the deal they'd worked out. Moreover, there must be plenty of hot moaning brunettes in Brazil.

Tottenham Court Road and people, dreary bloody people, pushing their way out and pushing their way in. And off again—sway, rattle, bang, bang, rattle, sway. A long thin woman, loaded with parcels, dug an elbow into his ribs, and he used his own elbow, with some force, to knock it away. She glared at him over her parcels, but all he did was to raise his eyebrows at her. After a moment or two she was able to move away a few inches. It was then that a curious thing happened. Through the gap she had left between them he saw for the first time a small figure sitting down. It had the face of an old-looking boy or a rather young-looking dwarf. He stared at this creature, who then met his stare with a widening of the eyes, odd eyes, yellowish. Next, the little oddity closed his eyes and moved his

head slowly from side to side, almost as if he was giving a 'No–no
–no' signal. As soon as the eyes opened again, Ray gave them a
hard scowling look. But now there was no sign of recognition in
them. It was just as if Ray was no longer there at all. The boy-or-
dwarf might have been looking *through him*. A silly idea. Ray began
to think how he would deal with Mum and Cherry.

At Euston there was a lot more pushing out and shoving in,
twerps on the move. The little monster had gone, and in his place
was a fat suet-faced woman who stared angrily at anything or
nothing, just to prove she had a right to a seat. Rattling and swaying
on again, Ray told himself how he ought to deal with Mum and
Cherry this time. Very different, he decided, from last time when
he'd been all solemn, very much the business man, explaining again
why Cherry had to stay with Mum, now that he'd got rid of their
flat, and why he was staying in an hotel to be near the two Frenchmen who'd agreed to let him buy into the big property development
just outside Nice. This time, everything being settled now they
were giving him their cheques, there'd be no point in going on with
the solemn business thing. It would have to be all merry chit-chat
about Nice and the Riviera, how they'd be joining him down there
quite soon, how he'd be arranging their flights, booking a posh
double-bedded room with bath for Cherry and him, with a good
single nearby for Mum, and at least one balcony the three could
use for breakfast—all that bullshit. Yes, there he'd be, egging them
on, the stupid cows, maybe taking them out to a pub if Mum hadn't
got anything in to drink.

Somebody touched his arm. This was deliberate. A woman was
smiling at him. She was an oldish woman, white-haired but with a
plump red-cheeked face and bright blue eyes; and he'd seen her
before somewhere. 'You're Ray Aggarstone, aren't you ?' she said,
smiling away.

It seemed as if he hadn't time to think before he heard himself
saying, 'No, I'm not.' He said it sharply too, as if really telling her
to mind her own dam' business.

It wiped the smile off her face and narrowed and darkened her
eyes, almost turning her into another person. 'I think you *are* Ray
Aggarstone, y'know,' she said; and though the train was making a
lot of noise, somehow she managed to say it quietly. 'And you must
remember me. I'm an old friend of your mother's.'

She must have been too, he realised now. But he hadn't to be bothered with her, when he was busy with his own thoughts and plans. He shook his head at her. 'Got this all wrong.' And he had to shout because the train might have been grinding its way through rocks, the noise it was making. 'I don't know you. And you don't know me.'

'Yes, I do. Or I did do, once,' she went on steadily. 'She thought the world of you, Ray. Her only son—so good-looking, so clever!'

He found a snarl coming out of him this time. 'Do you mind! Just turn it up!' And he looked away, to get rid of her. But when he turned his head again, she was still there, though not quite so close, having managed to back away from him a little. And now she seemed a lot older and was giving him a long sad look. He couldn't return it—he suddenly felt he had nothing to return it with, not even a scowl—so he looked away again and was relieved to find the train was stopping at Camden Town. This time not many got in, but then not many got out, so he was still forced to stand, even though he'd a bit more space round him. And this suited him all right because if there was one thing he didn't like it was being jammed among all these idiotic, bloody disgusting people, staring old cows, smelly bitches and stupid buggers of all ages and sizes. When he got to Brazil and the money was rolling in, as Karl swore it would, he'd work it so that there was no more of this horrible caper. The only people allowed near him would be the ones he could enjoy seeing, hearing, smelling and touching.

As the train started rattling and banging off again, he started thinking again. Working out how he'd deal with Cherry and his mother, chatting them up about life on the Riviera, breakfasts on balconies, drinks to welcome the wonderful new life, laughs and hugs and kisses and all that female crap, he realised he'd overdone it, not for them but for himself. For what he'd gone and done, if only for a minute or two, was to go soft and feel a bit sorry for both of them, considering that he was about to skin them down to their last fifty quid each. No time for that tonight! He'd got to be as sensible and hard as he'd been when he worked out the plan. Serve 'em right for not having more sense! He'd to look after himself, so they could look after themselves—and women always managed somehow. And he began to remember and light up every grievance he'd ever had against the pair of 'em. He'd deal with them the way he'd planned, pretending to be as silly as they were, and when they laughed then he'd laugh too, even, just for a private giggle, bringing out and flourishing his wallet, which already had in it his Air France ticket to Rio.

It was just past Chalk Farm when the man tapped him on the shoulder. He was a tall man, so tall he had to bend over Ray, and he had very sharp grey eyes and a long chin.

'Better get out at Hampstead,' the man said, almost in Ray's ear.

'Can't do,' Ray told him briskly. 'Going as far as Hendon Central. Unless of course I have to change. Is that it?'

'You might say that's it.' A solemn reply.

This sounded idiotic to Ray. 'I don't know what you're talking about.' This tall fellow didn't look a chump, but then, like so many people now, he might be round the bend.

Two women pushed past them, getting ready for Belsize Park. The man waited but then he tapped Ray on the shoulder again and bent closer to his ear. 'Just a last word. Most people think this line's at its deepest at Hampstead. What they don't know—and I don't suppose you do—is that there's a second line, starting at Hampstead, that goes deeper still—on and on, deeper and deeper—'

'Oh—come off it!' Ray was impatient now. This was obviously a crackpot.

'I'm not on it.' The man gave a short crackpot's laugh. 'But you may be *if* you don't get out at Hampstead and then take a taxi or a bus—*and go back.*'

'That's enough,' Ray told him. 'I'll mind my own business and you mind yours.'

'No, it's not as simple as that,' said the tall man quite mildly. 'You're part of my business now. That's why I'm telling you—not asking you, *telling* you—to forget Hendon Central and get out at Hampstead—'

Ray lost his temper. 'And I'm *telling* you—not asking you—to piss off.'

The train was slowing up. Belsize Park now. There were sufficient people getting out to push between Ray and the tall man, but then there was quite a gap between them now. Only a few got on, and Ray saw that he could have a seat at last if he wanted one. But somehow he didn't. Perhaps he felt he might go soft again if he sat down. Better to keep on standing and be hard and tough. The tall man, easily seen, had moved down and was now near the far door, ready to get out at Hampstead, where the big daft sod thought everybody ought to get out. All these mental hospitals and yet a crackpot pest like this was allowed to wander around loose, making a bloody nuisance of himself! Anyhow, as soon as the train pulled up at Hampstead, out the chap went, followed by nearly everybody else. This left the carriage almost empty. Ray could have taken as many seats as he wanted now, but he didn't make a move, not for the moment trusting himself to let go of the strap he was clinging to, for he had to admit that he felt a bit faint, probably because of all the clattering and swaying and what so many stinking people had done to the air had combined to make him feel faint.

This was an unusually long wait. He closed his eyes, just for a few moments, and when he opened them again he was both surprised and alarmed to discover that he had the whole long carriage to himself. Nobody else at all in sight. Had they shouted, 'Hampstead—all change!' and he'd missed it? Even dim as he felt, he was about to make for the door when, with an unpleasant jerk, the train started again. Then two things, equally unpleasant, happened together. There were several loud bangs and the lights went out. Badly shaken, there in the dark with the train obviously gathering speed, he made up his mind he would get out at the next stop, which would be Golders Green, and find a taxi to take him up to Mum's place. The lights came on again, and though they seemed bright enough at first, after the dark, he soon realized that in fact they were much lower than they'd been before. Ten to one some power-cut frigging nonsense!

Then quite suddenly—and it came like a hammer-blow at the heart—he *knew* that this train was going nowhere near Golders Green. At the same time he felt that it wasn't moving like all the others, which went more or less level or climbed a bit to rush out into the open air. No, it was *going down and down*. And what had that tall crackpot said? Something about a second line going deeper still—*on and on, deeper and deeper*—? He tried to forget this but he couldn't, and he began to wish there was somebody else with him who could explain what was happening. The train went rattling on, faster now than the usual underground train. There was nothing to be seen of course, and with this poor lighting he could hardly catch a glimpse of his own reflection. He tried cursing and blinding, to stop himself feeling frightened; but it didn't work.

However, bringing a flood of relief, something happened he never remembered seeing before on an underground train. Some sort of conductor chap, wearing a dark uniform, had come through a door at the far end of the carriage and was now walking towards him—that is, if you could call this slow shuffle a walk. Enjoying his relief, Ray took a seat at last and began rehearsing the indignant questions he would ask. 'Now look here,' he called out, 'what the hell's the idea—?' But there he stopped, terrified. He was staring at something out of a nightmare. The man hadn't a face, just eyes like a couple of blackcurrants, and nothing else—no mouth, no nose, no ears. In his terror Ray huddled into his seat and shut his eyes tight, hoping feverishly that the lard-faced monster wouldn't stop, even to put a finger on him, but would go shuffling past him. And this indeed he did, so that when Ray risked opening his eyes he was alone again. That was something, and what happened next was better still. At last the train was slowing down. There must be a station soon—certainly not Golders Green—but whatever the station was, however far it might be from Hendon Central, it was where he would get out of this nightmare train.

He caught glimpses of an enormous packed platform. As soon as the train stopped he reached the door, but even then it was too late. He was swept back by a solid mass of people, who pushed and shoved like maniacs and closed round him so that he couldn't move and felt he could hardly breathe. And what people! All the faces he'd ever looked away from, disgust blotting out compassion, seemed to be here, and the train was already moving again. He felt he was hemmed in by ulcers, abscesses, half-blind eyes, rotting noses, gangrenous mouths and chins. And how far, how long? Even out of the depths of his nausea, he'd have to say something.

He put his question to the face nearest to him, a twisted slobbery caricature of a face, but all he got in reply was a senseless gabble.

'No use asking him,' a voice said over his shoulder. 'He's forgotten how to talk. What you want to know?' The voice belonged to a bull of a man with a face like a volcanic eruption.

'Where—' and it was a shaky question, 'where are we going?'

'Where we going?' the bull roared. 'We're not going anywhere, you silly sod.' Now he roared louder still. 'Time to push around, shove about, all you bastards!'

Ray found at his elbow an old creature whose nose and chin nearly met: she could have been a witch out of an ancient fairy tale. 'I'll tell you where you're *not* going, young man,' she said, cackling

[93]

and spitting. '*He–he–he!* You're not going to Rio in Brazil. Not now and not ever. *He–he–he!*'

His heart turning into ice-water, he understood at last that he might never know anything again except this underground journey to nowhere, wedged beyond any chance of escape among these malicious jeering monstrosities . . .

. . . 'Full name's Raymond Geoffrey Aggarstone, but liked to call himself just *Ray*,' said the first man. 'Got that? Okay. Now—effects. Silver cigarette case, inscribed *Darling Ray from his loving Cherry* . . . Posh lighter . . . Diary, gold pencil, three fivers and four pound notes in small notecase in one inside pocket. . . .'

'Not too fast,' said the second man. 'And what about trousers pockets—keys and change and all that?'

'Come to them in a minute, chum,' said the first man. 'And if I'm going too fast, why ask for more? . . . Wallet in right inside pocket. . . . Contains credit cards, two letters, and something from Air France—'

'Hold it! Yes, sir?' But this query was addressed to the new arrival. He was a tall man, with a long chin and sharp grey eyes, and he was obviously top brass authority, not the kind of bloke to be asked what he was doing there and where was his warrant card.

'I'll take the two letters,' this tall man said pleasantly but with assured authority. 'Not needed for the next of kin. I must look at that Air France booking too. Thank you!' He examined it, took out a pen and made an alteration. 'Yes, as I thought. There's a mistake here. Should have been Nice not Rio. Here you are, ready for the next of kin, but I'll keep the two letters, they'd only bewilder a couple of miserable women.' He gave the two men a sombre look. 'You know, this is a world where the guilty all too often go unpunished and the innocent are increasingly victimised, robbed, ruined, maimed or murdered.'

'That's true enough, sir,' said the first man. 'As I've said more than once to the wife and kids.'

'Well, now and again,' the tall man told him, 'we have the chance to change that. Just now and again. By the way, what are the facts here?'

'Found unconscious in the Northern Line train at Hampstead, sir. Major heart attack. Never recovered consciousness. In fact, died in the ambulance, sir. Finish!'

'Thank you! Possibly *finish*—possibly not. We don't know, do we? Goodnight!' And he left them so quickly, he might almost have vanished, a trick some of these top blokes seem to have mastered.

The Pavilion of Masks

A Comedy in a Romantic Setting

Prologue

DR A. F. D. PERKISSON arrived at the exact time I had asked him to come—three o'clock. I knew he was Senior Lecturer in Latin-American studies at the University of Brumley. I also knew, because his letter told me, that he was not *a fan of mine* (his actual words) but that he would like to see me *on a matter of some importance*. He had given me the date when he would be visiting Stratford to see one of the Royal Shakespeare Company's productions; and in my reply I had offered him three o'clock. So now here he was.

He was one of those men whose eyes are out of key with the rest of their features. Fifty-ish, he was long-nosed, long-chinned, bravely moustached; but his chocolate eyes were uncertain, tentative, looking out of a melancholy inner world. Academics have a wide range of conversational styles: some of them never stop talking, and some at the other extreme are hesitant and reluctantly pay out phrases as if they were banknotes. Dr A. F. D. Perkisson was one of the hesitators.

'Mr Priestley, *this* has brought me here.' It was a thin box file that I hadn't even noticed. I regarded it with immediate misgiving. It suggested a manuscript—the autobiography of his father, probably a civil engineer, or the memoirs of the uncle who had been a doctor in Singapore—and he would want me to read it, write an introduction to it, and then find a publisher for it. Even while my face fell, if it did fall, I was beginning to sketch my excuses. However, I said nothing. It was still his move.

He opened the box file and began tapping its contents with a

[99]

forefinger. 'My Great-Aunt Dorothea left me this—among other things. . . . Her wish that something could be made of it. . . . She was the granddaughter of the hero and heroine of this romantic tale—no, no, not fiction . . . all of it true, that is, if we make some allowance—for any lapses of memory—on the part of the three people concerned . . .'

I was beginning to find his slow-motion manner irritating, and rather brutally I changed the subject. 'Yes, yes, no doubt. But, Dr Perkisson, if you're looking for somebody to edit your family memoirs then you're talking to the wrong man. However romantic they may be, they can't turn me into their editor. And I'm surprised you didn't realize that before you wrote to me.' I don't think I was downright rude, but I certainly wasn't encouraging him. 'In short —why me?'

His manner was the same as before, all hesitations and pauses, so I will give the gist of his reply. The material he had brought along was very sketchy in places. Indeed, it contained some episodes that could only be roughly indicated, simply because not one of these 'three people concerned' had actually taken part in them, though they were well acquainted with the various characters involved in such episodes. Apparently his Great-Aunt Dorothea had tried to collate three different accounts, remembered after years had passed, of what had happened on one decisive day. All he, Perkisson, had done was to translate the whole thing into English, out of a mixture of German, French, Spanish, and laced in one narrative with some idiomatic Italian not easy to understand. All this took me some way but was no answer to my question, 'Why me?'

'I thought of you—after reading a few of your novels—and some of your plays. . . . You are not very artistic,' he continued nervously, not looking at me. 'Some of our Latin-American writers are very artistic . . .' Now he did look at me, rather severely too, as if something might be my fault. 'They are largely unknown here, such writers. . . .'

After waiting a few moments, I said, 'Well, let's agree that I'm not very artistic. But surely you were about to make a point and then it escaped you.'

'That is true, Mr Priestley—and I apologize. . . . The point is that—that after reading some of your plays and novels, I saw that you had a certain gift. . . . You are able to *shape*—to put everything in order—to construct and develop convincingly. . . . I tried to do something with this material myself—but I soon realized that I don't possess this particular gift. . . . so I thought of you . . .'

'Very flattering, Dr Perkisson. But it's one thing to put in order what one has dreamt up oneself. It's a very different thing to weave together, into one seamless fabric, various sketchy reminiscences, which, as you warned me, must have some gaps in them. There's another objection, really more important. The setting itself, the whole *locale*. I've visited Chile and Peru, but I've only dropped down into the airports on the Atlantic side of South America—'

He interrupted me for the first time. 'No, no—please! They went to South America—to Uruguay, in fact—there to enjoy a very happy marriage—afterwards with two sons and three daughters—which is why it is so romantic, this story. . . . But what made it possible were the events of a single day—and on this day they were still living in Mexe-Dorberg. It was a small South German principality. One day in the early autumn of 1847. With everything happening in the Pavilion of Masks.'

'A Pavilion of Masks ?'

He saw that he had really caught my attention now, that we were in a different atmosphere. Hastily he removed the manuscript from the box file and brought out a large envelope. 'Look,' he cried, 'here are drawings, engravings, even some early photographs. Exterior and interior of the Pavilion of Masks, destroyed by fire—deliberately of course—during the next year, 1848 . . .' He was emptying the envelope into my hands. 'Actual early photograph of Prince Karl and Princess Louise—very faded of course. . . . Another of Nicolo Novelda and Cleo Torres—no better but you can see what they looked like . . . And here is Suzanne Belsac—daguerreotype, taken in Paris . . . wonderful, wonderful—a great unknown romance —now what do you say, Mr Priestley ?'

All I could say was that I would keep the manuscript and the various illustrations for a week or so, and then I would either return them or agree to make something out of them, with my agent sending him a contract. If I did agree, however, it must be understood that what I wrote would be something that pleased myself—I always write to please myself first of all—and that if it displeased him and any surviving members of his family, then they must make the best of it.

Just a week later, I telephoned him—he had left me a number— to say that I proposed to write a novella called *The Pavilion of Masks*, and that a contract from my agent, giving him 25% of all rights, publication, film, TV and radio, was already in the post. Oddly enough, I never saw Dr A. F. D. Perkisson again; he dwindled, as the Epilogue will disclose, into a telephone voice.

Meanwhile, after poring over the manuscript and those drawings, engravings, early photographs, this is what I made of it all.

One

ON A BRIGHT warm morning in the early autumn of 1847, a cab
arrived at the front entrance of the Pavilion of Masks. The driver
having opened the door, a shortish elderly man stepped out, looking
very hot, almost steaming in his thick black suit. He wiped his
spectacles and then asked, 'How much?'

'Two thalers, gracious sir.'

'Too much. A thaler a mile? Ridiculous! Far too much!'

'It *is* too much,' said the driver with a frank and friendly air. 'But
that is the tariff now. Look for yourself, gracious sir. Here it is.
*From the Golden Lion to the Palace or the Pavilion of Masks—2
Thalers.* We can't argue against that, can we, sir? So—two thalers
if you please.'

After paying him, the elderly man saw two grotesque figures
making large gestures as they came weaving on their way. 'Who are
these fellows?'

The driver turned. 'Idiot students. *And* drunk.' Hurriedly he
climbed to his seat, gave his two horses a touch of the whip, and
drove away.

Feeling uneasy now, the elderly man moved closer to the Pavilion
door but before he could pull at the bell there, a young man came
charging out to wave and bellow at the two drunken students, sending them away. He looked at the visitor. 'Sir, I am sorry if you have
had any trouble out here—'

'No, thanks to you.'

'The fact is, our students' corps had a great beer evening last night, and I'm afraid those fellows are still drunk.'

'But what are you students doing here?'

'We take it in turns to provide a guard for the Countess of Feldhausen, our beautiful Cleo Torres. Today I'm Captain of the Guard. Wilhelm Glubfer—student of philosophy.' He had long fair hair and a long and rather foolish face, and the gaudy tunic he wore didn't fit him. However, there in his belt was an enormous pistol.

'And you are—er—?'

'I am Dr Stockhorn of Zurich, the German–Swiss representative of a famous financial house—'

'Ah—a financier—'

'A financier—certainly,' said Dr Stockhorn with some complacency. 'And my business here is very important, young man.'

'So. But this is not the Palace, where you will find Prince Karl or some of his officials. This is the Pavilion of Masks, the home of the Countess—'

'I am aware of that, Mr Glubfer. But I wish to see the Countess first.'

'You are acquainted with her? I ask, you understand, as Captain of the Student Guard. We have to be very careful, these days—'

'Not all of you apparently,' said Dr Stockhorn drily. 'Those fellows, for example—'

Glubfer suddenly turned himself into a Prussian. 'They will be dismissed from the Student Guard by this evening,' he shouted. 'And already I have apologized for them, Doctor.' Still wary but taking an easier tone, 'I asked if you were acquainted with the Countess.'

'She will remember me. I knew her long ago, before she was the Countess of anything. And may I remind you that I am here on important business—'

'She is still out riding but may return at any moment.' Glubfer was immensely dignified. 'Please to enter, Dr Stockhorn.'

He was ushered into a large entrance hall, well furnished with comfortable chairs and various odd tables but also having an ornate staircase on its way to other and more intimate rooms. He stared about him. 'Picturesque no doubt but I would say—gimcrack,' he muttered, more to himself than to Glubfer.

'Entirely rebuilt, specially for the Countess, only three years ago, and designed by a leading architect from Munich,' said Glubfer, a guide now. 'The style of decoration was chosen by the Countess

herself. You will notice the recurring comic and tragic masks, also
the various suggestions of dancing girls everywhere. A brave free
spirit, she is not ashamed of her origins. You can wait in comfort
there, I think, Dr Stockhorn.' He waved a hand towards one of the
larger chairs, and then, as the visitor sat down, he began walking on
his way out.

'One moment, please, Mr Glubfer.' It is not easy to call out and
yet at the same time create a confidential atmosphere, but Dr
Stockhorn, an old hand, could do it and brought Glubfer to stand
close to his chair.

'We financial men, Mr Glubfer, are always in need of information
and are always ready, if necessary, to reward our informants. Now
tell me,' he continued, lowering his voice, 'why does the Countess—
Cleo Torres—seek your protection?'

'She has never sought it. But we students felt it might be necessary.'

'Quite so. But why?'

This question turned Glubfer into a divided young man. How
could he combine the confidential manner with his own oratorical
style? 'Why does Cleo Torres need our protection, Dr Stockhorn?
I will tell you.' He took a deep breath and launched into oratory.
'Because she is Prince Karl's mistress and he built this Pavilion of
Masks entirely for her. Because she is a bold free spirit, lighting a
beacon—'

'Yes, yes, yes, I can imagine all that. But how does she stand
politically?'

'She has offended our two strongest political parties. The Jesuit
Reactionaries don't object to her morals but detest her political
views. The Radical Party, which is bourgeois and puritanical, dislikes her morals—'

'And thinks she costs too much,' Stockhorn put in neatly. He
waited a moment. 'So now she's extremely unpopular—'

'But not,' cried Glubfer, 'with those of us—young, pure in heart
—who worship beauty and freedom—'

'Quite so—she's extremely unpopular—'

'No, sir. I said—'

'I heard you. But we were talking politics, in which the young
and pure in heart are of little or no importance. A shade closer, Mr
Glubfer, please. Now tell me—is there any truth in the rumours
that Prince Karl may soon dismiss her?'

The student of philosophy now emerged, together with an air of profundity. 'There may be. There may not be. It is not impossible. But is it probable? Let us say that it is possibly probable.'

'Go on. Unless,' Stockhorn added drily, 'you feel you've exhausted the subject. Perhaps if you told me what has been happening—um?'

'Lately there have been stormy scenes—both here and in Dorheim—'

'Involving Cleo Torres?'

'Directly or indirectly—yes, Dr Stockhorn. What can you expect? She is a fearless, proud, untrammelled soul—indifferent to public opinion—'

'Which public opinion always resents, even in Mexe-Dorberg. I think you would hate to admit that Cleo may not last much longer here, so I won't press you but will draw my own conclusions. But I thank you all the same.' He waited a moment and then when he continued, his voice had lost its hard dry tone. 'Ach!—I knew her ten years ago—first in Prague, then in Petersburg—still young, still innocent.' He took off his spectacles to wipe them. He would have said something else but Glubfer stopped him. There were sounds, various noises, voices, coming from outside.

Glubfer was impressive. 'She is here.'

Two

THE TWO RIDERS who were now dismounting were not badly matched. Cleo Torres, Countess of Feldhausen, was wearing an emerald-green riding habit that set off her dark beauty and eyes that still glittered with anger. A first glance would have kept her in her middle twenties, but a closer examination would have added some years, perhaps reaching as far as the middle thirties. She had a splendid figure. Her companion, Nicolo Novelda, was a man nearing forty, as dark as she was except that he had greenish eyes, alight with humour, hardly in agreement with his black moustache and short pointed beard, suggesting a compromise between a diplomat and a sorcerer. He wasn't really dressed for riding, though he was in fact an excellent horseman, for he was wearing a loose and not long brown coat and light peg-top trousers. His manner, unlike hers, was easy and careless. But he opened the door for her, and she hurried into the Pavilion flourishing a short whip as if she would be happy to use it on somebody.

However, not on Glubfer, now officiously reporting as Captain today of her Students' Guard. She smiled and extended a hand, and at once he knelt and kissed it fervently. It was then she noticed Dr Stockhorn, who was out of his chair and was staring at her intently. To this she replied with a frown.

'Who is this?' she demanded of Glubfer haughtily.

Back on his feet again, Glubfer said hurriedly, 'A gentleman from Zurich on important financial business—'

'Dr Stockhorn, Countess,' he announced himself rather uneasily.

'And now I see—' but he hesitated.

Still frowning, haughtier than ever. 'Well sir, what do you see?'

'That indeed you are very beautiful, Countess.' His reply was humble enough, but then he went wrong. 'And that I was right to think that you and I had met before.'

'Rubbish! I don't know you.' She turned to Glubfer, awaiting orders. 'You may go, Glubfer. And tell your young men to be careful. A lout on the Lime Walk flung a foul name at me—and I slashed his idiot's face with this whip. There may be trouble later. Be ready for it, Glubfer. Be alert, man, be resolute, be daring. On guard now—go!' Waving Glubfer away, she turned to give another frown. 'You heard what I said? I don't know you. And if I thought you meant to be impertinent—' She left the threat in the air but flourished her whip.

The poor Swiss almost grovelled. 'Countess, I assure you—'

She was brisk now, cutting him short. 'Explain your business to Dr Novelda. He has my complete confidence in all matters. I must change. But if it should be really necessary, I could receive you in my boudoir later. Nicolo, find out what he wants.'

The two men watched her hurry upstairs. The atmosphere cleared at once. Novelda gave the other man an encouraging smile. 'Well—now, Mr Stockhorn—'

There was no reason why he should stand any nonsense from this fellow. 'Dr Stockhorn,' he corrected him sharply. 'Not medicine—political economy—Zurich. And you, Dr Novelda?'

'Doctor of philosophy—University of Padua.' The encouraging smile was still there. 'Join me in a glass of wine? No? The wine here is good. Cleo doesn't buy it, I do. But if you won't drink, at least sit down, Dr Stockhorn. Settle down in comfort, make your mind easy, and forget that whip.' He sauntered across to a side table and poured out a glass of hock. After a sip or two, he returned to give Stockhorn a long enquiring look.

'I must tell you,' said Stockhorn quietly, replying to the look, 'I am here as the German-Swiss representative of the House of Rothschild—'

'London?'

'No, Paris. Jacob Rothschild.'

'Not so good,' Novelda told him. 'At least, not just now. Paris is running into trouble, isn't it?'

'The House of Rothschild,' Stockhorn declared, 'has always been able to cope with that kind of trouble, my dear sir.'

'You're right of course.' Novelda perched himself on the arm of a solid chair, drank more wine, and looked down and across at the visitor amiably. 'And I'm impressed. I don't remember anybody from Rothschild's coming here to little Mexe-Dorberg. If there is anything I can tell you, don't hesitate to ask me.'

'Very well, Dr Novelda.' He waited a moment. 'I wish first to know about her—Cleo. Is she always like that nowadays?'

'The grand manner?' He offered a slow mocking smile. 'We vary. We have our moods, you understand. But after face slashing with our whip, we prefer the grand manner.'

'Yes, yes, I follow you. It may explain something. For a moment, no matter what she said, I thought she recognized me, Dr Novelda.'

'Dr Stockhorn, I'm sure she recognized you.'

'You must be right. And I must say that after that eloquent and romantic student, it is a pleasure to talk to you.'

'Hardly a compliment, though,' said Novelda. 'These students are probably the biggest donkeys in Europe.'

An approving nod, even a smile: 'I can well believe you have Cleo's confidence, Dr Novelda, but if you aren't her physician— what then?'

'She's never ill. Strong as a horse. But if you'll forgive me and wait half a minute, I'll explain what I do.' He drained his glass and returned it to the side-table, took a long dark cheroot out of a box there, lit it, and this time, puffing away, stretched himself out in an easy chair. 'Now what I do, Dr Stockhorn, is to minister to her mind, to her soul. I read her horoscope, stare into the crystal ball for her, lay out the fortune-telling cards. I keep her clear of evil magnetic influences.'

'And what exactly are evil magnetic influences, Dr Novelda?' A very dry enquiry.

'They are anything a woman wants them to be.'

'I would never have taken you for a charlatan.'

'And I wouldn't have thought you could be bad-mannered.' No smile now from Novelda, just a stare under raised eyebrows.

'I beg your pardon. But crystal-gazing—astrology—how can you take them seriously?

Novelda smiled. 'I do exactly as you do with high finance. As soon as fortune-telling is mentioned, I look solemn.'

'Yes, yes,' said Stockhorn impatiently, 'but our modern world couldn't exist without high finance.'

'Two hundred years ago the world thought it couldn't exist without astrology. You're jeering at me merely because I'm out of fashion in your circle. But here—you see—with Cleo, I am in fashion and indeed in high favour.'

'But if a man has a certain relationship with a woman,' Stockhorn began dubiously.

'No, no, I take your point,' Novelda told him. 'But this isn't a sexual relationship. I am no more her lover than you are Jacob Rothschild's. Now where did you meet her before, Dr Stockhorn?'

After some hesitation: 'Some years ago, in Prague, I was asked to help a beautiful girl who had lost her engagement as a dancer. She had, in fact, no talent. I was moving on to Petersburg and she persuaded me to take her with me. In Petersburg of course she soon found a protector. Her name then was not Cleo Torres but Fanny Donovan—Spanish mother, Irish father. But I recognized her at once. After all, I had seen her every day for many weeks. But she wasn't my mistress. It was not that kind of relationship—'

'No,' said Novelda cheerfully, 'just a sentimental friendship between a middle-aged businessman and a good-looking girl—eh?'

Stockhorn frowned at him. 'A friendship—but not sentimental, Dr Novelda, if you please. I'm never sentimental. I'm a man of hard facts and figures.'

'Are you sure?' Novelda asked softly. 'You probably came here just to take another look at her—'

'Nonsense!' The Swiss was annoyed. 'You are not telling fortunes now, Dr Novelda. I came here because Jacob Rothschild has been asked by Mexe-Dorberg for a loan. So we need information. After I have talked to Cleo, I must try to see Prince Karl. There is unrest here as there is almost everywhere. So what will happen?'

'That will depend on Cleo, not on Prince Karl. She is a far abler politician than he is—'

'Oh—come—come—my dear sir! I know his reputation in diplomatic circles—'

'And now you are beginning to talk nonsense, Dr Stockhorn. I know nothing about his reputation in diplomatic circles, but I *know* him.'

'Possibly. So?'

'The Prince is really a bad German minor poet. He ought to have been sitting every day in a café, writing atrocious verses for the local paper. Instead, he gives a third-rate performance as a master of intrigue and diplomacy, a kind of touring company Metternich. Cleo has more political sense in her little finger—and in any event will be advised by me—'

But Dr Stockhorn had now closed his eyes and was wagging his head in disbelief.

'You don't believe me, Dr Stockhorn?'

Opening his eyes to look contemptuous, Stockhorn cried, 'Of course not. Such rubbish. We're not crystal-gazing and reading the stars now. If you can't afford to tell me the truth, kindly say so. But no fairy tales. I'm here for information—facts—'

Novelda jumped out of his chair. 'Say no more, Dr Stockhorn. I've caught a glimpse of the upper realms of finance. I've had my lesson. And now, if you'll excuse me, I must go through some bills, here.' Still smoking his cheroot he went across to a small desk on the opposite side of the hall to its large windows, sat himself down and took no further notice of Dr Stockhorn.

After a few minutes, during which Stockhorn made some uneasy movements, 'I am afraid I have offended you, Dr Novelda.'

'Not at all,' Novelda replied coolly, without looking up from his bills. 'But I've much to do and can't afford to waste any more time telling you fairy tales.'

A pause. 'Am I wasting *my* time waiting in the hope that Cleo will see me?'

Novelda still didn't look up. 'Oh no, she'll see you any minute now. Sheer curiosity. But while she'll have changed her clothes, she may not have changed her mood. You'll have to risk that.'

Stockhorn contrived something that was not quite melancholy, not quite complacency, but somehow suggested both at once. 'I have had to take many risks. Ach—yes!' He made several of those vague noises that elderly men seem to enjoy, but he did not succeed in attracting Novelda's attention.

After an empty few minutes, a woman came down the staircase. She was grey-haired, plump, a few years past fifty. However, she was also trim and energetic, and her good plain face suggested a keen intelligence. Like so many Frenchwomen of her age, she was dressed in black and she was carrying a black mantilla. As she reached the bottom stair, she said, 'Dr Stockhorn?'

'Yes?' He was now on his feet.

'Allow me,' said Novelda, who had made a quick move from his desk. 'Dr Stockhorn—Madame Suzanne Belsac, Cleo's companion, housekeeper—'

'And now personal maid, cook—and if the last old woman leaves —bedmaker and dishwasher—' she added, rather grimly.

Stockhorn was astonished. 'You have no servants here?'

'In reply to Cleo's grand manner, they have now made a grand exit,' Novelda told him.

'And when or where we'll find any more, God knows,' the Frenchwoman muttered. Now she looked at Stockhorn and spoke up. 'I have a message from the Countess, Dr Stockhorn. She does not see why she should receive you, but she will do so if Dr Novelda should think it really necessary.' She turned to Novelda. 'Nicolo— what?'

'Yes, Suzanne, I think it is important.'

'Then, Dr Stockhorn, I will take you to her boudoir.'

Novelda gave their backs, climbing the stairs, a glance of sardonic amusement, and then returned to his desk. He did not look up from the bills he was sorting out, not even when she came down the stairs, still carrying the mantilla. She didn't speak for a few moments, just smiled at his bent figure in an affectionate semi-maternal fashion.

'Nicolo—stop pretending to work. Attend to me.'

He turned his chair round. 'For once you're wrong, my dear. I really am trying to work. I must deal with these bills today. However, if you want to talk to me—'

'I do. Nicolo—I'm surprised at you.' She was obviously about to give him a fond scolding. 'Apart from me, you're the only person in this idiotic German principality who isn't a fool—'

'You are nearly right—'

'Yet now even you go and behave like a fool. Last night's gambling! Cleo has just told me.'

Novelda pulled a face. 'Did she also tell you she lost over three thousand thalers?'

'Yes, but who cares? She has this gambling fever—for her it takes the place of love—but why do you allow her in infect you— *you*, a clever man, not one of these idiots. Yet you throw your money away at the tables—over five hundred Cleo says—all you had. So why, Nicolo—*why*?'

He got up and went closer to her, speaking very quietly. 'I went there hoping to turn five hundred thalers into five thousand. No doubt that was foolish. They say a man never wins when he plays in

that spirit. I took the risk because I can do nothing with five hundred
—but with five thousand—' But there he stopped.

She knew this was serious. 'Yes? With five thousand—what?'

'I can start again,' he told her very quietly. 'A new life.'

She stared at him, went closer, put a hand on his arm. 'Nicolo
my friend—if you knew something I ought to know, you'd tell me,
wouldn't you?'

'I would indeed, Suzanne. I might need your help.'

'You can depend upon it. But you must tell me everything you
know.'

'It's still impossible to make a plan,' he said softly. 'But the ice
is cracking and soon we may be in the water. So last night I gambled,
not to amuse myself, but because I must have money.'

She gave him a long hard look. 'Who is the woman?'

'We're not talking about women—'

'Money for starting again? A new life? And you are certainly not
entering a monastery, my friend. So there must be a woman in it
somewhere. I've felt for some time you must have one hidden away.
It's many months since the little dancer left Dorheim—'

'Ah—the delicious little Maria!' cried Novelda, overdoing it.
'What charm! What—'

'Rubbish! You're trying to change the subject. Delicious little
Maria—fiddlesticks! Good dancer's legs—a nice little bosom probably—and then what?'

'A passion for sweet wine and macaroons,' said Novelda, ruefully
reminiscent. 'And endless chatter about the ballet mistress at La
Scala and her uncle who is clerk to the Bishop of Pisa—'

'Of course—a stupid little thing! This woman you make your
plans for is quite different,' she added slyly.

'Quite different, because she doesn't exist.' He moved away a
few steps, but then turned to shake his head at her. 'My dear
Suzanne, if there was anything to tell you, I wouldn't keep it from
you. We must wait—but not long.' They were standing not very
far away from the bottom of the staircase. He touched her arm to
move with him much nearer the windows. 'That staircase has big
ears. Now then—how was Cleo up there?'

'Impossible!' She showed him the mantilla. 'I nearly threw this
mantilla in her face when she told me to mend and press it. Nicolo,
I'm so tired of this boring Cleo Torres. What *is* she? What *has* she?
No talent. No taste. No real feeling—'

'But a great performer,' said Novelda, smiling. 'Not on the stage of course—and, I'm told, not in bed—'

'It is really true, Nicolo, you never went to bed with her?'

'Most certainly, my dear. It explains the respect she has for me. She thinks that every man who insists upon bedding her is a fool.'

'I know that. But what has she to offer? Flashing eyes and a good figure—and all the rest is just impudence.'

'Yes,' said Novelda. 'But unlimited impudence is a kind of talent—perhaps genius—'

Suzanne was too busy being indignant to value that observation. 'The great Spanish dancer—my God! Even now she's never learnt how to wear a mantilla properly—like this.'

As she wore the mantilla, defying her years and comfortable size Suzanne began a spirited sketch of a Spanish dance while Novelda quietly laughed and applauded her. But then a great noise outside hurried them to the window.

An enormous travelling carriage, dust-stained and weighed down with baggage, had arrived. A young man, probably a courier, jumped out, said something to Glubfer and waved him away, then held the door of the carriage wide open for somebody important to alight. As soon as this somebody got out—a shortish man with a fine large head—he flung aside the rich cloak he had been wearing but stopped a moment or two to speak to his courier.

'Name of God!' cried Suzanne. 'It's Victor Vatannes.'

Glubfer looked in. 'Count Victor Vatannes—the great French poet,' he announced.

'Yes,' said Novelda. 'Go away.'

Not to be caught staring out, he and Suzanne hurried away from the window and took their stand half-way between the staircase and the entrance, which they faced, Suzanne still wearing the forgotten mantilla. Count Victor came in and waited a moment to display himself. He was wearing a splendid cravat, a waisted cutaway dark coat, and striped light trousers to make his legs, obviously rather short, look longer. Then he rushed across to Suzanne, dropped to one knee and seized her hand, kissing it fervently.

'I have travelled eight hundred miles, day and night, to kiss this hand,' he declared passionately.

'Nonsense!' And she snatched away both her hand and the mantilla.

'Madame, my apologies. I thought you were Cleo Torres—'

'No, I'm the cook,' she told him brutally. She moved quickly towards the far end of the hall, but then turned. 'I'm Suzanne Belsac. We met in Paris, Count Victor. At Emile de Girardin's. Be careful—you're putting on weight.' Then she opened a door at that end of the hall and closed it smartly behind her.

The poet stared at Novelda, still horrified. 'Putting on weight! Surely not!'

Novelda smiled at him. 'Come, Count Victor, you must know women say anything when they're annoyed—'

'But is she the cook?'

'She is today. Normally she's Cleo's companion and housekeeper, but all the servants here departed in a body early this morning. And it looks as if I'll be a superior doorman instead of the resident magician. I am Dr Novelda, Count.'

'Of course, of course—I have heard of you, Dr Novelda.' If Cleo had an imperious grand manner, Victor Vatannes had a romantic-poetical grand manner and now swam into it. 'Yes, of course—you are the confidential adviser of our radiant Cleo Torres. You claim supernatural knowledge. I shall value your friendship, Dr Novelda. The poet and the magician should be allies.'

Novelda, an old hand, could adopt this style too. 'I am honoured, Count Victor. The fame of the greatest romantic poet in Europe— and his noble works—are known and treasured here.'

The poet flashed his fine eyes. 'She reads my verses, knows my dreams?'

'She does.'

'She has spoken to you of my genius, my passion for freedom, my endless quest of the ideal, my tragic destiny?'

'She has,' Novelda said emphatically, though he couldn't remember how or why or when.

'Then soul has cried to soul across the wastes?'

'No doubt,' said Novelda, who had had enough now of the grand style. 'But what wastes?'

'Ah—you think I exaggerate.' Taking his cue the poet also abandoned the grand style. 'But I don't. I've just crossed the wastes of White Russia and Poland. Damnable country—flea-bitten—no wine worth drinking—nothing to eat but eggs. And a fast journey there, day and night, is hellishly expensive. My publishers in Paris, who will have to pay for it, will never believe what it costs. But the thought of Cleo Torres has haunted me these past weeks. Though

we have never met, I have long felt that our destinies are inter-
twined. She *is* here, I take it?'

'Upstairs, talking to a Swiss financier.'

Victor was about to ask a question but stopped himself. He looked
around for the first time. 'German work of course. Heavy—tasteless.
The Prince should have engaged French architects and decorators.
However, I don't propose to live here. But, Dr Novelda, you and I
need a quiet private room in which to exchange our ideas. Perhaps
through that door over there where Madame Belsac went—eh?'

'That leads to the dining room,' said Novelda, 'and then through
to the kitchen. I would take you upstairs to my room, but then I
wouldn't know what was happening down here—and I have no
man on duty to warn me. Come—this is the best I can do for you,
and you can take a glass of wine with me.'

He led the way to the side-table that held the wine and glasses.
It was well removed from the entrance and the staircase, and was
not far from the dining room door. He began pouring out some more
hock and indicated a chair close to his own. 'This isn't too bad. If
we don't shout at each other, we shan't be overheard.'

Victor nodded, drank his wine, and became at once a partner in
conspiracy. 'A Swiss financier—eh? Cleo needs money?'

'Who doesn't? But she didn't send for the Swiss. *He* came to her
here.'

Victor half-closed his eyes, lowered his voice. 'There are also
rumours that the Prince is about to banish Cleo. Is there any truth
in them?'

'I wonder,' said Novelda blandly.

The two eyed each other for a moment. Then, looking away,
Victor, after some hesitation, finished his wine as if he had come to
a decision. 'I'll be frank with you, my dear Novelda. I need an ally
here.'

'For what? You have some plan?'

'Yes.' He leant forward. 'Suppose I persuaded Cleo to fly with
me to Paris—'

Novelda's eyes, which might be said to have been twinkling,
widened and lit up. He returned to the grand manner. 'It would be
the romantic sensation of the age.'

'That is how I see it. The poet of love flings open the door of her
golden prison—'

'Cleo Torres abandons power and wealth for a poet's devotion—'

Victor wagged a triumphant finger. 'And we cross the frontier only a few minutes ahead of the Prince's cavalry. It could become the great legend of our time.'

'It could. And if you hadn't been a poet, Count Victor, what a journalist you'd have made. Do you happen to have any important new work ready for publication?'

'Only awaiting my return to Paris. My masterpiece—*Semiramis, A Tale of Assyria*—an epic in six parts.'

'Perfect! After this sensational affair, all Europe would resound with it,' said Novelda smoothly.

'Something tells me so,' the poet replied, not without complacency. 'But that isn't what has brought me here. I've been blown here, a leaf in the wind, by my emotions. I'm entirely a man of feeling—'

'Naturally—'

'And surely I may depend upon Cleo—'

'Certainly.' Novelda was smoother than ever. 'Cleo is entirely a woman of feeling. You will set her on fire at once—'

'You think so?'

'I guarantee it. *But*'—and now he held up a warning finger, gave Victor a hard searching look, and changed his tone—'but to elope with her, to abduct her, with the Prince's dragoons in hot pursuit—and I'm sorry to say all his cavalry is short of good remounts—all this means that officially she must be still under his Highness's protection. If she's been dismissed, then she merely takes another lover—accepts the poet, failing the Prince. The affair looks almost shabby. No romantic sensation there.'

Victor nodded gloomily. 'I must say I find it profoundly distasteful to consider the matter in such terms—'

'Of course,' said Novelda with smooth irony. 'But I speak as an essentially prosaic character.'

'But you're undoubtedly right. As I said before, I need an ally here.'

'You have one.'

'I ask for no better, my dear Dr Novelda.' They shook hands solemnly. 'You know, if you follow us I could make you the rage of Paris, with every woman of fashion clamouring to consult you.'

'I will help you to take her to Paris,' said Novelda calmly. 'But I may not follow you myself. So far I have other plans. But we shall see.'

'What about Prince Karl? He has the reputation of being hard—a ruthless man, cunning in diplomacy—'

'You don't have to believe it. He hasn't that reputation here in the Pavilion of Masks. In my experience few of us are what we seem —or even what we imagine ourselves to be. As for Prince Karl—'

But he stopped there, and both men sprang up and looked at the staircase. Dr Stockhorn came clattering down it, closely followed by Cleo, very angry and flourishing her whip.

'But I assure you, Countess,' cried poor Dr Stockhorn, over his shoulder.

'Get out—get out—you wretched money-grubbing creature—*out*,' Cleo was shrieking as she tried to hit him.

'But—please—please—you're mistaken—' This came from Stockhorn as he made for the front door and the open air. But Cleo just had time, before he vanished, to let her whip fall across his back. However she didn't pursue him but turned away from the closed door and stood for half a minute to catch her breath. Her eyes were bright; her colour high; she had changed her riding costume for a light-grey close-fitting upper garment, against which her breasts seemed to be straining, and a full tiered skirt of pale pink; and she looked splendid indeed.

'Magnificent!' cried Victor with enthusiasm. 'Truly magnificent!' He was moving closer.

She stared at him. 'And who are you?'

He bowed, smiled, then quoted in his grandest manner:

> *In desolate lands and on the trackless sea,*
> *I burn my time till I have sight of thee.*

At once Cleo was all excitement. 'Yes, yes—of course. You are Victor Vatannes—the great French poet—'

'Who has travelled a thousand miles, day and night, to kiss this hand.' And he kissed it rapturously, to Cleo's obvious delight.

'Count Victor,' she began, rising to his style, 'I am one of your most ardent admirers. You are a man—a true man—as I am a true woman, who defies the miserable conventions of this age—'

'We spurn the chains offered to us—'

'The air most people breath only stifles us—'

'We live on mountain peaks,' cried Victor.

'And now at last salute each other—the poet of love—the woman starved of the love of an equal soul—'

[118]

'Yes, yes, yes—and what would I not dare for you?'

'Dare all then—dare all!' Cleo opened her arms, though without moving closer to him. 'Victor—my poet—'

'Cleo—spirit of the South,' he proclaimed. 'Passion and freedom incarnate—Cleo!'

They ended this rhapsody, breathing deeply, gazing at each other as if about to fall into each other's arms, but not in fact making any move. By this time Novelda had shrugged them away and gone back to his desk.

Cleo was now brisk and businesslike. 'Victor, where is your baggage?'

'In Dorheim now—at the Golden Lion—'

'I can't have you staying there,' she told him, 'surrounded by those German oafs and listening to the vilest gossip. You must stay here. Cancel your room—send for your baggage.'

'But the Prince?'

'He is one of your admirers too. But that is not the point. It is I, Cleo, who insist upon your staying here, in my Pavilion. Nicolo, explain to him while I speak to Suzanne about lunch.'

As she made for the dining room door, Novelda left his desk and as he moved across to Victor he softly clapped his hands together. 'I congratulate you, my dear Count. She is nearly yours already. It's years since I heard such passionate rhetoric—outside a playhouse. But you must do as she commands you—and stay here.'

Victor brought his shoulders nearly up to his ears. 'But the Prince, my friend, the Prince—'

'What about him?'

'He rules this country. And I can't take her away from him if he puts me under arrest.'

'He won't. Cleo knows exactly how far she can go with him. And he'll be delighted to see you here. Now off you go—settle your bill at the inn—'

'I'll do that of course. But remember—I'm depending on you, my friend.'

'You couldn't do better. By the way, this elopement may be expensive, and we're out of funds here. How much money have you?'

'I'll cash a large draft at the bank.'

'Do that—and then hurry back, my dear Count. Cleo's catching fire already.'

'So am I. What a woman!' He looked as if he were about to go, but then hesitated and finally beckoned Novelda closer. He used a whisper now. 'But—er—this whip business. I thought all those stories mere inventions.'

'So they are, most of 'em,' said Novelda, also in a whisper. 'You must take her by storm.'

'Well of course in the ordinary way that's what I'd do. But what with one thing and another—finishing my epic—Russia—the journey here—not much sleep—'

'Naturally you're feeling exhausted,' said Novelda smoothly, 'not quite ready for storming—'

'Could you—perhaps—drop her a hint—'

'Leave everything to me.'

'I'm most grateful to you—'

'Then don't forget to call at the bank,' said Novelda, taking him to the door.

Three

NOVELDA WAS BACK at his desk, still trying to sort out the bills, when Cleo returned from the dining room, followed by Suzanne, who was wearing an apron now and carrying an open bottle of champagne, which Cleo, glass in hand, had already sampled.

'This is to drink to our poet,' said Cleo. 'Suzanne says she doesn't like him.'

'Well, she doesn't have to like him,' said Novelda, leaving his desk to find a glass on the side-table. 'What's for lunch, Suzanne?'

'Blue trout—and *vol-au-vent*—'

'Good! Better cook enough for four—'

'Six—if Victor Vatannes eats as much as he used to do—'

'It's obvious you don't like him. Why?' said Cleo.

'I used to adore Byron when I was young,' Suzanne began slowly, 'and I used to weep over broken hearts, despair, and great souls doomed to wander. But Victor Vatannes is too late—and still too artfully busy in the doomed-soul-and-despair business.'

'If he makes money, so much the better,' Cleo remarked briskly. She smiled at the other two. 'Thank God the three of us have the place to ourselves for a little time. But listen, Nicolo—this can't be the man you said would arrive to change everything. You said *he* would come from the East.'

'Count Victor *has* come from the East. He's just arrived from Russia—'

'Just to see me?'

'That's what he told me. And I believe him.' Novelda held up his

[121]

glass. 'I give you Count Victor Vatannes.'

Suzanne drank to him with the other two, but ended by shaking her head. 'Not worth it. Well—back to the kitchen. Butter sauce with the trout?'

'Certainly,' said Novelda. 'And plenty of it. One of the few good ideas the Germans have ever had.'

'Soon we'll be too fat to run away.' And Suzanne left them.

'Now Cleo, we may have little time,' said Nicolo, very briskly indeed. 'I know this poet wants you. Do you want him?'

'Aren't you going too fast?'

'No. He wants to elope with you—to abduct you—preferably with cavalry in pursuit—'

'Oh—what a wonderful idea! Where—to Paris?' Cleo glowed with enthusiasm.

'To Paris.'

'It would be a romantic sensation.'

'That's what we told each other. He arrives with you in Paris, just as his new masterpiece comes from the press—'

'I care nothing about that.'

'I know, but don't tell him so. The point is—*you'd* return to Paris in the most romantically sensational circumstances. A ruling Prince thrown away for love. If you choose to be witty, you could say you'd exchanged an amateur minor poet for a professional major poet.'

'I could be wittier than that—'

'So could I—but we're pressed for time. What do you want? More champagne?'

'Yes, of course.' As he filled her glass, 'But why all this talk about time? It's not like you, Nicolo, to sound panic-stricken. Nothing has happened.'

'Not yet. But the kettle's coming to the boil. A great many things, mostly unpleasant, may happen at any moment. If we're not ready to juggle with them, they'll juggle with us.'

'What things?'

'I'll come to them. But first—have you any money?'

'No, of course not. You know what happened last night.'

Novelda gave her a hard look. 'Cleo, you owe me between three and four thousand thalers.'

'And what if I do? You know I'll pay you as soon as I can. I always have.'

'Not good enough. I need the money today,' he said sharply.

She couldn't hide her alarm. 'Nicolo—you're not leaving me?'

'I hope *you* will be leaving *me*, Cleo. We can't have an elopement for three.'

'No, but you can follow on afterwards.' She twisted his sleeve in her urgency. 'You mustn't leave me, Nicolo. You're the only man whose judgment I believe in. I think you're the only man I've ever known that I've really respected—'

'Because most men imagine you have nothing but sex. I saw from the first you had almost everything—except sex.' Now he gave her another hard look. 'Cleo, I can't carry out any plan without money—and you owe me thousands—'

'Oh—take this then,' she cried. She pulled at the diamond bracelet. 'It must be worth ten thousand.'

'Thank you, Cleo. I shan't get ten thousand for it, but it'll help us out. Now to business. You are ready to elope with Victor Vatannes?'

'Of course. It settles everything.' She clapped her hands. 'I can dance again. I'll be the rage of Paris.'

'Dream about that later. We're still talking business. Now Vatannes won't carry you off unless you're still in favour here. The cavalry must be pursuing you and not escorting you to the frontier.'

'I can keep Karl by my side for another day or two.' She was thoughtful now. 'And we could complete our plans for running away in twenty-four hours.'

'We may not have twenty-four hours. We may not have twelve—'

'Ridiculous! I can hold Karl—'

'I tell you,' cried Novelda harshly, 'not even twelve hours if the pressure on the other side's too great. First, there's the Dorheim mob whose face you keep slashing—'

'Pooh! I'm not afraid of them.'

'No, but Karl will be if he hears them howling outside these windows tonight. And if he *isn't* here tonight, then you'll have lost him anyhow. No, be quiet, Cleo. One of us must think.' He wandered slowly across to the side-table, but took a cheroot instead of more wine. 'Next,' he said, after lighting the cheroot, 'there's this financial man, Stockhorn. Why the devil didn't you make a friend of him instead of threatening him with that idiotic whip of yours?'

'Because he tried to humiliate me,' she replied. 'Pretending that years ago in Prague he'd almost kept me out of the gutter!'

Novelda fingered his moustache. '*Pretending?*'

'I'd made it quite plain I'd no intention of recognizing him,' she continued haughtily. 'A *gentleman* would have taken the hint.'

'Why expect him to be a gentleman? Jacob Rothschild would no more send a gentleman on an errand like this than he'd send a bassoon player. What did he say to you?'

'Oh—he reminded me that he'd helped me once. Then he said that if things turned out badly for me now, he'd be ready to help me again. Without any conditions—he was never my lover, you understand—'

'So you had to fly at him in a fury.'

'I felt he was trying to humiliate me—'

'It's just as I thought.' Novelda sat down, made himself comfortable, took a pull or two at his cheroot. 'This man Stockhorn pretends, even to himself, that he's nothing but a hard man of business. Actually, he's a German–Swiss sentimentalist, seeing himself helping beauty in distress. He enjoyed doing it once. Now he'd enjoy doing it all over again.'

Cleo wasn't impressed. 'Why should we care?'

'You aren't thinking, Cleo. You must be suffering from that theatrical balderdash you exchanged with Count Victor.' He waited a moment, pointing his cheroot at her. 'Stockhorn's duty to Rothschilds and his own secret inclinations now run all one way. He's prepared to ruin you so that you'll be helpless again. He'll tell Prince Karl there can't be a loan while you're still here. You'd then be dismissed and there could be no dramatic elopement with Vatannes. This means we can't allow Stockhorn to see Karl anywhere but here in the Pavilion of Masks, where we can control events. Therefore we must bring Stockhorn back.'

'How can we when I drove him out?'

'You must send an urgent message to him. Write it now.' As he saw her hesitating, he left his chair to lead her towards the writing desk, still talking as they moved. 'Remember—he's not what he thinks he is, but a sentimentalist, choked with unused sex turned into sentimentality.'

Cleo sat at the desk but still looked bewildered. 'But what can I say to him, Nicolo?'

'Try this.' He began dictating very slowly. '*My dear Dr Stockhorn ... What you said this morning brought back the past ... and hurt my foolish pride . . . so I behaved very badly to an old friend and benefactor . . . I have been feeling very unhappy about it . . . and so dear friend I beg you to come and see me early this evening . . . so that I can ask for and receive your forgiveness . . . please—please !*

He waited for her to catch up, then said, 'Underline the second *please*—and if you can manage a tearful smudge somewhere, all the better.'

'But I don't see,' Cleo objected, 'how you can expect a hard-headed man of business, clever enough to represent Rothschilds, to swallow such stuff.'

'If *I* offered it to him, he wouldn't,' said Novelda. 'But you meet him at the point where he's busy deceiving himself. And there a man's completely vulnerable—he helps you to deceive him. You know this as well as I do. The trouble is, you're really thinking about being the rage of Paris. But this won't happen unless you and I use our wits and make it happen. Now seal the note and we'll have it delivered at once.' He went to the door and called out, 'Captain of the Guard! Mr Glubfer!'

By the time that Glubfer, looking immensely self-important, had entered and come forward, Cleo had the note ready for him. Bestowing a smile upon him, she said, 'Please ask one of your young men to take this at once to Dr Stockhorn at the Golden Lion.'

'And choose a sober one,' Novelda told him.

Glubfer bowed. 'It shall be done at once, gracious Countess. It is an honour to serve you.' Another bow and off he went.

'They're rather sweet, those boys,' said Cleo.

'All students are idiotic,' Novelda declared. 'But these are the biggest boobies of all time. God help Germany!' He laughed but then sharply changed his tone. 'Well, so much for Stockhorn. Now —Prince Karl. If he calls this morning, you must keep him here, out of harm's way. If he doesn't call, send him a message, tell him you're miserable, ask him to explain the political situation abroad—'

'Don't be stupid, Nicolo. Telling me how to handle Karl!'

'You're quite right, my dear. I'm wasting time. But you agree that we must keep him here, where the politicians can't get at him. It only needs one strong Radical deputation talking to him officially in the Palace, then you might be dismissed. And if you're dismissed, you can't elope with the poet—'

'I know, I know, I know.' Cleo was all impatience. 'What is the matter with you today, Nicolo? You are not yourself at all. No

[125]

longer quiet and calm and clever. All hurry-scurry. And if you're seriously thinking of leaving me, why are you so anxious that this precious eloping plan should succeed? Why—Nicolo—why?'

'Perhaps it would be best for you—and best for me. And perhaps I want to leave everything neat and tidy before I go. If I'm not being as calm and clever as I ought to be, then I apologize, Cleo. The trouble is, that while you still think we have plenty of time, I know we haven't. If midnight finds us all as we are now, we're trapped—and done for. So there is some reason for hurry-scurry, though I agree I must collect myself. Yes, what is it, Glubfer?'

Not only had Glubfer marched in but he had also closed the door carefully behind him. 'Councillor von Marstein, the politician, leader of the Radicals, is outside and wishes to see the Countess.'

'Not until I'm ready to see him,' said Cleo hastily. 'Guard the door yourself until then, dear Mr Glubfer.' She watched him go and then took Novelda to the far end of the hall. 'Listen, Nicolo! It's this man, von Marstein, who has turned the Radicals against me. He's convinced them that I must go. And I hear he's asking for an official audience with Karl to tell him so. You've not met him, have you?'

'No, unfortunately—'

'He's one of those cold heavy calculating men that a woman can do nothing with. An ambitious puritan. He's always spoken against me, even when I was popular with the Radicals. He hates me.'

Novelda opened his eyes wide. 'Now why should he hate you?'

'Because I'm Cleo Torres of course—the wicked extravagant mistress—'

'Yes, yes, but a calculating man, an ambitious politician, ought to regard you as just another piece on the chessboard. There must be something personal in such hatred.'

'He hates me because he doesn't want me.'

'No, that won't do,' said Novelda. 'I don't want you, but I don't hate you. What if he hates you because he *does* want you. Probably he doesn't know it, but that's what is wrong with him. He's probably a sensualist—a puritan with fire down below—'

'You don't know the man.'

'Do you? Have you ever been in a room alone with him? No, I thought not. Well, let's try removing the jumping hot lid. Ready, Cleo?' He hurried across to the door and as he opened it, an angry voice could be heard.

'And *I* tell *you*—I am Councillor von Marstein—and I *insist*—you hear me—*insist*—'

'Come in, come in, Councillor,' cried Novelda. 'I'm sorry you've been kept waiting.'

Four

VON MARSTEIN, WHO was wearing heavy boots to show he was a man of the People, came clomping in. Ignoring Novelda, now regarding him with some distaste, he clomped straight across to Cleo. He was a bulky man about fifty, and had enormous eyebrows, rather bulging eyes, and the loose-lipped mouth often found among professional orators.

He gave Cleo a stiff little bow. 'Councillor von Marstein. I must speak to you, Cleo Torres.'

'One moment. If I am Torres, then you are simply Marstein.'

'Councillor von Marstein, if you please.'

Cleo was in good form. 'The same authority that created you Councillor von Marstein created me the Countess Feldenhausen. So either we are Countess and Councillor or we are Torres and Marstein. Please yourself.'

Another man might have been amused, but this one was surly. 'Oh—if you must have your title—Countess then.'

'This is Dr Novelda. He is completely in my confidence.'

'So I have heard. The fortune-telling charlatan—um?' He threw Novelda a contemptuous glance.

'Certainly,' said Novelda loudly and cheerfully. 'And you, being a politician, are the fortune-*promising* charlatan. But I am more amusing and less expensive.'

'You don't amuse me.' But the Councillor was already frowning at Cleo. 'Some of us are very narrow provincial folk, Countess, so narrow that we object to the money we earn and pay in taxes being flung into the lap of a—well, let us say a Spanish dancer—if you *are* Spanish—and *can* dance. Reports seem to vary—'

Cleo was furious. 'I don't care what you think about my morals but let me tell you I am a true artiste—'

'Then you ought to know when to make your exit—'

'When I've finished my performance—and not before—'

'I suggest *tonight*,' said the Councillor heavily. 'I came here to tell you so. The anger of the decent people in Dorheim grows every day. It has now reached the point where it must find an outlet. That outlet will be *here*. You understand? Here—at your trumpery and lascivious Pavilion of Masks.'

'Councillor, for once I am ready to agree with you,' said Novelda. 'Cleo, don't think we can ignore what he says.'

But she was ready now for the grand manner, as if she had heard a cue on the stage. 'He may frighten you, Nicolo, but he can't frighten me. I've faced mobs before—cowards, louts, idiots—all beer, sausage and wind.' Looking bold and magnificent, she flashed her eyes at the Councillor. 'Cleo Torres isn't one of the whining snivelling creatures *you* call women.'

Not without reluctant admiration, von Marstein replied, 'I'll grant you that much, Countess.'

'Tell your fat-bellied followers I not only have a whip but keep a pair of pistols here and know how to use them.'

Novelda put in hastily, 'Don't do anything of the kind. It's probably only a line from an old play. We must talk politics not pistols.'

'Now you are talking like a sensible man—'

'I *am* a sensible man—'

'Then allow me.' The Councillor addressed them both, speaking very carefully. 'It's quite simple. Even if Prince Karl wished to protect her, he won't dare to put his army to the test. Look at it. He knows already that most of his officers belong to the Church Party—your old enemies, Countess. He will learn from me tonight that most of the common soldiers are now with *us*, the Radicals. History shows us that it is fatal to give soldiers orders they will almost certainly disobey. It's asking for revolution.'

'Which is what you Radicals want,' said Cleo.

'Not I, Countess, not when I'm within sight of attaining power quietly and peaceably. Anything can happen in a revolution.' He broke off because there was a lot of noise outside. 'What the devil's this?'

'A small revolution perhaps,' said Novelda. 'Or a famous French poet.'

It was the poet. 'I am here and all is settled. I have brought back my travelling carriage with all my baggage—called at the bank too, Dr Novelda. Ah!—my Cleo—'

'Victor! My poet! At last!' cried Cleo, delighted to see him.

He was about to kiss her hand but this time she flung her arms round him and embraced him passionately, with as much display of herself as she could contrive. Then, still holding him, she regarded him fondly. 'My darling poet!'

Victor adopted the same style at once. 'My beautiful dark angel!'

'My darling,' said Cleo, 'this is Councillor von Marstein, our chief Radical politician. He came here to frighten me but is only frightening himself. Councillor, this is Count Victor Vatannes, the illustrious poet—and a *man*.' Then, to Victor, caressing him and appearing to be very wanton, 'Victor my darling, let's leave them to go droning on. I'll show you the rest of my Pavilion—and you shall choose your room.'

She gave von Marstein a glance that was at once scornful and provocative, then took Victor's arm to climb the stairs. While von Marstein stared after them, saying nothing, he in his turn was watched closely by Novelda.

'Bare-faced impudent lechery. At this hour of the day too!' But Novelda thought he could detect a certain envious gusto in the Councillor's outcry. 'Well, she's had her warning. After I've talked to the Prince tonight, he'll tell her to leave the country. What a wanton! She looked as if in another minute she'd be tearing off her clothes. This poet, I suppose, is her latest lover—'

Novelda put a hand on his arm. 'Councillor, I'll tell you a secret.' He was impressive and confidential.

Von Marstein released himself, apparently wanting to go. 'Well —what is it?'

Novelda looked him in the eye, and then spoke softly: 'That performance of hers was staged entirely for your benefit.'

'If you mean she deliberately attempted to shock me, to anger me—'

'No, no, you don't understand this woman. I do. She did it not to repel you but to attract you—'

'If she imagines that the mere sight of her—'

Novelda cut him short. 'Remember, she is all Woman—born to

charm, to seduce. And a man like you—upright, hard, stern, the complete male—fascinates her. You are a challenge.' He refused to be interrupted. 'No, Councillor, allow me to make my final point. Such a woman knows in her heart that a man like you, restraining himself with an iron will, has depths of sensuality and reckless passion beyond the reach of these princes, poets, elegant dandies.'

'Quite true,' said the Councillor coming close to a smile. 'If some of us should choose to abandon our habits of self-discipline—'

'Of course. You're men, not triflers. And that provocative display of hers was a challenge. Why do you think she took the poet away at once?' Novelda continued softly. 'You saw her look at you. She left us alone so that I could explain the situation. I've done it before.' He gave the other man a long hard look.

After a moment or two. 'But if—let us say—I accepted this challenge, as you call it—what then?'

About to play his ace, Novelda spoke carefully now. 'Then you would come here this evening, to see her alone, instead of going to the palace.'

'But I've asked to see the Prince. He's expecting me—'

'And he'll be delighted if you postpone the talk. Believe me, Councillor. I am now very well acquainted with Prince Karl.'

The politician still protested. 'But I feel it is my duty—'

'Duty can wait, unlike a woman. In a day or two Cleo will have gone, and then you'll never see her again. What a woman—what an experience—to have missed!'

'A man might regret it, certainly.'

Seeing that he was weakening, Novelda pressed him. 'And even in the line of duty, there's much to be said for spending an hour or two alone with her. At these times, with a man who pleases her, a woman will reveal many secrets—important state secrets, if necessary—'

'Yes, there's that of course,' the Councillor admitted, about to give in. 'But won't this poet be here?'

'Leave him to me, Councillor,' said Novelda confidently. 'Now then—I suggest you put off the Prince and return here this evening, a little after dark. What do you say?'

Obviously indecisive, von Marstein didn't want to say anything. But he muttered, 'One moment. Let me think.'

'If you would prefer it, Councillor,' said Novelda, smoothly persuasive, 'I could take a message from you to the Prince this afternoon—'

'You mean to the palace?'

'Yes, he wouldn't be here. Prince Karl no longer comes during the day—'

'Which is probably very fortunate for you, my friend.'

'We still have our small pieces of luck, Councillor. And one of them is—no Prince Karl before nightfall.' He might have gone on, but this was the very moment when Glubfer, at the height of his importance, threw open the door.

'His Highness Prince Karl'—at the top of his voice.

Astounded and crestfallen, Novelda cried softly: 'Damn and blast!'

Five

PRINCE KARL CAME shambling in, a tall but slack man in his fifties, not unimpressive at a distance but giving everything away when close to anybody observant. He spoke sternly, for he could put on a stern manner at times, as Novelda and the Councillor, looking uneasy, gave him a dutiful bow. 'Good morning, gentlemen. I realize this is an unexpected call. But I have an important duty to perform.' As he paused impressively, the other two exchanged looks of consternation, safe enough because Karl was notoriously short-sighted.

'But where is the Countess ?' the Prince asked. 'Still out riding ?'

Novelda tried to cover his uneasiness. 'No, your Highness. She is showing the Pavilion to a distinguished visitor—Count Victor Vatannes—'

The long whiskered face of Prince Karl cleared like an April morning. 'Splendid! Splendid! That's why I am here. I had a police report that Count Vatannes had arrived in Dorheim. I feel it is my duty to welcome him. A great poet, gentlemen—undoubtedly a great poet—the Byron of France. And if I can find time from international affairs, I must ask him to look at some trifles of mine in verse. But I'm pressed—hard-pressed—gentlemen.'

Only a keen ear, which the Prince certainly did not possess, would have detected the faint flavour of irony in this question of Novelda's. 'Your Highness is finding the international situation difficult ?'

At once the Prince went into his routine as another Metternich, as if he were ruling an empire and not a tiny principality. 'Very, very

[133]

difficult, Novelda,' he sighed. 'Prussia troublesome again . . . Austria enigmatic—Metternich of course . . . more disturbing reports from Paris . . . Bavaria impossible, quite impossible . . . every factor to be taken into consideration . . . so many things to be weighed against one another . . . all very *very* difficult. . . .' His voice trailed away into a longer sigh. Then he returned from some muffled labyrinth of international misunderstandings to notice that the Councillor was present. 'Councillor von Marstein, I hardly expected to see you here.'

'I've been having some talk with Dr Novelda, your Highness.'

'Indeed! You surprise me. You have an official audience this evening, I think?'

Anticipating this moment, Novelda had moved out of the Prince's line of sight but had stayed within the Councillor's. He pointed aloft, where Cleo Torres was somewhere, and the Councillor caught the signal.

'Your Highness, I was on my way to ask the Chamberlain if my audience tonight could be postponed. Certain urgent Party matters—'

But the Prince interrupted him. 'Yes, of course, Councillor.' His tone was all relief. 'I might have asked for a postponement myself. And as I know you are a busy man, you have my permission to withdraw.'

No sooner had von Marstein bowed and then turned to leave, than Prince Karl had wandered away until he came close to the champagne and the glasses. 'Champagne already—eh?' He began to pour himself a glass.

'This evening then?' said Novelda softly as he kept pace with the Councillor towards the front entrance.

'You are sure she will be here?' It was an anxious whisper.

'Of course. Where else would she be?'

'This evening then.'

Returning, Novelda saw Cleo and Count Victor coming down the staircase, chattering and laughing. Cleo was in high spirits, and she almost ran towards the Prince, who was now drinking his champagne.

'How sweet of you to call so early!' she cried. 'I was longing to see you. May I present Count Victor Vatannes?'

Making the best of his rather long body and short legs, Count Victor bowed low. Prince Karl awarded him a most gracious smile. 'Mexe-Dorberg,' he announced, 'is honoured by the visit of so illustrious a poet.'

The illustrious poet bowed again. 'Your Highness is too gracious.'

Sardonically attentive to these solemn proceedings, Novelda remained a little apart from the bowing and smiling pair but had a chance to raise his eyebrows at Cleo, who seemed to him to be in one of her reckless moods. 'Let us drink a heavenly glass of champagne,' she was exclaiming gaily, clearly not including him in the invitation, so that he made no move and kept silent, his mind busy with plans.

After a minute or two, the dining room door opened to admit Suzanne Belsac, who was still wearing an apron.

'Ah—Madame Belsac—you have a domestic air this morning,' said the beaming Prince, out of his international labyrinth with the help of the champagne.

'Today she has to be cook,' said Cleo. 'You see how we live here, my friend. What did you say you were giving us for lunch, my dear Suzanne?'

'Blue trout with butter sauce,' Suzanne told her. 'Then—*vol-au-vent*. And now asking to be eaten.'

'Suzanne is a wonderful cook,' Cleo added.

'Capital, capital!' The Prince clapped his hands. 'At these moments, my dear Madame Belsac, I find it possible to forgive your fellow countrymen their unrest and turbulence. Cleo—gentlemen— I will stay to luncheon.'

'Of course,' cried Cleo, taking his arm fondly and at the same time exchanging a fervent glance with Count Victor. All this gave Suzanne the chance to signal wildly to Novelda, indicating there would be little or nothing left for him.

'If your Highness will excuse me—I still have one or two appointments—' he began.

'Of course, Novelda. But don't expect to find any trout left—ha ha!'

'Ha ha ha!' went Novelda. Left to himself, with the dining room door now firmly closed against him, and feeling uncertain about his next move, he sauntered absent-mindedly across the hall to the front entrance and then found himself outside, enjoying the sunlight and fresh air. He stared about him idly. There, on the lawn to his right, was the temporary shelter erected by Glubfer and the idiotic student guard. Beyond was a spur of the forest that stretched for twenty miles at the back of the palace, the former rulers of Mexe-

Dorberg having had a passion for boar-hunting. In front of him was the junction of the broad old road to the palace, with carriages and horsemen moving along it even at this hour, and the new and much narrower road constructed for the Pavilion of Masks. The sun was still warming but an autumnal haze, with a touch of cold in it, was spread over the whole wide scene. Novelda let go of his planning and lost himself in a rather melancholy reverie. Also he was beginning to feel hungry.

A dilapidated carriage, drawn by one dilapidated horse, now arrived at the Pavilion, and Glubfer rushed across to challenge its passenger, who proved to be a fat and rather shabby man.

'It is Mendelheim, director of the Folk Theatre, Dr Novelda,' said Glubfer. 'He is very anxious to talk to you.'

'Very well. And ask him to keep the carriage. It's a wreck but better than a two-mile walk to Dorheim.' A few moments later he was staring at Mendelheim's rather greasy moon-face, that of an old actor. 'Yes, Herr Director, and what can I do for you?'

'Dr Novelda, they have closed our Folk Theatre,' Mendelheim began in a deep tragic tone. 'The Chief of Police is now working with the Radicals. He says it is because they are afraid of public disturbance, but really it is because they know we have been supporters of Countess Cleo. So we appeal to her—and of course to you, Dr Novelda—to have our theatre opened again.'

Novelda nodded several times. 'I'll do what I can for you, my friend. No, no, keep quiet a moment. I have an idea.' He was quiet himself for another moment or two, then looked as if he had arrived at a decision. 'Was it you who produced Shakespeare's *Coriolanus* a few weeks ago, with that tremendous crowd scene?'

'My own production—yes, Dr Novelda. The crowd scene has always been much admired.'

'How soon could you call your company?'

'They are already called for this afternoon,' Mendelheim replied. 'Just in case I have some news for them.'

'Good! I may have some useful work for them to do, for which they will be well paid.' Smiling, Novelda raised a hand to stop the other man speaking. 'Herr Director, could you eat some blue trout with me at the Golden Lion?'

'I could indeed. Wonderful!' And Mendelheim did an eye-rolling and lip-smacking act.

'Then over the trout I'll explain what I have in mind. We'll take your carriage back to Dorheim. Let's go. I'm hungry.'

'Dr Novelda. Dr Novelda, please!' This was Glubfer, hurrying towards them. 'It is very important.'

'And it just might be,' said Novelda. 'You get into the carriage, Mendelheim. I shan't be long.' He turned and walked towards Glubfer and now saw that a girl was there too. She was a pretty girl who was wearing the charming old peasant costume worn by all the girls in the palace.

Glubfer was all confidential solemnity. 'I thought you'd wish to know about this, Dr Novelda,' he whispered. 'This girl, her personal maid, has been sent by her Highness, Princess Louise—'

'Sent? Sent? To Prince Karl? To Cleo? To me?'

'I hadn't thought of that,' said Glubfer apologetically. He turned to the girl, who came nearer. 'Who were you told to ask for here? Make yourself clear.'

The girl tossed her head at him and then looked at Novelda. 'Her Highness wishes to pay a visit to the Pavilion of Masks later today, and of course she knows this could be rather difficult. She mentioned you, Dr Novelda sir, and a Frenchwoman—a Madame—Madame—'

'Belsac,' Novelda prompted her.

'Yes, her. But her Highness said she didn't want to write anything or to receive anything in writing.'

'A woman in a thousand, evidently,' said Novelda dryly. 'Very well. Now listen carefully, both of you. On the right hand side of the Pavilion, as we face it—indeed, over there,' he added pointing, 'there is first the dining room, then the pantry and kitchen and larder, and beyond them is the housekeeper's room, now used as a sitting room by Madame Belsac. This room has a small green outer door, leading to the vegetable garden. Her Highness must go round the corner and then look for that green door and walk straight into the little sitting room. She will be quite safe from discovery there and she can explain to Madame Belsac what she wants. Glubfer, go round and make sure you can find that green door—I have a question for this pretty maid.' He waited for Glubfer to leave them. Then he smiled at the girl. 'You must see a good deal of your mistress—um?'

'Yes, sir, I do.'

'We're all curious about her. She leads such a quiet life.'

'She does, sir, yes—except for riding in the forest.'

'Yes, I've heard she likes doing that. But tell me, how does she behave these days ? Is she happy ? Is she sad ? Or what ?'

'A bit mixed, I'd say, sir,' said the maid earnestly. 'Sometimes she smiles at nothing. Sometimes I've caught her crying a little. Sometimes she stares at books—more thinking than reading. Just like my older sister was at one time.'

'And what happened to *her* ?'

'Married him—head carter at the brewery—and now they've three children and a fourth on the way.'

Novelda laughed and gave her a thaler. 'And don't forget to explain to the Princess about the little green door round the corner there.'

'Oh no, sir, I won't. And thank you, sir.'

He was about to go, but hesitated. 'You like her—the Princess—don't you ?'

The girl was suddenly quite fierce. 'Like her ? She's worth a hundred of this woman here. Begging your pardon, sir !'

'No, please don't apologize.' He smiled at her. 'You're probably quite right.' And off he went to the waiting carriage.

Six

AT THE PAVILION of Masks, with Novelda still absent, the whole afternoon slipped quietly away; and it was already dusk when a woman, heavily cloaked, arrived at the little green door and quietly knocked on it. 'You are Madame Belsac,' she said to the woman who opened the door. 'Dr Novelda sent a message through my maid that I must come to this door.'

'If he said so, then you are welcome. Please come in. Yes, I am Suzanne Belsac, companion and housekeeper to Cleo Torres, Countess of Feldhausen. And you?' They were now well inside the room with the door closed behind them. The visitor did not answer the question but lifted her veil and removed her cloak. Suzanne saw a rather tall slender woman, in her later twenties or perhaps even thirty, who had darkish golden hair, long eyes that might be a light hazel with flecks of green in them, and a rather wide humorous mouth. She had never been as close to Princess Louise before, and she hesitated a moment before sketching a curtsey. 'Your Highness—'

'No, please, Madame Belsac,' said the Princess, smiling. 'We can't possibly be formal. Officially this visit doesn't exist. It's entirely a private indiscretion. Let's sit down, shall we?' Having sat down, she looked about her. 'I like this room of yours. It may be rather small and dark, but it's so—so—sensible. When I was hardly more than a schoolgirl my father took me to France with him, and I remember there were inns with rooms like this in the provincial towns—plain and sensible, not like Paris, much better. That clock,

[139]

for instance, and those old maps of France—and those great fat dark old bottles! You must have done all this yourself, didn't you, to remind you?'

'I did, Princess Louise,' said Suzanne, glowing. 'And you are the very first person who has understood it.' As they smiled at each other, they were now cosily together, ready for a gossip.

'It is only curiosity that has brought me to this Pavilion of Masks, Madame Belsac. Everybody is saying that Cleo Torres will not be here much longer, and we have never met of course, and I should like to talk to her for a few minutes before she goes. But alone, naturally—I believe my husband is here—'

'Prince Karl called to greet Cleo's guest—the French poet, Count Victor Vatannes—'

'Oh yes—do you admire him?'

'I don't and never did,' said Suzanne firmly. 'He and the Prince drank far too much at lunch and almost emptied a bottle of Armagnac with their coffee—the idiots! Now they're asleep but very soon they'll wake up to find themselves in a bad temper. And the one person who would know how to manage them—Nicolo Novelda—isn't here. I couldn't spare enough lunch for him, so he went away, God knows where.'

'And I know where he is,' cried the Princess in amiable triumph.

'*You* know, Princess Louise?'

'It seems odd but is really quite simple,' the Princess replied. 'I sent my maid, Charlotte, with a message, and she happened to catch Dr Novelda, who was about to leave the Pavilion. Now Charlotte, who must have the roundest and bluest eyes in Mexe-Dorberg, isn't very clever, but she is always able to overhear talk about other people's business. So she told me that Dr Novelda was taking the director of the Folk Theatre, Mendelheim I think he's called, to lunch at the Golden Lion in Dorheim. Perhaps he too has drunk too much—'

'No, he wouldn't do that. Besides I know he is trying to plan something. He wants to leave this place. He said to me yesterday: "It's hard to be honest with yourself in Dreamland, harder still in Germany, harder even still in Mexe-Dorberg, and hardest of all in the Pavilion of Masks, Mexe-Dorberg, Germany, Dreamland." '

The Princess laughed. 'I like that.'

'Yes, but this morning he was serious about going away, to begin a new life.'

'But surely this Dr Novelda shouldn't talk about honesty. Isn't he some kind of charlatan? Though of course he did say, "honest with *yourself*".'

'He did,' said Suzanne firmly. 'And it makes a difference.'

'But a charlatan—a man who's pretending to be some sort of magician—can he be honest with himself?'

'He can if he's not telling himself he's a magician. Nicolo Novelda is in fact the ablest and most intelligent man for miles and miles around.'

The Princess smiled. 'I can see that you are friends.'

'Yes, I am devoted to him.'

'Then you must please explain to me why an able intelligent man should be content to play the charlatan in the entourage of an adventuress. Is he—or has he been—her lover?' No longer smiling, she gave the older woman a direct long look.

'No, never. Of that I'm certain. Nicolo has never been interested in her in that way, though he is himself, you must understand, very much a man. But he saw at once that Cleo, like many successful courtesans, has no real sexual feeling.'

'That was clever of him.' The Princess waited a moment. 'But, dear Madame Belsac, you've still not explained—'

'Why he's here,' Suzanne went on quickly. 'At first I think it was cynical amusement—a man watching the strings move in a puppet show. But when he was tired of that then something else—a woman perhaps—kept him here. But now he has finished. Whatever happens to Cleo, he says he is leaving, to begin some other life—that is, if he can collect enough money. Did you say something, Princess Louise?'

'No—not really—please go on.'

'I felt this morning,' Suzanne continued, 'that he was about to try manipulating everybody and everything. And I can only hope, because I am fond of him, that he knows what he is doing.'

'Well, wasting a whole afternoon with the director of the Folk Theatre—'

'I know, I know—and I am worried about him. But will you please tell me one little thing, Princess Louise. What is your interest in Nicolo Novelda?'

'Why—none that I know of,' she replied hurriedly. 'He has not even been presented to me. Surely we were just two women idly talking—weren't we?'

'As you please, my dear,' said Suzanne quietly. 'I'm a French-woman—and more than old enough to be your mother—but if you say so, then we were just idly talking. Ah—excuse me.' She opened the room's other door, the one leading to the kitchen and the rest of the Pavilion. Both women could now hear Cleo calling for Suzanne. They exchanged a glance and then waited. Cleo burst in and at once recognized Princess Louise, ignoring Suzanne. As the two younger women stared at each other, they made the sharpest possible contrast. Cleo had dressed for the evening, in orange satin trimmed with dark crimson, and was glittering and flashing with jewels, and she glanced with contempt at the other woman's plain light-brown dress. Suzanne, who knew that these two were about to give battle, looked for a moment or two from one to the other with grim amuse-ment, then rose to move past Cleo on her way out. 'If I am wanted,' she announced, 'I shall be up in my bedroom.'

'Yes, I'll talk to you later, Suzanne,' said Cleo. She continued to stand, the Princess to sit.

'If you've come for your husband, he's asleep,' Cleo began, with more force than the statement demanded. It was like the opening shot in a battle.

'So I understand,' the Princess replied coolly. 'And the poet too. Too much wine and Armagnac, Madame Belsac says. However, I didn't come for Prince Karl. After all, if I was going to do that, I ought to have done it nearly three years ago. I came,' she went on, in the same easy manner, 'because I felt I ought to meet you at least once before you left Mexe-Dorberg.'

It was this manner that fed Cleo's anger. 'Very well—you're here,' she cried fiercely, 'so we meet. But understand this, Princess Louise. If I leave Mexe-Dorberg it won't be because Prince Karl or the Jesuits or the Radicals tell me to go. I'll go only because passion or art or freedom call me.'

'Then you're a most fortunate woman.' This was said with a little smile intended to infuriate. 'Though somehow you don't sound and look as if you are.'

Cleo tried the grand manner. 'I am Cleo Torres—a free soul—responsible to nobody—a true woman—'

'I think true women *want* to be responsible to somebody—and generally are unhappy if they're not.'

'You consider yourself a happy woman?'

'No,' Louise replied, 'I do not. Do you?'

'Not now.' Cleo waited a moment, then went storming on. 'I'm bored with this petty principality—this absurd pavilion—this stupid German life—'

The Princess widened her fine eyes. 'You're not very kind, are you? You take our money. You take our titles. You take our husbands. And then tell us we bore you.'

Cleo managed a hard little laugh. 'Shall I tell you why I am able to take so much?'

'Yes, please. How do you do it? What would you recommend?'

'A sensible woman *uses* her sex instead of allowing it to use her.'

'That may be sensible but is it really wise?'

Cleo was still angry but was now able to sharpen her anger to a point. She spoke now as if she were holding a dagger. 'I can tell you what is really *unwise*, Princess Louise.'

'Then do, of course. There may not be another opportunity.' That infuriating little smile again.

'What is *unwise* is—riding in the forest.'

For the first time Louise sounded as if she might be out of breath. 'Oh—surely—that's harmless—'

Whip and dagger now: 'Not if you go there to make love in a darkened hunting lodge—'

'Oh—come—you've been reading too many bad novels.' But the laugh was forced.

'No, no, don't waste time denying it,' Cleo told her sharply. 'One of the foresters is in my pay. He's often seen you entering and leaving that lodge. He's seen your lover too of course, but so far hasn't been able to identify him. I told this forester to waylay the man and take off his mask, but he's too big a coward. He says your lover carries a pistol and looks dangerous—pooh! I ought to have done it myself. However, I've kept your miserable little secret.'

'You've told nobody?'

No longer angry but simply contemptuous, Cleo sat down at last. 'Not a soul. Not even Novelda. Cleo Torres doesn't stoop to take advantage of such wretched folly—'

'Yes, of course it must seem foolish to you—'

'Foolish? Sheer feminine idiocy. To take such a risk for nothing, offering oneself like a chambermaid infatuated with a groom? I knew better than that when I was fifteen.'

'I'm sure you did,' came in a murmur.

'Men should be made to pay for their pleasure,' Cleo declared sternly. 'If you don't ruin them, then they'll ruin you. That's life.'

Louise shook her head. 'All life? Surely not. There must be other—and happier—kinds of life.'

'Not between men and women—'

'I was thinking particularly of men and women.'

'Sheer idiocy!' Cleo left her chair and made stabbing motions with a forefinger. 'Now you see what hypocritical rubbish finds its way into talk and print. You are the pure good Princess Louise, suffering in silence, because that notorious bad woman, Cleo Torres, has bewitched your husband. And yet in fact you do, of your own freewill and gladly, what I'd never forgive myself for doing—you offer yourself—'

'*For nothing,*' Louise cut in very sharply. 'And in a disused shuttered hunting lodge, when pavilions, diamond necklaces, titles, may be earned by reluctant acquiescence on a silk bed. Foolish, isn't it?'

'Idiotic!'

'But you forget that Nature doesn't always like to be cheated,' said Louise steadily. 'There may be compensations for not doling out your sex as a moneylender does his banknotes. If you sell your blood by the pint you may never know its ecstasies—'

'You talk as you behave—like a fool—'

'And you think as you behave—like a whore—'

'Whore?' Cleo was furious. She began to shout. 'I am Cleo Torres, who came from nowhere and is now famous everywhere, who ruled this country, snatching the reins out of your husband's fumbling hands, while you could do nothing better than open your legs to some actor, fiddler or hussar captain who wouldn't dare to speak to *me*—Cleo Torres.'

Louise treated this fiery oratory with demure amusement. 'He's not an actor, fiddler or hussar captain—though I wouldn't care if he were—and I'm certain he wouldn't be afraid of speaking to you—'

Cleo went closer, as if about to slap her face, but Louise did no shrinking, no eye-closing, no looking away, still appeared quite at ease.

'Who is he then—this man?' Cleo demanded fiercely.

'Come, come, you may think me a fool but you can't imagine I'm *so* foolish.' And now Louise did close her eyes for a moment.

'If you won't trust me,' said Cleo angrily, 'then I'll no longer keep your miserable secret.'

She stopped there because the door to the kitchen opened:

Novelda was staring at them. Then, recognizing the Princess, he bowed ceremoniously. 'Dr Nicolo Novelda, your Highness,' he announced himself as Cleo, stormily silent, obviously refused to present him.

Louise, now looking rather pale and shaken, gave him her hand to kiss as he went forward. 'I have heard a good deal about you, Dr Novelda.'

This little scene broke Cleo's silence. 'And he will now hear something about *you*, Princess Louise—if only to prove I don't make idle threats. Novelda, this is something I've kept from you. For months now the Princess has been meeting some man, obviously her lover, in an old hunting lodge in the forest. She admits it but refuses to tell me who he is.'

Novelda raised his formidable eyebrows and his mouth twitched. 'Well, Cleo, we know something about him.'

'I know nothing,' she replied sharply. 'What do *you* know?'

'I know that he has been supremely fortunate.'

Louise gave a happy little laugh, annoying Cleo, who said with some contempt, 'Don't allow that remark to flatter you, Princess Louise. Dr Novelda didn't mean it. He is completely cynical about all sexual relations, has no real interest in them.'

There was a touch of mischief in Louise's reply to this. 'That seems a pity. Especially as so many people assume that he is—or has been—your lover—'

'They are quite wrong,' said Cleo angrily. 'Stupid fools! Novelda and I have always had something better to do. In some ways ours is a stronger relationship.'

'Are you sure, Cleo?' Novelda asked smoothly. But then he had to stand aside for Suzanne, who came in hastily.

'You had better go up, Cleo,' she declared. 'The Prince and the Count are returning to consciousness. I could hear them stumbling around.'

'Both of them may be suffering,' said Novelda cheerfully. 'Try laudanum.'

'I am better than laudanum,' said Cleo as she left them.

Louise looked at Suzanne and then at Novelda. 'Will I be safe from discovery if I stay here?'

'Yes, you will,' Novelda told her. And Suzanne agreed.

'Somehow I'm reluctant to return to the palace. How do you explain that, Dr Novelda?'

[145]

'You know instinctively that if anything happens in Mexe-Dorberg tonight, it will happen here. So you might be curious.'

'I *am* curious, Dr Novelda.'

After three loud knocks, the door to the outside was opened, and Glubfer looked in. 'Councillor von Marstein and Dr Stockhorn have arrived and are waiting to be admitted.'

'Hold them a minute or two, my noble captain,' said Novelda. 'Then I'll be in the hall, ready for them. Hurry now!' He looked at Louise. 'Your Highness, I'm sorry I can't make myself responsible for you—'

'So am I, Dr Novelda,' she replied demurely. 'Everyone says how capable you are.'

'I am. But for the next hour or so I have set myself the task of juggling with a difficult woman, four self-deceiving men, and a possible mob—and I may have over-estimated my ability. Suzanne my dear, keep her Highness safe. She is probably the only treasure this country has. Now I must go.'

The two women sat in a comfortable silence for a minute or two. It was ended by Suzanne. 'Well, Princess Louise, you had your talk with Cleo. So—?'

Louise pulled a face. 'Imagine a cat and a dog trying to have a talk. Before we had done, she had called me a fool and I had called her a whore. I had rather discuss Dr Novelda. Obviously he's quick and clever, but—as he suggested himself—he may be over-estimating his ability. Do you know what he's hoping to do tonight?'

'No—and I wish I did. I think he wants to clear up everything here before he leaves the place. Also, while he's not greedy for money, he must be looking out for some, because he's not the kind of man who would want to face a new life with all his pockets empty. But then he told me this morning he was badly in need of money—for this new life of his.'

'What does he want to do?' Louise cleared her throat; she sounded rather husky. 'Where does he want to go—for this new life of his?'

'If he knows, he didn't tell me,' said Suzanne. 'But perhaps he doesn't know. Perhaps it depends on the woman—'

'Oh! There is some woman?'

'I told him there must be. But he said there wasn't. And somehow I felt he was telling me the truth.'

They exchanged long thoughtful looks.

Seven

USING HIS MOST important voice but one, Glubfer announced Councillor von Marstein and Dr Stockhorn.

Novelda, with a preoccupied air, rose slowly from his desk and turned to greet them. Nobody could have guessed that he had sat down at the desk only a minute ago. 'Ah—good evening, gentlemen.'

'Good evening, Dr Novelda,' said the Councillor. Then, pointedly, 'I'm keeping my promise, you see, as no doubt you are ready to keep yours.'

'But of course,' Novelda replied smoothly. 'Cleo is with Prince Karl at the moment—he's been asleep—but I'll see what can be done. Now—Dr Stockhorn?'

The Swiss gazed at him mistily. 'Cleo sent me a note—charming, very sincere, quite touching—asking to be forgiven for what happened this morning, and begging me to call and see her this evening.'

'Yes,' said Novelda, 'a quick temper but a warm heart. You feel that, don't you, Dr Stockhorn?'

'I do. And as, from the general look of things, she may soon need help—I am here.' He blew his nose as if sounding the first trumpet in a campaign.

Von Marstein had been frowning at these sentimental exchanges. 'Dr Novelda,' he began heavily, 'I need hardly remind you—'

'You needn't but you do,' Novelda told him. 'Now, gentleman, I'll go up at once and contrive somehow to let Cleo know you are here. A little patience, please.'

Standing rather close together they watched Novelda, an easy

[147]

mover, briskly mount the stairs. When he was out of sight, they looked at each other.

'Councillor,' said Stockhorn, 'do you trust that man, Novelda?'

'Trust him? About three paces, not more. A sly fellow, if ever I saw one.'

'Quite so. And an extremely bad influence on poor Cleo Torres,' Stockhorn went on. 'A cynical Latin type could never understand the suffering, the warmth, the tenderness I find in this note she sent me.' He brought out the note with some pride. 'It is too personal, too intimate, for me to share it with you—'

'You astonish me, Dr Stockhorn. But I haven't the least desire to share it with you.'

'I am a hard old man of business, but it brought tears to my eyes.'

'You still astonish me. The woman is a lascivious wanton.'

'I saw much of her years ago, and I don't—I can't believe it.' The little Swiss was almost glaring now.

Von Marstein was annoyed. 'Nonsense, my dear sir! She *must* be a lascivious wanton. Have you seen her, as I did this morning, fondling and toying with one man in order to provoke another? Shameless! Disgraceful!' And if there was a faint suggestion of lip-smacking, von Marstein himself can hardly have been conscious of it. 'In my opinion here is a woman whose erotic behaviour knows no decent limits.'

'In this matter,' said Dr Stockhorn stiffly, 'your opinion seems to me valueless. Only those—'

The other man ignored this, his mind probably still considering the extreme forms of erotic behaviour. He laid a heavy hand on Stockhorn's shoulder. 'You've been upstairs here, haven't you?' He had dropped down almost to a whisper. 'Do you happen to know how the rooms are arranged?'

'This Pavilion of Masks, Councillor von Marstein,' cried Stockhorn, stepping back to free himself from the Councillor's hand, 'is the residence of Cleo Torres, Countess Feldhausen. It is not a bordello.'

'It has been in the same business, only with bigger profits,' the Councillor shouted. Both men now turned away from each other at the same time. But both of them kept glancing impatiently at the staircase. Where was Cleo?

She was in fact playing the fellow conspirator in Novelda's bedroom, the only safe place for them to talk now that Prince Karl was awake and might wander into Cleo's boudoir.

'You must understand this, Cleo,' Novelda was saying, 'I have contrived to get these men here, so that we know where they are and can keep them out of mischief. But now, for the moment, I can do no more. They want you, not me.'

'I know what one of them wants and I would just as soon be chased round a room by a pig as by that filthy-minded puritanical politician—'

'No doubt, but if you want to elope tonight with Victor Vatannes and be the sensation of Paris—'

'Stop that. You are beginning to repeat yourself, Nicolo—a bad sign—'

'There'll be worse signs soon unless you play the game my way, go down there and take charge of those two. I have made my plans. I have lit the fuse and can do nothing now but wait for the explosion. And listen—if I'm attacked, don't defend me. Let the situation develop without any interference. I'm asking you to use your wits, probably for the last time.'

'No, Nicolo.' She was alarmed. 'You can't—'

'Never mind that now.' In his impatience he seized her by the shoulders and shook her. 'Get down there, Cleo. They've waited too long already. Hurry.'

As soon as she had gone, Novelda took a small table to the window, then a lamp and a chair. Though it was dark now, he did not draw the curtain for there might be torches to be seen below soon. Lighting a cheroot, he took out a notebook and stared at some figures he had entered into it earlier. There was nothing else he could do but wait. The comedy was now being staged elsewhere.

Cleo was a dazzling figure as she came slowly down the staircase. As she reached the last step she held out both hands and smiled sweetly. 'So here you are, my friends. Prince Karl is still half-asleep. He and Count Victor versified and guzzled half the afternoon. There never was a longer lunch. So nobody can see the Prince until he's thoroughly awake and I have coaxed him into a good temper.'

Both men started to speak but she silenced them with a pretty gesture, gave von Marstein a brilliant warning look and then took Stockhorn and led him towards the dining room door.

'Dear kind Dr Stockhorn,' she began, 'the only possible thing for you to do is to wait in the dining room through here. Come, let me show you.' She squeezed his arm before opening the door. 'Two lamps, you see. Quite enough light. Shutters closed—a nice snug room. Now you sit down here—' she indicated an armchair at the end of the dining table, well away from the door into the hall— 'while I take out of this special cupboard Suzanne Belsac's treasure —her kirsch, the finest in the world.' She placed the bottle and a glass in front of him. 'Enjoy that, as I'm sure you will, and as soon as I feel the Prince is in a good mood ready to receive you, I will come for you. Here, let me give you your first glass of this wonderful kirsch.'

'Very well, Cleo,' said Stockhorn on whom this sugary dialogue and attentions had not been wasted. 'I will wait and taste this famous kirsch. And remember,' he added sentimentally, 'if all is lost here, you still have a true friend in me.'

'Of course, of course—' not without a touch of impatience—'you are one of my oldest and truest friends. But please don't go and ruin me to prove how true a friend you can be. No, no, I was only teasing you, dear Dr Stockhorn. Now just sit there quietly and be patient a little while—for my sake.'

She returned to the hall to bestow a seductive smile upon the impatient von Marstein. There now began a performance that she was to describe later to many private and delighted audiences.

'So, Cleo Torres,' he began sternly, 'I—Councillor von Marstein, leader of your political enemies, am neglecting my duties—to be here with you.' His tone was stern but there was a gleam in his eye, and a very warm hand descended on her arm.

Cleo stepped back but remained provocative in manner. 'Such a stern cold Councillor,' she twittered, a feminine idiot, 'and so determined to frighten a helpless woman—a poor wild creature.'

'Wild no doubt, though exactly how wild—' He ended with a hopeful question.

'But timid too, like so many wild free creatures.' She took a risk now. 'Feel how my heart is beating.'

'Certainly,' he said, advancing. 'Now—keep still.'

Cleo eluded him again. 'No, you can imagine it. Now I will sit here—and you must sit there—and don't be too hard upon me in your thoughts.' With a generous display of her charms, with the orange satin sliding up her legs, she sat on the sofa, while he remained standing, ignoring the distant chair she had indicated. 'After all,' she continued, keeping the feminine-idiot look and tone, 'I can't help it if I am dedicated to art and love, not at all the kind of dull, barrel-shaped female you German radicals take to your kitchens and beds.'

'Respectable decent women, Countess.' But his eyes, busy with her charms, did not suggest he had such women in mind at the moment.

'That is what I am saying, sir.'

'Not lascivious wantons,' he continued, his voice saying one thing and his eyes another, 'who like nothing better than to arouse the passions—the *strong virile passions*—of men of my sort—' and as he went nearer—'to make even a determined and hard man like me forget his duty.' He was standing over her now, his eyes hopeful and bulging.

Not quite in control of the situation, Cleo took the risk of still appearing provocative. 'But you forget, Councillor, that with us passion and love *are* a duty.' A stupid remark, she decided as soon as she had made it.

And, to her dismay, he plumped himself down beside her. 'I warn you, Cleo, that we good German radicals are not easily seduced and bewitched.' He put his great fat right arm round her. She could only move away an inch or two.

Flustered, she said another silly thing now. 'You are very sure of your strength of mind—and arm.'

'They need to be tested of course.' His hot left hand was fondling her cheek. 'Not now perhaps. Neither the time nor the place is quite right. But later,' he whispered, 'in your room or another, and after a few glasses of wine, if you feel, as well you might, that I am too confident, that your charms are stronger than my powers of resistance, then we could put the matter to a test.'

'We will see.' Making a considerable effort, she removed the hand that was now pressing down on her left thigh, possibly leaving a sweaty imprint on her beautiful satin. It was time to drop the feminine idiot. 'Meanwhile, have you and your Party decided that Prince Karl must send me away?'

The hand returned, squeezing her knee this time. 'Of course. I was to have given him the ultimatum now—to tell you to leave this very night—but at some risk I have postponed definitive action until tomorrow morning.'

The hand was on the prowl above the knee. Cleo removed it with some force and tried again to edge away. 'You realize of course you are only doing what the Jesuits and the reactionaries attempted to do—and failed?'

'Of course.' His hand had come back to attend to her left breast. 'And they failed because their attempt to banish you was mere policy—a purely political move.'

'What is yours then?' Cleo began wriggling.

'Behind us, strengthening our resolve,' said the Councillor, his hand busier than ever, 'are all the outraged feelings of our good bourgeois folk—'

'You mean,' said Cleo, struggling away, 'jealousy and envy?'

'I mean,' he replied heavily, resisting her wriggles and struggles while turning her into a public meeting, 'the essential decencies of our good folk—the sanctity of the home and family—their ideal of frugality and plain living you have defied—their long tradition of pure undefiled womanhood—'

Making a supreme effort, Cleo escaped and jumped up, shouting angrily, 'Oh—do stop mauling me about!'

'Why, you cheating little harlot!' He rose ponderously, purple in the face.

'Clumsy, lecherous old hypocrite!' Cleo hurled at him. There was a warning cough from somewhere behind her back. She turned to see Novelda and Victor Vatannes coming downstairs together.

'I'm sorry to interrupt—' Novelda began smoothly.

'You couldn't have arrived at a better moment.' She smiled at Victor and held out a hand. 'Ah—Victor my love—did you have a pleasant sleep—happy dreams?'

After kissing her hand, Victor said, 'Perfect, sweet Cleo. We were together—in Provence—Italy—Greece—'

Von Marstein went storming across to Novelda. 'And you're as bad as she is, just another cheat. I'll denounce the pair of you.'

Novelda regarded him with grave mockery. 'But Councillor—what will you say we have cheated you out of?'

'Take me to Prince Karl,' von Marstein shouted. 'Say I insist upon an audience.'

'Certainly not,' Novelda told him. 'I daren't bring him out of dreamland to see your face.'

'There are people in Dorheim who want to see my face—people who are in an ugly mood—people ripe for revolution. I shall call for my carriage.'

He went charging out. Novelda followed him and caught hold of Glubfer just outside the entrance. 'This is very urgent, Glubfer.

Von Marstein mustn't return to Dorheim. Stop him. The Countess demands it. Do anything. Get your fellows to take the horses out of his carriage—anything so long as you keep him here. Hurry now!'

Back indoors he saw that Cleo and Count Victor were close together on the sofa, smiling fondly at each other. 'You don't want me here, I think,' he told them, and he crossed to the dining room. To his surprise, for he had forgotten about him, there was Dr Stockhorn, sitting at the far end of the table, drinking kirsch, a foolish smile now illuminating his dour face.

'Not yet—the Prince?' he enquired amiably.

'No, not yet, Dr Stockhorn. Stay there a little longer.'

'Not for your sake, Novelda. Frankly, I have turned against you. But if it is for Cleo's sake—'

'It is, it is. Entirely for Cleo's sake—'

'Then I will stay here a little longer. The kirsch is *beautiful*—the best I have ever tasted. And I have been thinking of old times—in Prague and Petersburg when I was able to help Cleo. Do you ever think of old times, Novelda?'

'Never,' he replied promptly. 'I have to think about new times. Excuse me.' He went through the kitchen and found his way into Suzanne's little sitting room. She and Princess Louise were still there, quietly talking as if they were intimates now.

Louise simply looked at him enquiringly but Suzanne told him bluntly, 'We want your news, Nicolo.'

He explained the disappointment, indignation and angry exit of von Marstein. 'Cleo and her poet are sitting close together, gazing into each other's eyes.'

'With love?' asked Louise.

'Love—yes,' said Novelda, 'but love of notoriety, the press and percentages. Prince Karl of course hasn't come down yet. Oh—Suzanne—Dr Stockhorn is sitting in the dining room—Cleo put him there—drinking our best kirsch and becoming heavily sentimental. Rothschilds wouldn't recognize him. But I don't know how long he'll stay in there.'

'He can stay all night for all I care,' said Suzanne. 'I hope your plans don't include a nice hot supper for everybody, Nicolo, because I've finished cooking for today. Unless I made an omelette just for us three,' she added thoughtfully.

'It may work out like that,' said Novelda slowly. 'But it is too early to be certain. Stay here, please, both of you. The plans I have made include food, though no hot suppers. Wish me luck!' He glanced at Suzanne, who nodded, and then he exchanged a long look with Princess Louise. 'Now I'm sneaking up the backstairs here to my room.'

The two women said nothing for a minute or two after he had gone. Then Louise: 'Is he always so mysterious?'

'He often pretends to be—though not with me,' said Suzanne. 'That is just his nonsense. But today he is different. If he can raise the money, he will go away. And unless he absolutely forbids it, I shall go with him.' She waited but Louise said nothing, though neither of them looked away. 'I was never blessed with children,' Suzanne added slowly. 'And to me Nicolo is like a son. A woman my age must have somebody to worry over. And Nicolo Novelda is all I have.'

Eight

CLEO AND HER Victor were deep in loving talk.

'My dark angel,' he said, after kissing her hand again, 'you are still ready to be abducted—carried off to Paris?'

'Of course, my noble Victor. It will be a sensation—'

'It will. People will talk of nothing else for months.' He said this with such enthusiasm that what followed seemed rather perfunctory. 'And what bliss will be ours, my love!'

'Unutterable bliss, my darling. But has Novelda made the necessary arrangements?'

'He has explained everything to me. The carriage is there already, quite close but not where it will be easily noticed. Relays of fast horses to take us over the frontier. Even a picnic basket with some champagne—and ham. I'm particularly fond of ham—'

'Not the local ham, I hope—' Cleo spoke sharply.

'No, no, some Westphalian ham. I tell you, my love, Novelda has thought of everything. An invaluable man. He must join us later in Paris.'

'Of course he must. I couldn't do without him. I shall have so much more business to transact—contracts for the Theatre, articles and interviews in the press—'

'Naturally.' Victor hesitated a moment. 'By the way, so long as we are obviously devoted to each other in public, I am not the man to play the Turk in private. So if you and Novelda have some satisfactory arrangement—'

'No, we don't go to bed—and never have. He's not a great lover—

[155]

like you, Victor my darling.'

He hesitated again. 'Well, as to that—of course I have been a great lover, made some famous conquests—but just now, what with the Russian journey and my headlong ride here, for the time being I'm not quite—'

She stopped him by placing her fingers across his lips. The move was playful, almost as if she felt a certain relief, but when she spoke she sounded quite solemn. 'My darling, what does that matter? Nothing, so long as the whole world sees that our hearts and souls are united—in freedom and love. And after all this excitement, I ought to be able to obtain a theatrical engagement on first-class terms.'

'Undoubtedly, dear heart. I know several enterprising managers, and I might write some piece, not too difficult, for you to appear in.'

'For a substantial advance, I hope, and then a percentage of the gross—'

'Possibly up to twenty-five per cent between us, if you'll agree to one of the smaller vaudeville houses, my jewel.'

Cleo frowned. 'I'd prefer one of the larger regular theatres, my dearest.'

'We shall see, my beautiful dark angel, but there's much to be said for a smaller house that sells out every performance.'

Cleo was about to object to any small theatre when she saw that Glubfer had come in and was staring at her. 'No, Glubfer,' she called out sharply, 'nobody can be admitted.'

'Quite so, gracious Countess,' said Glubfer rather shakily. 'But this is something else. One of our fellows has just come back from Dorheim, and he says the townsfolk are talking wildly.'

'Pooh! What do I care? Let them talk.'

'But it is not only talk,' Glubfer went on. 'He says a mob of low ruffians—the scum of the town—are coming here—and may be already on their way.'

'If they do come, tell them Cleo Torres defies them—miserable cowards, pigs, rats. Now return to your guard, Glubfer.'

'We will do what we can, Countess Cleo,' he said dubiously, 'but there are only a few of us. And if a whole angry crowd arrives—'

'Then if you can't deal with them, *I will*. I—Cleo Torres.' She waved him away and turned to Victor. 'We can decide the size of the theatre later. Now if I agreed to write my memoirs, what kind of offer do you think your publishers might make? Fifty thousand

francs for the French edition alone? Or more?' When he didn't
reply: 'Aren't you listening?'

'I couldn't help wondering about this mob—'

'You're not afraid of these louts, are you?'

'My dearest Cleo,' said Victor, 'if they were French I wouldn't
care, because even an angry mob in France still has taste for oratory.
But these aren't French.'

'A German mob is even more idiotic and cowardly. I'll attend
to them with my whip—or a pistol if necessary.'

'It is a scene I would enjoy on the stage, but real life is so untidy,'
said Victor thoughtfully. 'But aren't you forgetting something, my
brave love? What about Prince Karl?'

Cleo pulled a face first, but then spoke slowly. 'Yes, dearest. I
wasn't being very clever. They could frighten Karl.'

'And remember, as Novelda has pointed out all along, I can't run
away with you—the Prince and his cavalry in pursuit—if he's
already dismissed you. No abduction, no pursuit—no European
sensation.'

She nodded her agreement. 'I can make sure Karl doesn't disown
me publicly so long as we go tonight.'

'But will he pursue you? Will he call out a squadron of cavalry?
It would give the final satisfying touches of movement and colour
to the romance—our carriage hurrying through the night—the outraged Prince galloping at the head of his dragoons.'

'Yes—yes—yes.' Cleo sounded impatient.

'But now that I know the Prince,' Victor continued, 'I find it
difficult to imagine him galloping in pursuit, through the night, at
the head of his dragoons. My love, have you any plan—'

She cut him short. 'No, but I'll think of something—'

'Novelda perhaps—'

Cleo jumped up and moved away. 'Novelda may be very useful,'
she said haughtily, 'but you're quite wrong if you think he's absolutely indispensable. I know Karl better than he does. I can think
of something.' But then she turned, put a finger to her lips and
indicated the staircase. Prince Karl was bringing himself very carefully downstairs. He was not looking his best. His long suety face
was longer and suetier than ever. It was obvious he was not in a
good temper.

'Really, Cleo—I dislike complaining, as you know. I'm easy to
please. But for once I *must* complain.'

[157]

'One moment, please, your Highness. I am sure you would like me to withdraw.' Victor threw in a bow or two.

'An excellent suggestion, Count Victor. I wish others here were as tactful,' the Prince added peevishly.

Victor mounted the stairs briskly, no doubt on his way to visit Novelda.

'Well now, in the first place,' the Prince said to Cleo, 'my head aches abominably. You shouldn't have encouraged me to drink so much at luncheon, Cleo.'

'Encouraged you? I warned you at least twice, Karl.'

'Then you were very tactless, Count Victor being present. And —in the second place—you don't seem to have managed things very well here. Those students out there have been making a terrible noise. They woke me up—shouting about carriages and that sort of thing—and here I am, wide awake and obviously threatened by a liver attack.' He sank into the largest chair. 'Really, it's too bad, Cleo. I come to your Pavilion of Masks to escape for a while from the palace and all my round of duties for a little peace and quiet— and what happens?'

He closed his eyes. She stood behind him and lightly caressed his forehead. 'I'm sorry, Karl my love. Really it's all Novelda's fault.'

He opened his eyes as if he had leaden lids. 'I'm not surprised, not at all surprised. And you can't say I've not warned you against that fellow.'

'I know you have, Karl dearest.' She brought up a light chair fairly close to his, sat on it, then looked hard at him, shut eyes or no shut eyes. 'Karl, dear—'

The eyes opened. 'Yes, Cleo?'

'If I were to vanish,' she began earnestly, 'you would miss me, wouldn't you, Karl? And I don't mean just miss me in bed or at the supper table—for our relationship has meant more than that—'

'Has it?' he enquired dubiously. 'I'm not quite clear what you mean, Cleo.' Eyes going again, though.

'Really, Karl!' She was so indignant that she lost sight of tact. 'What were we doing most of the time when all your stupid people thought you were drinking champagne out of my slipper or trying to snatch my garter? We were controlling the affairs, both domestic and foreign, of Mexe-Dorberg.'

This brought Prince Karl to life because it immediately annoyed him. 'Oh—come—come, Cleo—I may have given you an occasional glimpse of my problems—the simpler ones. But after all I've made a deep study of public affairs, especially, as most informed people recognize, our foreign relations. Metternich himself once congratulated me. Didn't I tell you that?'

'I think you have mentioned it, dearest.' Cleo had now to regain lost ground. 'And being a woman, all heart and no head, it isn't easy for me to appreciate your true political stature. Naturally, I think of you as the tender loving friend, a poet as well as a prince.'

'That too of course, my dear Cleo,' he said complacently.

She fondled his cheek. 'You are feeling a little better now, Karl, aren't you?'

'A little, perhaps. And I'm wondering if a glass of brandy—'

'No, please, Karl, not yet.' She paused and then went on dreamily. 'I was remembering something, dearest. You told me once that when you were young and your father was alive, you were attached to the cavalry—'

'*Attached* in the purely military sense. In every other sense, anything but attached. I dislike all branches of military service, but the one I particularly detest—is the cavalry.'

Cleo tried eagerness. 'But can't you imagine yourself, if the situation demanded it, galloping through the night at the head of your dragoons?'

'Certainly not.'

'But surely *you*—a true romantic—'

'There's nothing romantic about the cavalry,' he declared firmly. 'It consists of hard-riding, swearing louts, all reeking of sweaty leather and horse dung. When I succeeded my father, I immediately disbanded more than half the cavalry.' He stopped, to stare. 'But —what's this?'

Dr Stockhorn had come in from the dining room. He was not drunk but he could not be said to be completely sober. Solemn at all times, he now had that extra solemnity which can follow several glasses of kirsch.

'Well, sir—and who are you?' Karl was now very much the Prince.

After contriving a rather precarious little bow: 'Dr Stockhorn, your Highness, representing the Paris house of Rothschilds—'

'Rothschilds? Are you sure?'

'Absolutely positive, your Highness.' He wagged his head. 'Dr Stockhorn—their Zurich representative for many years, many years.'

'Ah—yes, we were told you had arrived in Dorheim, Dr Stockhorn. Something about a possible loan. But why didn't you apply to the Chamberlain for an audience? You should be at the palace, not here.'

'He came to see me first,' Cleo said hastily, 'because we are old acquaintances.'

'Possibly, but this is most irregular.'

'I am sorry, your Highness, very very sorry,' said Stockhorn. 'But Dr Novelda said—'

'I have no wish to know what Dr Novelda said. Dr Novelda holds no official appointment in this principality, Dr Stockhorn. You will be well advised to ignore his existence. Go now—but come to the palace at noon tomorrow and you shall have an official audience.'

Stockhorn managed another bow. 'I thank your Highness, thank you very warmly.' He hesitated. 'Pardon me, but I have just heard a lot of shouting in the garden at the back. There seems to be some trouble.'

'It is nothing,' Cleo told him. 'All nonsense.'

'Allow me, Cleo,' said the Prince gravely. 'I will be frank with you, Dr Stockhorn. There is at the moment some unrest in Dorheim, but I assure you we are quiet people˙here in Mexe-Dorberg. You may ignore rumours. You will be as safe here as you would be in Paris, Munich or Berlin.'

'With all due respect, your Highness,' said Stockhorn, 'I should like to feel very much safer than I would do in Paris, Munich or Berlin, all within sight of revolution.'

'It will not happen here. You will be perfectly safe,' the Prince assured him. 'We meet tomorrow at noon at the palace. Goodnight, Dr Stockhorn.'

'Goodnight, your Highness.' He moved closer to Cleo and gave her a look compounded of kirsch and sentimentality. 'Remember, Cleo, whatever happens you have a friend in me.'

'And what did he mean by that?' Prince Karl asked as soon as Stockhorn had gone.

Cleo produced a contemptuous and unladylike sound. 'Once, years ago, when I was penniless, Stockhorn befriended me. There was no sex in it—all pure sentiment. Now he would dearly like to see me ruined so that he could play the same part all over again. Outside business he's the complete old sentimentalist—as Novelda saw at once—'

'Don't tell me what Novelda saw.' The Prince was annoyed.

'There has been too much Novelda here. You have spoilt that man.'

'A little perhaps, Karl dearest. I must light two more lamps here, otherwise it will begin to look dreary.' As she went lamp-lighting, 'But Stockhorn was quite right, wasn't he? I mean, in all three cities—'

'Yes—yes—yes!' He sounded impatient. 'I read my bulletins, and I know more about these things than you do.'

Perhaps excited by the two extra lamps, Cleo suddenly cried, 'Oh—to be in Paris if the barricades were going up again! What a moment to be a people's heroine!'

'Nonsense! Why do you talk this stuff, Cleo?' the Prince demanded peevishly. 'You despise the mob and yet you will insist upon spouting mob oratory. Why? Why?'

She came towards him and spoke for once as if she were no longer playing a part. 'I'm sorry, Karl. There is something in me— a little ragged man perhaps—that suddenly takes charge of me at these moments.'

He began peevishly again but then worked himself angrily. 'You should learn to control yourself as I've had to do. It's not always easy, I admit.' He was nearly shouting now. 'I'm not finding it easy tonight, when I'm here at considerable personal inconvenience, only to discover that everything has been arranged in the most stupid tactless manner—thanks to your friend Novelda—with all kinds of unnecessary persons walking in and out of the place. It has been left to me, only here for a little peace and quiet, to get rid of these fellows—'

'Surely, Karl dear, you are not referring now to Count Victor Vatannes.' A dignified reproach.

'I am not, Cleo, and you know very well I am not.' He was still angry. 'But what about that little Swiss financier, who didn't seem to me quite sober—?'

'He wasn't.' Cleo had to giggle. 'I let him have Suzanne's best kirsch.'

'Then you were very foolish, Cleo. I hope there's some left. Now that I'm feeling rather better and we have this place to ourselves—a little peace and quiet at last—I could enjoy some of that kirsch.'

It was then, before Cleo could make a move towards the dining room, that a ruffled Dr Stockhorn and a desperate Councillor von Marstein, without even an announcement from Glubfer, came bursting into the hall.

Nine

PRINCE KARL DREW himself up to his full height and glared at these unseemly arrivals. 'Gentlemen, I regard this as an unpardonable intrusion. Leave us at once.'

'With respect, your Highness, it is impossible,' said Stockhorn.

'We had no alternative, your Highness.' Von Marstein stopped for breath. 'Many apologies—but—'

Recognizing him now, the Prince was astonished. 'Councillor von Marstein, what were you doing here?'

'I was here earlier, your Highness, at the suggestion of Dr Novelda—'

Almost dancing with rage, Prince Karl cut him short. 'Novelda —Novelda—Novelda! This is intolerable.'

'It is, your Highness.' Von Marstein could be angry too. 'I left some time ago, but there was trouble with my carriage. The horses had been taken away. Now Dr Stockhorn and I have been turned back. Those students tell us—'

'Don't believe them,' Cleo told him impatiently. 'They're idiots.'

'Possibly, but I'm not. And I have eyes and ears.'

'And with all due respect, your Highness,' Stockhorn added mournfully, 'and even bearing in mind what you told me, there are some people here in Mexe-Dorberg who are not at all quiet.'

'Drunk, probably,' said Cleo.

'Be quiet, Cleo. If you keep interrupting,' the Prince continued, 'it will be impossible for me to understand the situation and do what is necessary. Now what about these noisy people?'

'They are on their way here,' said Stockhorn.

'They've been heard shouting, "To the Pavilion of Masks",' von Marstein added.

'What does it matter?' Cleo was scornful. 'Let them come. Are you afraid?'

'Certainly I am,' Stockhorn told her.

'I asked you to be quiet, Cleo. Now I *command* you, Countess Feldhausen. Yes, Councillor?'

'We thought it our duty to warn your Highness.'

'Yes, quite right.' The Prince looked troubled and was anything but decisive. 'And of course you must remain here now ... all very difficult ... most complicated.'

'I must stay here now.' Von Marstein put on an appealing look. 'Even so, I can't afford to be discovered here by an angry mob.'

'You can't—eh, Councillor? No, I suppose not.' Prince Karl looked even more troubled and sounded even vaguer than before. 'We must take—er—precautionary measures of some kind ... Though you gentlemen may possibly be exaggerating the seriousness of—er—the ...'

His voice trailed away and there was a silence finally broken by Cleo, who adopted a humble manner at first. 'Will you please allow me to say something now, Karl? After all, I have probably seen more mobs than anybody else here.'

'Very well, Cleo. What is it that you wish to say?'

She now dropped the humble manner and was vehement. 'Of course these two are exaggerating the seriousness. The idiotic students have infected them with panic. We are not in Paris but in Mexe-Dorberg. What will they do, these terrible desperate revolutionaries from Dorheim? I'll tell you. They'll hang around out there for five or ten minutes—call me a few dirty names—and then slink back to their beer cellars and fat wives.'

'Thank you, Cleo,' said the Prince. 'But whether you have given us a realistic point of view ... I am in no position at this moment to decide. Yes, Councillor?'

'Your Highness, I cannot accept this misleading feminine egoism for a moment. It is simply frivolous. I know the poorer citizens of Dorheim much better than she does. To dismiss them in terms of beer cellars and fat wives is arrogant nonsense, typical of a woman who has left far behind the class she originally came from—'

'Shut up,' Cleo demanded at the top of her voice. 'I've never

[163]

denied my humble origins, even if beauty, talent and a high spirit have raised me far above them. Because I come from the People, I know the People, without making a lot of hypocritical speeches to them. I know when and where they have to be taken seriously, and when and where they haven't. And here they are nothing but a bad joke. I've faced them over and over again—cracked my whip in their fat foolish faces—and watched them slink away.' She pointed to the staircase. 'Ask Novelda—and he'll tell you.'

'No, Cleo,' said Prince Karl, 'there has been too much Novelda already. But perhaps Count Victor may suggest something.' The poet and Novelda were coming downstairs together.

'Your Highness,' said Victor gravely, 'something is happening out there. And I have heard sounds like these before. For example, seventeen years ago in Paris.'

'This isn't Paris and these aren't Frenchmen,' Cleo told him sharply. 'Nicolo, help me to convince them it's all nothing—just a few drunken oafs—'

Novelda lengthened his face and wagged it. 'I'm sorry, Cleo, but this time I can't.'

Staggered, she cried, 'What—you too?'

'This could be serious.' He shook his head at her and then at the others.

Von Marstein was angry at once. 'And whose fault is it I find myself here, Novelda?'

'Your own.'

'You cheated me.'

'You cheated yourself,' Novelda retorted, with more than a suspicion of a smile.

This was too much for von Marstein. 'I appeal to your Highness,' he began angrily. 'I'm one of your three Councillors of State, leader of the Radical Party, and I'm being insulted by this charlatan, this fortune-teller—'

For once Prince Karl spoke with some authority. 'Dr Novelda, you have offended Councillor von Marstein, you have taken advantage of Countess Cleo's misplaced confidence in you, you have greatly displeased me. Your company is no longer welcome, sir. Withdraw at once.'

Novelda looked at Cleo. 'You're still mistress of this Pavilion—do you agree?'

'Yes, I do, Nicolo. You've tried to be too clever. Leave us now—'

'And at once, sir, at once.' Prince Karl was no thunderer but he was doing his best. 'I am still hereditary ruler of Mexe-Dorberg. I can still have you put under arrest.'

'I wonder,' said Novelda mildly. 'I really wonder if you could tonight. However, as you and the company don't want me here, then of course I must leave you.' His little bow was all mockery. 'I can only hope you will have a pleasant evening.' There was now an awkward silence as they watched him climb the staircase.

Prince Karl felt he ought to say something. He tried a light tone. 'Impudent fellow, like so many Italians. Never cared for him, as you ought to have seen from the first, Cleo. However, I think you're probably right about this situation. Nothing of importance is likely to happen. Even the few precautionary measures we had in mind won't be necessary.'

'Your Highness has some plan ?' Victor asked eagerly. 'Perhaps, hidden close by, some cavalry ?'

'Certainly not.' And his distaste was obvious.

Cleo gave her poet a sharp look. 'His Highness particularly dislikes the cavalry.'

'A great pity,' Victor murmured, pulling a very French lower-lip face.

'I don't know about the cavalry,' said von Marstein, 'but I must impress upon your Highness not to attempt to give any orders to the infantry.'

His Highness took this badly. 'Indeed—why ? If, Councillor, you will remember that I am in command of the armed forces—not you. However, I shall be interested to learn why I must not attempt to give any orders to my own infantry.' He used his haughtiest tone.

'Because if you do,' the Councillor replied, roughly for him, 'they will not obey your orders. And this will develop into a revolutionary situation. It has happened before, in more than one country.'

'It has,' said Dr Stockhorn, feeling it was time he said something. 'Though, in any event, I fail to see how any message could be passed to anybody at the present time.'

'Not even to the cavalry ?' said Victor hopefully again.

'Karl,' cried Cleo urgently, not troubling to stand on ceremony, 'believe me they are all talking nonsense. What is really happening ? Nothing—except that we are all standing here fussing away like a lot of old women. When we might be enjoying ourselves too.'

'Speak for yourself,' von Marstein told her sourly.

'No, Councillor, I think Cleo is speaking for me too.' He looked around, forcing a smile. 'Well, my dear Cleo—gentlemen—as apparently no excitement is to be imposed upon us, perhaps we might create a little pleasurable excitement of our own. A glass or two of good wine perhaps, or that excellent Armagnac—eh, Cleo?'

Whitefaced, dishevelled, terrified, Glubfer burst in and hurriedly bolted and locked the big front door.

'Beg to report, Countess,' he gasped. 'No students' guard on duty now. My fellows have left. Great murderous mob coming—'

Before any of the men could speak, Cleo asked promptly, 'How many are there?'

'Hundreds—thousands—'

'Rubbish! I don't believe a word of it. Go away.'

'But how—where—?'

'Oh—go to the kitchen and ask Madame Belsac to give you a drink.' She looked around as he scuttled towards the dining room. Prince Karl and Victor looked uncertain: von Marstein and Stockhorn were exchanging uneasy glances. She alone had any confidence.

'Students' guard!' She made a rude noise. 'All quite useless. I only allowed it because it amused them—and gave me a free doorman—'

Prince Karl liked this outburst. 'There is something in this, my dear Cleo. These young men are Romantics—and of course exaggerate.'

'They can't help it,' said Cleo. 'They hear three drunks shouting —and imagine they're in the French Revolution. You'd like some wine and brandy?'

'I think so, my dear. A glass or two, gentlemen, over which we can discuss at leisure—*not*—ha ha!—an imaginary crisis here but the very real situation we find in international affairs, which are of course my special study. I think we'll be left in peace to do that, don't you, gentlemen? Ha ha!' He smiled complacently.

As if reality outside had devised an instant retort, a large stone came crashing through the upper part of one of the three windows, above the meeting of the shutters. Following the noise of breaking glass came threatening shouts and yells from the mob. While the men were staring at one another with the mouths open, Cleo in a fury rushed to a drawer and took out a pistol. 'Louts—idiots—apes —jackasses—swine!' she was shouting. 'Do you think you can frighten *me*?'

Before the men could stop her, she jumped on to the window seat, yelling, 'Yes, I am here—*Cleo Torres*,' and then she fired the pistol into the air, through the broken window. There might have been an enraged demon behind the huge furious bellowing that went up outside.

While the men were still silent, merely exchanging bewildered or fearful looks, Cleo bustled about trying to find one of her whips. Finding one, she was now in great form, a whip in one hand and the pistol in the other, her colour high, her eyes sparkling. As the huge noise outside had died down to a few occasional yells, she took a deep breath or two, glared round accusingly and scornfully, then turned the men into an audience.

'What's the matter with you?' she began. 'You're behaving like miserable cowards. Very well, I was wrong. The mob's here and is angry. But I'm ready to open that door and dare them to lay a finger on Cleo Torres. I'm not afraid of them. Why should I be? Who are they? What are they? The People? Pooh!' She made a spitting noise. 'The riffraff and sweepings of Dorheim's back streets. Grooms and postboys, knifegrinders, bakers' drudges, and sausage-mixers. Out-of-work waiters, bad fiddlers and street cleaners. They are the People. You've read about them in newspapers and history books. But I'm not afraid of them because I know them for what they are. For me they have faces and voices and smells. I'm not like you—as I've told you already—*I come from the People*. I became Cleo Torres to have done with them for ever. And I would rather kill myself than live with such stupid animals again.' Drawing a deep breath, she looked at Victor and appealed directly to him. 'You are a poet—you are a man—you can't be content to shiver there—'

'Cleo, I am not shivering. If these people were French, I would talk to them. But they are German—not my kind of animal at all.'

'There's no real difference. Mobs are mobs. Oafs are oafs. Idiots are idiots.'

'And if there are enough of them and they are angry,' said Stockhorn dryly, 'they can pull down a Bastille.'

'Very true, Dr Stockhorn,' said Prince Karl. 'Cleo you are being childish and I must ask you to put down that pistol. I cannot think when it may go off at any moment. Please put it down.'

Muttering something, she turned her back on them scornfully.

'Well, gentlemen—the immediate situation is—er—undoubtedly

very difficult.' Prince Karl was very hesitant and dubious. 'If this
—er—demonstration were taking place outside the palace, I
wouldn't hesitate—er—to show myself—appeal to their loyalty—
make some—er—promises of some kind—ask them to disperse
quietly—go home. But unfortunately—well, this isn't the palace.
... Quite a different thing discovering me here—notorious Pavilion
of Masks ... Might easily—er—inflame—lead to regrettable—even
revolutionary ...'

As his voice died away in a sad murmur, a fierce yell came
through the broken window. This was enough for Cleo. 'Hogs!
Rats! Cockroaches!' she shouted. 'I'll quieten you!' Pistol in hand,
she made a dive for the nearest window.

'Stop her,' cried Stockhorn. 'She'll have us all murdered.'

Victor and von Marstein were already struggling with her.

'Be careful of that pistol.' This was Prince Karl. 'Careful now—
careful, gentlemen!'

As von Marstein released her: 'You're behaving like a lunatic,
woman.'

'Better a lunatic than a coward.' She glared at him. 'This mob's
packed with your supporters. Why don't you go and take charge of
them?'

'Because I can't be discovered here. I'd lose control of the Party.
What am I supposed to be doing here?'

'You let them see you,' Cleo told him, 'and they'll soon tell you
what you can do here. And quite different from what you expected.
Oh—Victor!' She collapsed, breathing hard, into his arms.

'My dearest angel,' he murmured, half-caressing and half-tidying
her. 'Please remember what we planned.'

'Hopeless now—'

'I still don't think so,' he muttered. 'We had some talk upstairs.'

Suzanne came in from the dining room. 'There are still some of
them at the back door,' she announced, quite cheerfully. 'Enough
anyhow to make plenty of noise. But it's all safely bolted, barred,
shuttered. If we can't get out, at least they can't get in. I've left that
student in the kitchen.'

'Glubfer?' said Cleo. 'What's he doing?'

'Drinking schnapps and crying.' She looked around. 'Where's
Nicolo Novelda?'

'In disgrace,' said Cleo.

'I felt compelled, Madame Belsac,' Prince Karl told her, 'to order him to leave us. I must confess—that was—er—before the demonstration began to be—er—really hostile—otherwise perhaps—in view of the situation . . .' As his voice trailed away, he looked enquiringly at the others. Dr Stockhorn shook his head.

'Your Highness, for my part I have no confidence in that man. Councillor?'

'I am of the same opinion. No possible degree of confidence,' von Marstein concluded.

'Then you're a pair of imbeciles,' said Suzanne. She turned away and walked slowly towards the dining room door.

'Where are you going, Suzanne?' Cleo called.

Suzanne turned at the door. 'To my room, to start packing. Enough is enough. You're behaving like an imbecile too, Cleo, and there's even less excuse for you. What can you do now without Nicolo Novelda?' And the dining room door answered the question with a slamming sound.

Prince Karl looked round helplessly and wandered into one of his vague monologues. 'Really this is very difficult. . . . If any danger of general uprising—arrangement to be in communication with Saxony and Bavaria—mutual advantage. . . . Impossible to do anything here and now of course. . . . Not possible to leave either, apparently—very delicate situation. . . . Any suggestions? Councillor?'

'I have walked into a trap,' said von Marstein with savage emphasis, 'and now like a trapped creature I can't think properly. All I can suggest is that you speak to the crowd yourself, Prince Karl, and tell them you have dismissed Cleo Torres—'

'No—never!' she cried. 'What an idea!'

'A typical politician's idea,' said Victor. 'Typical—mean—cowardly—miserable!'

'And utterly stupid.' She pointed her whip at von Marstein. 'They'd never believe him. If Karl had dismissed me, why is he here? You were quite right. You can't think properly. So stop trying, you big fool.'

'Not acceptable, I'm afraid, Councillor. Though Cleo must moderate her language.' The Prince sighed so deeply that it seemed to shake his whiskers. 'Yes, Dr Stockhorn? You have a plan perhaps—eh?'

Stockhorn had. 'Count Victor is a Frenchman. The crowd will let him pass through, so he can go to Dorheim and summon the police and the military—in your name, your Highness—to disperse the crowd.'

'No, no—a dangerous bad plan,' von Marstein told them. 'As I have said before, if the troops disobey orders and then fraternize with the crowd, you have at once a revolutionary situation.'

'You are quite right, Councillor,' said the Prince unhappily. 'It would be madness.'

Victor went at once into the grand manner. 'And I would never consent to go on such an errand. What I—Victor Vatannes—the poet of liberty—the prophet of freedom—go running for the police, the dragoons, the instruments of tyranny and repression? Why I could never live it down. It would mean humiliation, obloquy, ruin—'

'It would, would it?' said Prince Karl in a tone of mild interest. 'Great pity. I am sorry, Dr Stockhorn, but your plan is not acceptable. We are not making much progress, gentlemen.' There were now more yells, taunts, loud threats, and all four men looked uneasily at the windows. Cleo now claimed their attention. 'Yes, Cleo? You have an idea?'

'The only one left. Novelda.'

'You are quite right of course,' said Victor warmly. 'This man is our only hope.'

There were three murmurs of disagreement.

'Oh—for God's sake!' And Cleo almost screamed at them. 'Another two minutes of this idiotic Emergency Council—and I'd jump through the window. Nicolo Novelda could do better than this—even without trying—in his sleep.' She looked round, her eyes flashing defiance. 'I'm bringing him down.' Without another word or look, she marched upstairs.

Ten

'RATHER AWKWARD OF course,' Prince Karl sighed. 'But she may be right.'

'With respect, Highness,' said von Marstein sourly, 'I've never found it good policy to recall a man after dismissing him.'

'The same thought was crossing *my* mind,' said Stockhorn.

'I do not find them very helpful,' Victor began, 'these thoughts that are crossing your minds. Here we are, besieged. Every minute probably the crowd is larger and angrier. We must do something quickly. So it would be better to keep these thoughts about administration policy for your memoirs, if you live to write them.'

'I began my memoirs some years ago,' Prince Karl told him quite blandly, 'but I found it impossible to get past my childhood, which was so tedious I couldn't keep awake describing it.'

Encouraging this mood for the moment, Victor said, 'Invention is necessary, even in autobiography. In my first chapter I have invented an encounter, at the age of five, with Napoleon during the Hundred Days that will be quoted for generations.'

'Indeed, Count Victor.' But there the Prince stopped, for now there were not only more angry shouts but there was also a thumping or banging at the front door. When it ceased for a moment, Prince Karl continued: 'I think you were quite right about the crowd, Count Victor. It sounds larger and angrier. Most unfortunate.' But now Cleo was running downstairs. 'Yes, Cleo?'

'Novelda is coming,' she said. 'But I warn you he may be difficult.'

'*Difficult?*' Von Marstein was angry. 'This is no time to be difficult. Did you hear them trying to break the door down?'

'You talked them into this,' Cleo told him. 'Why don't you try talking them out of it?'

'I tell you, if they found me here, you foolish woman, they'd never listen to me again.'

'That I can understand, you foolish man,' said Victor sharply, 'for *I* found you here and never want to listen to you again.'

'Nothing is gained, gentlemen,' said Prince Karl, 'by these heated exchanges. As I heard Metternich on one occasion—' But Novelda was coming downstairs. He had changed his clothes and was now dressed for travelling.

Obviously glad to see him, Victor called, 'Ah—Dr Novelda, we need you here. We haven't a good idea between us.'

Novelda gave him a nod. Then he addressed the Prince in a smoothly ironical tone. 'I have your Highness's gracious permission to rejoin the company?'

'Yes—yes, Dr Novelda—er—in the circumstances. But you look as if you are dressed for a journey. Have you one in mind?'

Novelda sat down at ease. 'It is as well to be prepared, your Highness. Why don't we all sit down?' He looked round blandly. 'You know, from the upstairs window, the scene outside is rather impressive. The savage glaring faces. The cudgels and threatening fists. Even a few old muskets. Torches too—a theatrical touch—but impressive. All they need now to complete the picture are some tumbrils.'

There was no reply at once. Then von Marstein: 'Well now that you *are* here, what have you to suggest?'

Novelda threw him a mocking glance. 'Councillor, you are behaving badly. His Highness is present. Unless of course you know that he's already been deposed—'

'What? What? What's this?' cried Prince Karl. 'Don't tell me, Councillor—'

He cut in swiftly. 'I assure your Highness that although certain extreme Republican elements in my Party—'

'Oh—shut up! Don't waste time. Nicolo, is there anything we can do? Have you a plan?'

'Certainly, Cleo,' he replied, smiling. 'I've had time to work it out very neatly. It takes care of everybody. Almost, you might say, a little work of art. Incidentally, it takes care of *me* as well as of everybody else. But we'll come to that shortly.' He smiled at them all.

'Well what is it? Hurry up!'

'Yes, indeed—I share Cleo's impatience,' said the Prince. 'Your plan at once, sir. This is an order, Dr Novelda.'

'But, with all respect, an order you can't give me, Prince Karl.' Novelda held up a forefinger. 'If you are still ruling this principality —and of that we can't be sure at this moment—you can order me to leave this room—or return to it. But you can't order me to take off the top of my head and show you how my brain is working.'

'It might be a point,' said the Count dubiously. 'But my dear Novelda, you said from the first, this morning, that you and I could be allies.'

'Certainly, my dear Count, and so we are, as you'll see. But as yet you have made no contribution to the Novelda Travel and New Life Fund.' He held out his right hand and rubbed his forefinger against his thumb, a gesture no Frenchman could fail to understand.

'Oh—how stupid of me!—of course,' Victor produced a handful of large banknotes. 'Thalers or francs?'

'Francs might be more useful, if you can spare them.'

'Of course. It is a pleasure.' But as he handed over a bundle of notes, 'You feel sure you can guarantee our plan will work, my dear Dr Novelda?'

'Barring any terrible accident, I can. And thank you, my dear Count Victor. Now then. Cleo, you have made your contribution— the bracelet. Your Highness—gentlemen?'

'Cleo, I am not following this,' said the Prince. 'If you will kindly explain—'

'He wants some money from you,' she replied with brutal directness.

This shocked the Prince. 'Oh no—cannot undertake to do that kind of thing.' He looked at Novelda. 'The Order of Saint Bernard —second class?'

'No, thank you.'

'First class then.'

'I'm sorry but the style of life I'm looking forward to would offer me no opportunity for wearing the order. Money, please.'

Cleo said impatiently, 'Oh—give him some money, Karl—or a draft or something. If you haven't any money, let's go over to the desk and you can sign something.'

As they went, there was a different sound at the door, a steady thudding. 'Listen, they're trying a battering ram of some kind,' said

Novelda rather carelessly. 'It's a fairly stout door, though.'

There were alarmed exclamations from von Marstein and Stockhorn.

'I'll be opening that door before they break through,' Novelda continued. 'Oh—yes, I'm going to talk to them with the door open. Only thing to do. But we can't waste much more time. Cleo, bring pen and ink when you've finished there. Now, Councillor von Marstein—a contribution from you, if you please.'

'I have nothing but some banknotes belonging to Party funds—'

'Party funds are acceptable, Councillor.'

'This is very irregular—'

'It is an irregular occasion. How much?'

'Nine hundred thalers,' he replied, handing them over.

Prince Karl had now joined them. 'And here is a draft for two thousand thalers.'

'The Novelda Travel and New Life Fund thanks you both. And now—your Highness—Councillor—a little formality.' He brought out two documents. 'This is for you—and this is yours. Now please sign in your official capacities these safe conducts for Dr Novelda and party. The pen, please, Cleo. Both won't be wanted but one of them probably will.' As they took the documents and began to sign them, he turned to Stockhorn and stared hard at him. 'Now then, my friend, what's your contribution to the Fund?'

'Not a penny,' he replied promptly. 'I can't believe that Rothschilds would authorize any payment to an agent as unreliable as you are.'

'Forget Rothschilds. I strongly advise you to make a contribution yourself—'

'I cannot accept your advice. Not a penny.'

'Then you're a stingy old fool,' Cleo told him.

'You're also outside the agreement and I accept no responsibility for you.' Novelda now addressed the others. 'In a minute or two I must talk to the people outside this door. But first I shall ask those outside the back door to join them. That will give me a larger audience out here. It will also leave the other door clear for us to use when we need it. I'll borrow your pistol please, Cleo.' He took it and went out through the dining room.

There were still some yells and banging on the door, though the battering ram seemed to have been abandoned. The noise was not continuous, so that low-toned talk was possible.

'Surely Novelda's no intention of opening this door, has he?' Prince Karl said uneasily to Cleo.

'I hope so. Why not?'

'There seem to be several hundred good reasons out there,' said Victor, pulling a face. 'However, unlike Dr Stockhorn, I have confidence in our friend Novelda.'

'It is entirely misplaced,' said Stockhorn. 'Once a charlatan, always a charlatan.'

'Perhaps we need a charlatan,' Victor told him. 'Sound finance and experienced statesmanship haven't been much help so far.'

Cleo, who had been turning down several lamps, sounded cheerful. 'Nicolo has thought of something. I can tell. I've made plans with him too long not to know he has something. You'll see.'

Novelda came back to address them in a masterful style. 'I shall open this door and make a speech to the mob. There will be no swarming in here, I promise you that. But now you must promise *me* something. I shall announce that all of you have done—or are doing—certain things. They are things, I'm sure, you are willing to do, perhaps have been wanting to do. But I must have your assurance.'

'I trust you, Nicolo,' said Cleo.

'I too,' said Victor.

'Good! Your Highness? Councillor?'

'We will see,' the Prince replied. 'But you can't expect from me, head of a ruling house, an exact promise. We never make exact promises.'

'And I try to avoid them,' said von Marstein. 'But I will do my best, though you understand, Novelda, they must not learn that I am here. I cannot be seen.'

'Not one of you four must be seen. Otherwise my plan miscarries.'

'But, Nicolo, they know I am here,' Cleo objected. 'They must have heard me shouting when I fire the pistol.'

'Never mind that. Keep well out of sight of the door, all four of you.'

'What about me?' asked Stockhorn uneasily.

'You're not included. You wouldn't join in—Rothschilds must look after you. Now then—'

He waved them well away from the door and they began hiding themselves behind the sofa and one or two of the larger chairs.

Stockhorn remained where he was, so within easy reach of Novelda who now placed a wide low stool facing the door. 'And not a sound from any of you four, remember? One yelp from you, Cleo, will throw us to the wolves. Now for the door. Ready?'

'No.' The Prince popped up, looking and sounding very shaky. 'Wait a moment. Is there no other—safer—way?'

'Tell me one.'

'But once that door is opened—'

'We sink or swim,' said Cleo. 'Stop dithering, Karl.'

Victor had popped up too. 'Novelda, my friend, you are either a fool or a very brave man—'

'I am neither. I am something different—a desperate man. This door can open upon the other side of the world—and a new life. Quiet now. Not a sound. Not a movement. Here we go.'

Holding the pistol in his left hand he used his right hand to unbolt and unlock the door and fling it open; he then hastily took his place on the stool. A yell of triumph had gone up from the mob and they surged forward, several of the foremost, ruffians to a man, filling the doorway. The one most prominent, bulkier and older than the rest, a ferocious left-over pirate wearing a black eye patch, suggested a leader.

'Stand back,' Novelda roared, using a tremendous voice. 'Back —back—or I'll spill your brains over the doorpost—back—back— I tell you.' He even bent forward and gave the piratical leader a push. Those in the forefront of the mob were now only occupying the doorway again.

It was time for Novelda's speech. 'Now listen my friends, I have news for you. Quiet! Quiet!' He waited a moment. 'I'm sorry you've been kept waiting here, but I wanted to be able to give you some news. Now I can tell you the news, so you needn't waste any more time hanging about here when you might be celebrating the night of your lives back in Dorheim. Now listen—friends. Cleo Torres has gone.'

There was an excited buzz from the crowd, and one voice shouted, 'Gone where?'

'She's run away with the great French poet—Count Victor Vatannes—who's taking her to Paris hell-for-leather.' There were cheers. 'No, you won't see Cleo again. And friends, if you're wondering where Prince Karl is tonight, I'll tell you, though this is all in strict confidence, mind. The Prince is chasing Cleo and the

Count with a squadron of cavalry—on their way to the frontier. So you're the first to learn about what will be a great European sensation. And that's not all the news, my friends. Quiet now! I've two more items of the greatest importance. First—Councillor von Marstein is to address a special mass meeting at the Burg Hall in one hour's time. You should all be there—to give him your support.' That was cheered. 'Now wait. That's not all. Wait now—a big surprise.' He jumped down, grabbed hold of Stockhorn, and with the help of the piratical mob-leader held up the little man so that the crowd could see him.

'This is Dr Stockhorn of Zurich who is here representing Rothschilds, the great international bankers. And I've persuaded him to offer Mexe-Dorberg a new loan on the most favourable terms.' Cheers again. 'He's on his way now to shake hands with the Burgomaster—give him another cheer, lads.' A tremendous cheer, to which Stockhorn, who was terrified, responded with a sickly grin.

Novelda looked at the anachronistic pirate, who had let Stockhorn down but had still hold of him. 'You look after Dr Stockhorn, my friend, and see him safely to Dorheim.'

'Depend upon it, I will, your honour,' the ruffian growled.

'He wants to offer free beer and sausage to everybody who attends the Councillor's meeting.' More cheers. 'And that's all I can tell you. But what more do you want?'

'Nothing,' the ruffian-in-chief bellowed. He turned: 'Come on, lads. Dorheim for us.'

He disappeared, along with the helpless Stockhorn. They could hear the mob still cheering as they streamed away, just before Novelda closed and bolted the door. Cleo was turning up several lamps; Novelda was mopping his face.

'A model political speech, in my opinion,' he said when he had dried himself. 'First I persuade them that a lot of things have happened that we're all hoping will happen. Then I send them away happy by promising them something for nothing that they won't get. The very essence of successful political oratory.'

'My dear Novelda, you were wonderful. Now, you think they have all gone?'

'I'm certain of it. And you and Cleo must go too.'

'You are not as clever as you think you are,' said von Marstein sullenly. 'To give them Stockhorn was a blunder. He will tell them you were lying.'

'No, he won't,' said Novelda. 'By the time he's allowed to tell anybody anything, my lies will be the truth. The man I told to look after him will see to that. He was there for that purpose.'

'Humph—you are cleverer than I thought.' He turned to the Prince. 'It is all right about Stockhorn, your Highness.'

'It's not all right about this cavalry nonsense—' said Karl peevishly. 'What will Saxony think—Bavaria—?'

'They will admire your spirit,' Novelda told him. He paused to take in all four of them. 'You have just been rescued from what you felt was a dangerous situation. The mob has gone. You feel safe now. But if you think now you can begin to make difficulties, objecting to all the arrangements I've made for you, let me give you a warning. I've been patient all day, right up to a few minutes ago. Now I've very little patience left. Beware the fury of a patient man—remember? Yes, Suzanne?'

She was coming downstairs carrying a small travelling case and a cloak. 'Obeying your instructions, Nicolo.' She went towards Cleo. 'Nicolo told me to bring you these, Cleo, for your journey as soon as the crowd had gone.'

'Cleo—Count Victor—you have no time to lose. You must go now. The carriage I ordered for you is waiting under the trees, a hundred yards from the back gate. Now you must go.'

'At once—yes,' cried Victor. 'Cleo—my darling—'

But Cleo was furious. 'I'll go when I'm ready—and not before. So be quiet. Suzanne, you are a fool to think I can go with nothing at all like this. I want my things—not all of them but some of them—and I won't go until I've packed everything I want—'

'I have warned you, Cleo,' said Novelda in a quiet but dangerous voice.

'Shut up! I tell you, I won't go until I have everything I want. Why are you all so stupid?' In her fury she picked up her whip. 'I'll go when I'm ready and not before, d'you hear?' She cracked her whip, making Suzanne, Karl and Victor, nearest to her, jump back.

But her fury paled before Novelda's, which was terrifying. He jumped forward, tore the whip out of her grasp, took her by the shoulders, glaring at her like a madman.

'*Hell blast your soul, woman!*' he roared as he shook her. 'Get out —go—before I take the skin off your rump.'

'Dr Novelda,' the Prince protested feebly. 'You forget yourself.'

'I forget nothing,' Novelda replied, still glaring at Cleo though now releasing her.

She looked at him piteously, tears on her cheeks. 'Nicolo—are you coming to Paris?' Hers was now a small childish voice.

'No, Cleo.' He spoke quietly now. 'I told you.'

'But I didn't believe you, Nicolo.'

'Believe me now. I've finished.'

She tried another approach, giving a lift to her voice. 'You say that now because you need a holiday. You've had too much to do for me. In Paris it will be quite different.'

'I'm sure it will. But I shan't be there.'

She drooped and the tears came again. 'Nicolo, you will—you *must*—' And she put out a hand to him.

Novelda lightly brushed her cheek with the back of his hand. 'Courage, Cleo—courage. Remember, it's your greatest gift, and there are so many cowards about it makes you shine like a ruby. I have a present for you—' He went to the writing table, opened a drawer, and took out a crystal ball. 'Here, take it—something to amuse you on your journey.'

As she took it: 'Oh—Nicolo—the crystal ball!'

Novelda looked solemn. 'You stare and stare into it until it seems to be misted over. You stare harder still—into the mist—and you see the little pictures of places—the past or the future—'

'Just as you did,' she cried eagerly.

'Except you might have better luck. I never saw a damned thing.'

'Now you are laughing at me.' She smiled at him. 'I know I shall see you again. So we must go. Come, Victor. Karl, come and say goodbye. Not you, Nicolo, I won't say goodbye to you—just *au 'voir.*' She looked at von Marstein. 'As for you, now that I am going I think the Right, the uniforms and black cassocks, will defeat you. Don't forget—that fat old Bishop is their cleverest man. He once offered me a pension and a villa on Lake Como if I would leave the country. You never knew that, Karl, did you? Where is Suzanne? No, it doesn't matter. We always disliked each other. Come now— we must hurry.'

She went out followed by Victor and Karl. As if he had much to do in a short time, Novelda ignored von Marstein and sat down at his desk and began looking through bills, dividing them into two different heaps. Watching him curiously, von Marstein moved across to him.

'Dr Novelda, I don't understand you.'

'It's not necessary you should.' And Novelda did not even turn his head. 'I'm leaving the country.'

'You misjudge me. I don't think of politics all the time.'

Novelda turned to look at him now. 'You should. And don't forget you are addressing a meeting soon. They'll be expecting you now.'

'A clever move of yours. I'll be there.' He paused a moment. 'But I must know first what the Prince intends to do.'

Novelda shrugged it away. 'We shall see.'

'It's a good thing that woman, Cleo, has gone,' said Marstein, lowering his voice. 'But I won't pretend with you, Novelda. I wish I could have had her—if only just once.'

'You wouldn't have enjoyed the experience, Councillor. Any Dorheim waitress or chambermaid under fifty could probably offer you something more satisfying. I realized all that from the first. There was between Cleo and me the only relationship she could respect and enjoy. We were business partners—and fellow performers in a touring comedy.'

'Then that amorous French poet is about to gallop away to the greatest disappointment of his life—ho ho!'

'On the contrary, he'll feel immensely relieved. She can't be set on fire, and he's burnt out.' Novelda now turned round completely, resting his arms on the back of the chair, and began to enjoy what he was saying. 'In a few days' time, when this romantic sensational elopement explodes like a scented bomb in all the boudoirs, thousands and thousands of dissatisfied women will tantalize themselves conjuring up the erotic ecstasies of these great lovers. And by this time, Cleo and the Count will be sitting up going through each other's contracts and working out percentages. These two, never wasting a moment in each other's arms, are creatures of a new age, one that is just beginning, Councillor.'

'An age, no doubt,' said von Marstein who considered himself well-informed, 'of the cheap press, the type-casting machines, the new electric telegraph—'

'An age when appearance will defeat reality, when what is said is more important than what is done, when the shadow will be accepted for the substance, and more and more people will stop living their own lives to dream of living somebody else's life. In this age of make-believe, fraud, and journalism, you will see, the fame of Paola and

Francesca, Tristan and Isolde, Romeo and Juliet, will be eclipsed by that of Victor Vatannes, who in private is impotent, and Cleo Torres, who's frigid except in public. It's one reason why I want to leave Europe for ever. I prefer the air and the sun to life in a camera obscura.'

Von Marstein nodded, then said in a hurried whisper, 'I believe I'll be in power soon. What if I offered to appoint you Chief of Police?'

'Not for a'million a year. God made me the enemy of all chiefs of police and I respect His handiwork.'

Prince Karl returned, at first in his role of romantic minor poet. 'Well, gentlemen ... Cleo has gone ... a chapter of romance has ended ... a rose-coloured and perfumed interlude in a stern hard life ... a wonderful woman, all fire and imagination, all feminine passion and sweet surrender ... you can understand what I'm feeling, gentlemen ...' Then he stepped out of the role, 'But, look here, Novelda, this nonsense of yours about going after her with cavalry! Quite impossible! A terrible waste of time too.'

Smooth and deadly, Novelda said, 'What does your Highness want to do with the time?'

'Well—I ought to be communicating with Bavaria and Saxony —Vienna possibly—explaining developments here—'

As before, Novelda enquired, 'What would you tell them? What *are* the developments?'

Vague and rather miserable, Prince Karl said, 'Well of course— almost anything may be happening—'

'And where does your Highness propose to be while it's happening? In Dorheim? Of course not. In the palace or here? Risky. And after what the crowd's been told, it'll look as if you're skulking. Your castle at Markenburg? You'll be accused of running away.'

Peevish now, 'You're making it sound all very difficult. What do you think, Councillor?'

'Well, Highness, when one begins to look at it—er—it *is* difficult.'

'It is, is it? Yes—perhaps you're right—'

Novelda was immediately persuasive. 'There's only one thing your Highness can do tonight that'll keep you safe whatever happens. You can do what the people think you're doing—chasing Cleo and the Count with a squadron of cavalry.'

'But why *should* I?

'Because you'll be somewhere, doing something. You'll be with your soldiers—'

'But I don't want to be with my soldiers—'

'I'll come to that in a moment. You'll be heading for the frontier, apparently in pursuit. And not because of a possible revolution but for the best romantic reasons. "Prince Karl's still a devil of a fellow!" they'll say—even in Saxony and Bavaria.'

'Something to be said for this, you know, Councillor. After all, it's *something* I can be doing while the situation here's so uncertain.' He turned to Novelda. 'But must it be the cavalry? What about the artillery? No—it would look odd—you're quite right. But you don't expect me to be on a horse all night, do you?'

'No, sir. Outside the back gate, not where the Count's carriage was but on the other side, for the last hour the adjutant of the Second Dragoons has been waiting with a squadron—'

'One moment, Dr Novelda.' The Prince's interruption was quite severe. 'I have given no orders to this adjutant or any squadron of dragoons—'

'You will be able to do that shortly, your Highness,' said Novelda at his smoothest. 'I happened to see this adjutant lunching at the Golden Lion—and as I know him slightly and he's a pleasant fellow —I told him there might be a useful night exercise for one of his squadrons here tonight. But now, your Highness,' he continued rather hurriedly, 'your own travelling carriage is waiting for you there. And now, as I've still much to do here, no doubt the Councillor will see you into the carriage. By the way, at the Weisshausen cross-roads, please tell them to take the righthand fork—'

'Why? I must have some reason.'

'Because Cleo and the Count will have taken the road to the left, so you'll be in no danger of overtaking them.'

'Very clever,' said von Marstein.

'But I shall be reasonably comfortable, I take it? Could be a horrible long night.'

'In your own carriage, your Highness, and there's some excellent food in it, and two bottles of wine and one of brandy. So now I wish you a pleasant journey.'

'You're unquestionably a most capable man, Dr Novelda,' said the Prince, about to go. 'But as I find myself disliking you more and more, I trust you'll discover some opportunity of displaying your talents as far away as possible from Mexe-Dorberg.'

'About five thousand miles, I hope.' He held the door open for them. 'Goodbye, Prince Karl.'

Von Marstein in a hasty whisper: 'If we became a republic, you wouldn't change your mind?'

'Goodbye, Councillor.'

Eleven

NOVELDA CAME BACK rather slowly after closing the door, going to his desk again, separating the accounts there into two heaps. All was quiet. He worked steadily away for about ten minutes, but then Suzanne came in from the dining room. There were sandwiches, a bottle of wine, glasses, on the tray she was carrying. 'You must have something to eat and drink, Nicolo. An omelette later, perhaps.'

'Thank you, Suzanne.'

'You did everything you wanted to do?'

'I did.'

'Then why are you looking so melancholy?'

'I'm not. But it's been a long hard day.'

'Then why,' Suzanne persisted, 'are you still at this desk, working for Cleo Torres? She's gone. You've done with her.'

He tried the wine before he replied. 'I'm doing it for myself, Suzanne. I'm dividing these bills. On this side are the honest tradesmen who must be paid. On this other side are the scoundrels who've fleeced us all the time and deserve a bad debt. Prince Karl will have to tell somebody to settle up here.' He ate half a sandwich and drank some wine. Suzanne watched him and said nothing, which he found rather surprising. Finally, he said, 'By the way, when did Princess Louise go?'

'She went back to the palace just before the crowd surrounded us.'

'Very sensible.'

'She was not very sensible when she returned. She and her personal maid, Charlotte, had to hide until you cleared the men away from our side door. She was just in time to go upstairs and then hear you make your speech.'

Novelda stared at her. 'Why did she come back?'

'I can't tell you,' said Suzanne, looking rather smug. 'You must ask her.'

'Well, where is she?'

'Still upstairs somewhere, I imagine. Changing her clothes perhaps—'

'Why should she change her clothes? No,' he hastily corrected himself, 'that's an idiotic question to ask a woman about another woman. But I'm surprised she had to bring her maid to help her. Not a helpless kind of woman, I'd have thought.'

'And you'd have been right, Nicolo.'

'Then why—Oh! she's coming down—'

Suzanne turned, saw her, then said, 'I'll leave you to play your question-and-answer game. You don't need me.' And out she went.

Louise looked as if she had planned to take a journey. Both the cloak, which was merely hanging round her shoulders, and the dress it revealed were made of that rough English cloth favoured now by so many wealthy travellers. She wore no hat or bonnet, and as Novelda rose and went to greet her, he saw that she was smiling.

'Will you give me a glass of wine, please, Nicolo?'

'Of course.' He returned at once to the tray.

'You see,' she continued, her voice trembling a little, 'already I've learnt to call you Nicolo. That's because Suzanne Belsac has talked so much about you. I like her. And she's devoted to you.'

'We've shared many troubles here. We're good friends.' The hand that held out the wine glass was shaking a little, like her voice.

After a sip of wine, she didn't look at him but stared about her. 'This place seems sad—lost. Or don't you feel that?'

'I do. A place suddenly deserted by people and events—and perhaps by a little history. Probably I was feeling this when Suzanne came in with that tray and said I was looking melancholy.'

'Upstairs I overheard almost everything important. I think that woman, Cleo, loves you as far as she can love anybody.'

'Perhaps—just as a fellow adventurer—'

'I heard your speech to the crowd. You were very brave as well aş being very clever, Nicolo.'

'No, your Highness—'

'Oh—no!' she cut in furiously. 'How can you be so stupid? Or—are you trying to hurt me?'

'Of course not—'

'Then after all that's happened, how can I be your "Highness"? I'm still what I was in that hunting-lodge, a woman called Louise.'

'Louise then. I'm sorry.'

'And why are you telling me you weren't very brave and very clever?'

His smile was apologetic. 'It was fairly clever but not brave, Louise. There was no risk. Like everything here in the Pavilion of Masks, it was a performance. I was no hero, just for once an actor-manager.'

'But it helped everybody.'

'Incidentally—yes. It tidied things up here. But I did it chiefly for myself—and for money.'

'Suzanne doesn't believe that. She says you'd never have taken such trouble for yourself—only for some woman.'

'A woman's guess and not true. I told her she was wrong. There's no woman involved in my plan.'

'What is your plan, Nicolo?' She was almost severe with him.

'To begin with, I was tired of living by my wits.'

'How did you come to be such a cynical adventurer? Why the charlatan masquerade—and Cleo Torres—why, why?'

'More wine? A sandwich perhaps? No? Well, please allow me. And why don't you sit down, Louise?'

'Are you trying to be maddening, Nicolo?'

'Not at all.' He was now at the tray. 'But if I have to explain myself, we'd both be happier sitting down.'

'Oh—well, I suppose so.' She sat down and waited expectantly, her eyes very bright. 'Hurry up with that eating and drinking, which could easily be postponed.'

He shook his head at that, but after a minute or two he pulled up a chair closer to her and was twinkling at her over his wine glass. 'Louise, I was born, brought up, partly educated in Padua. I did well scholastically, but later was dismissed from the staff of three universities—two Italian and one German. There seemed to be no place in my world for a social philosopher but ample opportunity for a charlatan. I drifted into South Germany, heard about Cleo Torres, joined forces with her, as you know. But now I've had enough of it, more than enough too of Europe. The air's stale—too many people, too many steam engines, too many newspapers, too many bureaucrats.'

'But your plan—what is it?'

'I have an uncle—half-Spanish, half-Italian—who owns a vast *hacienda* or *rancho*—at least as large as this principality. There he raises cattle, and lives among his horsemen—the *gauchos*—like a prince—'

'No, not like a prince, please—not like a prince—'

'A simple Arcadian king, then,' said Novelda smiling.

'But where is this place—this country?'

'It is Uruguay, the southern neighbour of Argentina. Its capital is Montevideo. Politically, my uncle tells me, it is very unstable—frequent revolutions and civil wars. But my uncle is very rich and very cunning, so either he is on no side or on both sides and keeps out of trouble.'

'It must run in the family,' she murmured. 'But what sort of country is this Uruguay? Is it all steaming jungles?'

'A foolish question, Louise, when I've just told you my uncle raises cattle on a huge scale. It is a country with a temperate climate and *pampas* like those of Argentina except that they are more interesting, my uncle tells me, having more trees and little valleys filled with aromatic shrubs and brilliant wild flowers. He has described to me how you may ride all day, and then the men light a camp fire smelling of *pinon* and sage under the wide glitter of the stars, and then after all have eaten they sing to their guitars their songs of love and death.'

'Men sing it, women live it.' She looked searchingly at him. 'And this uncle wants you to go there?'

'Yes, he's old and lazy and has no son, no heir. He asks for no money of course, but there are some things he needs from Europe—'

'And that's why you wanted money?'

'And why I played the charlatan today. I hope for the last time. More wine?'

'No, thank you.'

'I want some.'

He was filling his glass when Suzanne looked in from the dining room. 'Are we ready for our omelette *fines herbes* now?' But Novelda's *Yes* was swept away by Louise's 'No, Suzanne. Certainly not.' After which, the women exchanged a look, and then Suzanne went back to her own department.

'So there's no woman involved in your plan?' Louise made it sound nearly like polite conversation.

'No, I told Suzanne Belsac the exact truth. She didn't believe me. Hardly anybody ever believes the exact truth,' he added lightly.

Louise now dropped any pretence of polite conversation. 'Perhaps now that we're in the light,' she began, with a very sharp edge on her voice, 'now that we can speak openly, and you are you and I am really myself, you're ashamed—or bored. Perhaps you only wanted a woman you could take in silence in a darkened room, just so much mischief, sensuality and vanity. Perhaps you're really in love with some woman you can't have.'

'Certainly I am.'

There was the usual bitter little laugh. 'And I thought you were an extraordinary man, not just another ordinary fool of a man.' She now produced that tone which in advance banishes all warmth and light from the creature that will emerge. 'And who is this woman?'

Novelda replied with a precision not without bitterness. 'She is Elizabeth Ingrid Louise, younger daughter of the Duke of Grunberg, and wife of His Highness Prince George Augustus Karl of Mexe-Dorberg—'

The sun might have risen in the room with all the birds singing. 'George *Wilhelm* Augustus Karl,' she corrected him gaily, 'and I'm Dorothea as well as Elizabeth Ingrid Louise. But I was right, after all. You *are* an extraordinary man. Kiss me.'

He did but soon released himself.

'No, again and longer, Nicolo. *Then* we can talk.'

'I can't. We'll talk now, please!'

'Very well. I'm not afraid of saying it first. I love you, Nicolo.'

'I love you, Louise. I'm half out of my mind with it. That's the final reason I'm leaving Europe.'

She waited a moment. 'Nicolo, I'm coming with you.'

'Louise, that's wonderful—but preposterous. It's not your mind talking but your blood.'

'All the better,' she cried. 'It's my blood that has been worrying you. A German princess on a cattle ranch! I know everything you're going to say—so let me talk now. But first, tell me this. Will there be a revolution here in Mexe-Dorberg? Will Karl be turned out?'

'Yes. Might be next week, next month, next year, but sooner or later Karl will have to go. He'll be much worse off now that he hasn't Cleo. He has no judgment, no sense.'

'He's never lived among real things,' she said slowly. Then, brisker: 'Now if we're turned out, it's been settled that we stay with Karl's sister in Mecklenburg. She's very mean. The castle's cold. Nothing there but gossip and needlework. Soon I'll look pinched, have a red nose, become a secret drinker on kümmel. By then you'll have married some dazzling Spanish creature, who'll share your *pampas* and glittering stars and fragrant camp fires and all the rest of it, bearing and bringing up your black-eyed impudent children. All this while I'm yawning and shivering over cold potato salad in Mecklenburg. *Never—never—never!*'

'But this would be life in a new country,' said Novelda, 'still wild —rough—'

'What's that? No women in Europe who aren't peasants have a more rigorous Spartan upbringing than the German aristocracy. You talk like that, and yet if I don't go with you, then you'll end by marrying some pampered plump Spanish girl who's been brought up like a pet kitten.'

Novelda laughed. 'But—remember—you and I can't marry.'

'Not until Karl divorces me—or dies. He'll do one or the other.'

'Meanwhile, if we have children?' said Novelda doubtfully.

'We are having children,' she declared firmly. Then she jumped up and stopped any reply from him by putting a hand against his mouth. 'No, Nicolo, if I hear another objection, then stupid pride won't allow me to answer it. I'll be angry. You'll be angry. We'll have no time to lose our anger, no place where we can discover each other again. This will be the greatest stupidity there ever was. You love me, Nicolo?'

'You know that—'

'Then I'm coming with you. Oh—and so is my little maid Charlotte. You don't object? She will be very useful. I will pay her passage—and mine—on the ship. I have money. And Suzanne is glad that Charlotte will be with us.'

'Then so am I.' But now Novelda stared at her. 'This doesn't make sense, though. How could you and Suzanne and Charlotte have made these decisions? What did you know? You didn't even know where I was going.'

'No, but Suzanne and I knew you were going *somewhere*, Nicolo my darling, and that we were going too—'

'But I might have been going to Timbuctoo or Greenland—'

'No, that wouldn't have been sensible and we both knew you were not only sensible but also a clever man.' She smiled almost pityingly at his bewilderment. 'We don't pretend to be clever of course, but we can also make plans—in our own way, Nicolo my darling—'

He offered her a comic groan, but had no time to say anything because Glubfer, looking bedraggled and terrified, came tumbling in through the dining-room doorway, followed more sedately by Suzanne and Charlotte, all round eyes.

'I thought you'd gone, Glubfer,' said Novelda.

Glubfer was impressive if hardly sober. 'Fell asleep in the pantry. Then suddenly woke up—and through the window where I'd pulled back the shutters—staring in—his eyes like burning coals—an officer of the Death's Head Hussars. I looked at him. He looked at me. He vanished. But I'm afraid he's not gone away. Ladies—Dr Novelda—sorry to say I think the Death's Head Hussars are here. What do we do?'

'We do nothing. You go home, Glubfer.' Novelda took him by the arm and led him towards the front door. 'Then take a cloth, some cold water—study Kant or Hegel for an hour—then go to bed and sleep for a day and a half.'

'I wish I could help you,' Glubfer stammered, as they reached the door, 'but—the Death's Head Hussars!'

'Of course,' said Novelda as he unbolted the door. 'Very disturbing. But off you go now—fast as you can.' He left the door unbolted and rejoined the others.

Troubled, Suzanne asked, 'What does this mean, Nicolo? Is the luck running out at last?'

'Was I being allowed too much happiness?' said Louise.

'Nobody punishes us for being happy, Louise,' said Novelda gently. 'We Latins know that. If God exists—and ever thinks about us—then it must be our determined unhappiness that annoys him. As for luck, Suzanne, we may have had a little—but mostly it wasn't —just cunning.'

There was a thundering knock at the front door. Charlotte screamed. The door opened to admit a tremendous figure, heavily moustached and in a Death's Head Hussar uniform. He announced himself in a huge voice. 'Colonel Shreckentaska—commanding the Death's Head Hussarrrrs—'

'Nonsense!' Novelda told him. 'Only an old actor ever made an

entrance like that, my friend. But come in.' He turned to the women.
'It's only Mendelheim, director of the Folk Theatre. We have a
little business to transact.'

Mendelheim had now removed his helmet and moustache. 'Not
a bad impersonation though, Dr Novelda. Fooled that student. My
apologies, ladies, if I alarmed you—' he bowed—'but coming out
here, I felt I ought to look like somebody else—'

'Besides you enjoyed dressing up,' Novelda told him.

'How was I as the revolutionary?'

'Excellent as it turned out, with nobody wondering how the
pirate make-up had found its way into Dorheim. What happened
about Stockhorn?'

'He finally decided, after some pressure, that he'd be wise to pay
for the beer and sausages. The Company were good, didn't you
think—even all the extras?'

'A most convincing and masterly production,' said Novelda,
pulling out some bank notes. 'I can't do anything about your
Theatre, I'm leaving early in the morning, but these—' he handed
over the banknotes—'will help you to keep the Company going.'

'Thank you, thank you, most generous! Well, I never thought
I'd have a production at the Pavilion of Masks—'

'The last,' said Novelda, as he moved Mendelheim towards the
door, 'and one of the best performances I've known here, Director
Mendelheim. Thank you. Goodnight.'

And the women called out their goodnights. This time Novelda
bolted the door and when he came back he was brisk and businesslike. 'Now this is the plan. I have ordered a big four-horse carriage
to be here before dawn, about five o'clock, to take us across the
frontier. We shall make for Basle by stages, and then take the railway
Basle–Lyons–Marseilles. The *Reina Isabella*—a new ship, I'm told
—will be sailing for Buenos Aires and Montevideo from Marseilles
in about ten days' time. Is that clear?'

'It is clear,' said Suzanne, 'and it is time I made that omelette.
Come, Charlotte.'

'It is also time,' said Louise, when they were alone, 'you kissed
me again.'

'Certainly, madame.' And now there was nothing hurried about
it.

Afterwards, Louise spoke first. '*Now* I understand why you told
me you were clever, making that speech, but not brave. That was

very honest, Nicolo. I would never have guessed it was all being done by actors. Perhaps you may have to be clever again in—what is it?—Uruguay—um?'

'Now and again—a little, perhaps. But I've stopped playing the charlatan for ever.'

The omelette was ready and they joined Suzanne in the dining room. After they had eaten and had enjoyed their wine, Suzanne said, 'We shan't be able to go to sleep at once, Nicolo. Could I have my fortune told, please? You could look into the crystal ball—'

'I couldn't,' he told her, beginning to laugh. 'I gave it as a good-bye present to Cleo.'

'A stupid thing to do,' said Suzanne. 'But you still have the Tarot cards, haven't you?'

He nodded, still laughing.

'Stop it, darling,' said Louise, looking at him solemnly. 'I want *my* fortune told too.'

Then he laughed and laughed and laughed, closing his watering eyes, while Louise and Suzanne told him not to be silly.

Epilogue

IS THIS EPILOGUE unique? There can't be many others that consist entirely of a telephone conversation. I had sent Dr Perkisson a typewritten clear copy of my novella, *The Pavilion of Masks*, and I had asked him to ring me up and tell me his opinion of it. At once it was clear that he was disappointed.

'Not sufficiently artistic of course,' I said, remembering our other talk. 'But then that was a risk you knew you had to take.'

'It is something else.' We had a bad line anyhow and Perkisson was the man to make it worse. I never caught what he went on to say, and told him so, raising my voice, hardly ever worth doing on the telephone.

'You have spoilt the story for me,' he declared angrily. He was rather better over the phone now that he was angry. 'It was a romance—you have turned it into a cynical comedy—'

'Not very cynical surely?'

'It was like a fairy story in real life.' I got that all right but can only put together bits of the rest of his speech. What it amounted to was that this Italian, Novelda, apparently a cynical charlatan but noble at heart, had won his way to a new life, had captured the love of a beautiful German princess, had taken her to the other side of the world, where, with five splendid children coming to them, they had lived happily ever afterwards. Wasn't that like a fairytale in real life?

'I don't know,' I told him. 'No doubt theirs was a good marriage. But nobody outside a fairytale lives happily ever afterwards. It can't be done.'

'You don't even suggest such a thing,' he said indignantly. 'It would have been more artistic and quite true to life—for it is there in Louise's memoirs—if you had shown them one bright morning gazing across the water at the new land that was to be their home. But you end with Novelda laughing and laughing at his beautiful Louise and loyal Suzanne, and this is not even true for there is no mention of it in their reminiscences. Why have you done such a thing—so very inartistic?'

'Because it brings a comedy to an end,' I told him. 'And there's no depth of malice in Novelda's laughter. All through the day he has been contrasting the men's self-deception with the clear-sighted realism of the women—'

'How do we know that? You don't describe his thoughts.'

'Quite true, Dr Perkisson. I deliberately chose a bare objective method of narration, never entering anybody's mind.' But then I climbed out of the Eng. Lit. department. 'Look what happens. The women, who have welcomed his decision to stop being a charlatan, now at the last moment want him to be one all over again—'

Perkisson broke in to say that I had made Novelda a more impudent and cynical charlatan than he appeared to be in his reminiscences.

'Every man—and think of the politicians—tones down his impudence and cynicism in his memoirs. If you don't like my Novelda, Dr Perkisson, then I'm sorry. I'm fond of him. And he makes a good hero of a comedy—the charlatan who doesn't deceive himself, so that he's the most honest and likeable man on the scene. Any princess, especially a German princess, ought to think herself in luck if she finds such a man in love with her. And particularly if she knows already he understands how to make love to her—'

He broke in again to tell me all that was low and vulgar and quite untrue, that in both their memoirs they said they met at the hunting lodge only to talk. That was part of the romance I had destroyed.

'But the romance you want,' I replied, 'is always moving well away from this world, into that of giants, witches, fairy godmothers, impossible castles and magical wishes. The story you take out of those reminiscences would not have been worth telling as a romance, only as a comedy. And in the world of comedy, beautiful dissatisfied women and ardent attractive men don't keep meeting in a darkened hunting lodge simply for conversation. Not that I made the mistake, all too common now, that making love is what it's all about. It's part of my real happy ending that when they're out of the dark and have their clothes on, Louise and Novelda find that they can talk. Happy lovers, married or not, are people who can talk and talk and talk and go to bed even later when they have no company. And that, I think, is enough, Dr Perkisson. I'm sorry I've disappointed you.'

'Well, you have, Mr Priestley. The story of these people—my family, remember—would have been different and much better if I could have written it.'

'But you couldn't. And I could—in my own way. Thank you for calling me, Dr Perkisson.'

DATE DUE		
MAY 1 9 1999		